FASHION VICTIM

Books by Chloe Green

GOING OUT IN STYLE

DESIGNED TO DIE

FASHION VICTIM

Published by Kensington Publishing Corporation

FASHION VICTIM

Chloe Green

KENSINGTON BOOKS
http://www.kensingtonbooks.com

To Ginna

FASHION VICTIM

Chapter One

The wind howled around the palace walls as I hurried through the courtyard garden toward the safety of the kitchen. He was late; and it was important. I didn't see anyone else around, just the black shadows of branches as they were whipped by the wind.

I paused in the light of a torch and looked at my watch. He was a good half hour late. I entered the dining room, which was totally dark except for the flashes of lightning outside that cast eerie shadows on the walls. I put my hand on the swinging door to the kitchen and opened it carefully, as I'd been instructed, in order to avoid flying knives.

"Hello?" I called, in Spanish and English. No one—the echoing silence of no other breath, no one else being in there filled my ears. But something was strange, I could sense it. This was not the way the kitchens usually smelled.

I felt along the slick tiled wall for the light switch and turned it on.

Well. *Late* certainly described him now.

My informant was stretched out on the butcher-block table as a bizarre sacrifice. The whole image was silver and white and red. The immaculate kitchen with steel shelves and pots, and the white tile floors and walls, the white of his uniform jacket and checkered pants, and the red of the blood that was smeared over everything. Especially the knife that had pinned him through the chest to the table.

He was dead—he'd told me he was going to tell me everything, but we had to do it someplace safe and secure. Like my room. I took a step closer to the body. This was why he'd been late. *Was* late. The blood was still dripping. He'd not been dead long, maybe a few minutes.

I raised my head in the sudden silence.

Where was the killer? Still here?

I looked over my shoulder.

There was a resounding crash—and the lights went out.

So much for my island getaway in Paradise.

"Fate of Paradise is their name," Lindsay, my agent, said to me on the phone. "A delightful band. All girls." Her voice was amazingly clear when you considered that she was in my hometown of Dallas, Texas, and I was in the Marais—in Paris. (The original, not the Paris in Texas.)

"Mm-hmm," I murmured. I've come to hate people talking on cell phones in public, and nothing seemed more ugly American than for me to be doing it in a broad Texan accent on the street in France.

"The job is really spectacular Dee, you get to style all five girls. Make the statement about who they are going to be and how they'll be perceived. If they like you, there's even talk of sending you on the tour. The concerts. Round the world. Doesn't that sound fab?"

"Mm-hmm."

"Shall I tell you the details?"

"Mm-hmm."

"I say, darling, is everything all right? You don't sound the least like yourself. Paris treating you well?"

I nodded, then mm-hmm'ed again.

"You haven't been kidnapped and I'm supposed to guess—"

"Lindsay, I'm fine," I said. "Tell me the details."

She did. There were five members of the band, the day rate was phenomenal, the budget was unlimited (my mm-hmm changed into a snort of disbelief there) and we were going to be on an island in the Caribbean. "Well, I don't know if it's actually, technically in the Caribbean," she said. "But it's in the general vicinity."

"Okay . . ."

"Owned by some crazy zillionaire who built a castle, or a palace, I'm not sure what the difference is between a castle and a palace; do you know darling?"

"Castle and palace? Uh, one is cold and made of stone, and one is luxurious and comes with royalty?"

"Sounds reasonable," she said. "Whatju think of it?"

"Sounds reasonable, as you said," I mumbled.

"What? Can't hear you darling."

"Good," I said louder, drawing a few looks from passersby on the street. "Sounds good."

"Is that a yes?"

Sure. "Yes. But when?"

"Well, that's the catch. You return in five days, right?"

I flew standby on American, thanks to my brother Beaumont's flight attendant status. But if someone else was going to spring for a ticket. . . . "I can."

"Are you willing to change your trip from vacation to shopping spree?"

"Lindsay, I don't have the funds—"

"Don't worry, darling. I'll ship you a little something to take care of everything."

Lindsay tends toward the dramatic. The longer and better I know her, the more convinced I am that she is a frustrated actress. Stage, not screen. And not a modern stage, but vaudeville. "Okay."

"I have this addy, correct?" She rattled off the friend's address where I was staying. "It'll arrive tomorrow. No, wait, day after tomorrow. Then you can shop until you drop!"

"Okay," I said. Writing off the last five days in Paris as work wasn't bad. "But—"

"Then they'll need you on the sixth day; in fact, would you like me to pack some clothes for you, from your house, and then you just fly direct from Paris to Miami?"

I stood, mouth agape while I reprocessed everything. "I'll leave a day early," I said. "I need to get to my house." I had a new renter and I wasn't really sure about him.

When "it" arrived, "it" was the Centurion, the new American Express black card. I'd only heard rumors about it, but apparently "it" came with private shopping hours at Barney's and The Store. Unlimited buying power. If ever there was a point in my career that I wanted to run away to Brazil, with someone else footing the bill, this was my chance.

But given the choices between a mountain hideout while being hunted by whichever hip-hop star this card belonged to (it just said: M. L. Diva) or spending thousands of euros on fabulous clothes while gorging myself on French cheese and bread, there was no contest. I stayed, and ate and shopped during the day, then danced all night. As the song says: Who needs sleep?

I got home to a soggy house: my intuition had been speaking to me. The washing machine had flooded and the grad student idiot who was renting the other half of my duplex had just "gone to Starbucks" to work on a paper. When he got home and found the mess, he put some towels down and continued working on his paper. He thinks he's going to be the next Great American Novelist. I'm not much for books, and (to the everlasting chagrin of my university prof parents: both Dr. O'Connors) I didn't go to college. But my boarder can't tell the difference between *its* and *it's*, so I'm not going to hold my breath for his Pulitzer.

Especially since I may have to kill him for stupidity.

Coming home was a bad idea. I packed while trying to straighten out the mess with its attendant insurance issues. I barely had time to glean through the stash of clothes I had and buy the others I needed, before flying to Miami. I got a business-class ticket and paid for my overweight bags, courtesy of the Centurion.

By the time I got on the plane to Bimini, I hadn't slept in two days (dancing all night in South Beach too—easier than checking into a hotel and checking out in the early a.m.) and I had more luggage than Imelda. I bought all the seats on the seaplane. (I'd learned from that Aaliya overweight plane crash.) Now all I had to do was settle back and watch the Atlantic below me, sprinkled with gem green islands like a sea glass necklace tossed on turquoise silk.

"There's your island chain," the pilot said, as we circled over Alice Town (we had to go through Customs here). He pointed past the two islands of Bimini to a spray of islands in the distance. "The Berries are mostly privately owned."

What a perfect place for a band called Paradise, I thought.

We took off from Bimini and skimmed over water so brilliantly blue-green it was almost neon. Scallops of land were identified by the pilot as this key and that key. We continued south, toward a larger slip of land, then came in low. A ruddy box surrounding a garden and flanked by towers was built in the center of an island bright with green foliage and surrounded by sand that looked like powdered sugar. A giddy bubble rose in my throat.

"The coves around here were used by the rum-runners during Prohibition," the pilor said, "and pirates before that. Now the DEA scours all these islands to keep the drug-runners out." He pointed. "See that ship out there?"

I nodded, looking at a boat perched on a rim of dark blue water.

"You're right on the edge of the underwater canyon we call the Tongue of the Ocean, TOTO for short."

The water was so clear I could see the bottom from the air. Landing on the sea was an unsettling feeling; I was glad to step onto terra firma. I breathed in: floral perfume filled the air, and the slightest sting of ocean salt touched my skin. White gardenias and orange hibiscus, purple passionflowers and red bougainvillea spilled over the walkway and climbed the low trees by the water's edge. Gorgeous men with white smiles and skin as dark as espresso welcomed me and unloaded the tens of thousands of dollars of clothes I'd brought. I smiled in return, enjoying the lilt of their English. Birds' music filled the air, and somewhere I heard singing.

Up a cobblestoned path, shaded by palm trees, fig trees, and fruit trees hung with their crops, I followed the men. The air was intoxicating, like stepping into Marc Jacobs's newest fragrance. Bees, fat and yellow, bobbled by the flowers; hummingbirds took their fill of nectar and were gone in an eyeblink. Butterflies in colors and numbers I don't think I'd ever seen before floated through the air.

Even my lightweight jacket was too much, so I stripped it off and bared my artificially brown shoulders to the sun.

"Welcome, welcome," a woman called to me in a musical voice as she gestured the men to put my luggage in a workroom. "Welcome to da island, to da castle. Yo' flight was good?"

"Yes, thank you," I said.

"Everyone, dey be workin in da studio, but dey said for you to get settled in and enjoy da day."

"Gotta love that," I said. "Thank you."

"We'll take your luggage, you will be in dat tower," she said and pointed to one of the taller of the four towers around the building. "Oh, here be Mama Garcia," she said as an older black woman walked up. "She is de keeper ob de house."

Mama Garcia's smile was broad and welcoming. "Welcome

to da castle," she said in the accent I'd come to expect from everyone.

"A pleasure to meet you," I said to her, then looked up at the castle. Palace? It was boxy and made of reddish gold brick with a dozen towers and walkways. But it definitely wasn't English or Scottish. Something warmer, like Moroccan or Moorish. "This is an amazing place," I said. "Your job must be a pleasure." I looked back at her with a smile.

Her face had gone gray.

"You!" she cried, pointing an accusing finger at me. "You!"

I looked over my shoulder, then touched my chest. "Me?"

"What is it Mama Garcia?" the younger woman asked. "Do you need to sit down?"

"Look at her, look at her face!"

I touched my face; did I have ink on it? Was it a shock seeing such a white person? Blonde hair? What was wrong?

"What Mama Garcia?" the younger woman said.

"Dat girl, she wear de face of Deat' imself!"

Welcome to Paradise, Dallas O'Connor.

Chapter Two

I'm a vegetarian; but it's not a religious decision and I do eat fish. So is conch an animal or a vegetable or a fish? I stirred it around in its coconut-scented base and debated. I was alone in the dining room, my "face of Deat' imself" having given me the immediate cachet of being an undesirable. My view was stunning. The sky was cerulean blue and the pool was framed in red and purple bougainvillea. I hadn't seen any other people, and I wasn't sure if it was because my reputation had preceded me or if it was just an accident. It was almost three o'clock in the afternoon.

I wanted to cry.

Most people would laugh off Mama Garcia's comment: These are the islands; voodoo and witch doctors are probably local color. Except Mama Garcia was right—I do know death pretty well, face to face.

I shuddered.

"Too strong for you, lass?" a voice bellowed at me. I turned.

The owner of the voice looked like a pirate, but one wearing white instead of black. His face spoke of berserking Vikings somewhere in his lineage, but his coloring was dark, and he had brown braids falling over his shoulder from beneath a toque. "Do you like it?" he asked as he approached me. I noticed a long-handled knife stuck into a knot around his waist.

I looked at my bowl as though I'd never seen it.

"You don't eat conch?" he accused. "You're allergic to coconut? You have an aversion to anything with flavor and texture?" He swooped down and swiped the bowl. "You want Cheerios instead? Perhaps a nice peanut butter and jelly sandwich on Wonder bread?"

His eyes were amber, blazing mad, and every other word he said started with an "f." F-words bring the remembered taste of lye to my tongue. I still held my spoon. He was halfway across the room before I shouted. "What are you doing?"

He spun on his heel, balancing my soup in one palm, the other hand on his hip. "What, you prefer my cooking to starvation? Why, James Beard, I'm so honored!"

The first and only time my grandmother heard me use that word, the one he so liberally sprinkled his sentences with, she'd washed my mouth out with soap. Lye soap. For real. I had blisters on my tongue for a week.

"What is your problem?" I asked. "Just because I haven't swallowed it whole doesn't mean I don't like it."

"Do you like it?"

"Um," I stalled. "Well. I haven't actually tasted it yet."

"Not tasted it! It's been sitting in front of you for at least fifteen minutes, getting cold and rubbery, and you haven't even tasted it! At least hating it is some form of passion! God's bones wench, you're as unfeeling as a corpse!"

My lunch and my attacker disappeared through a set of swinging doors. Presumably they led to the kitchen.

I'd been sitting here, staring at the view, for fifteen minutes? That's pathetic, Dallas. I was hungry, but I'd be damned if I'd tangle with that wacko waiter again. Then I remembered his outfit: checkered pants, double-breasted jacket, clogs. Puffy white hat.

He was the chef; I'd bet money on it.

"Hey lady," a man said, coming out of the kitchen. "What'd you do to piss off Bigshitman?" Another pirate, but this one wore banker's pinstripe pants and a bandana, and had a lot of facial hair and even more tats than hair. Beneath the costume was a Spanish speaker, about twenty, with flat brown eyes and an unfriendly expression.

"He swears a lot," I said.

"Yeah, he can't control himself, like some sorta dog humpin' everything in sight. He's loco. He's mad."

"Mad at who?"

"Whom," the object of our discourse said as he stepped out of the kitchen. He glared at the lesser pirate, who flipped him off. "I can't control myself? Is that what you're saying?" he asked the lesser pirate.

"I didn't say it, man, the lady did."

The chef glared at me.

"I just said you swear a lot," I clarified.

"You have to clean it up, man," the lesser pirate said. "Your madre, she said you're gonna get thrown off the boat. By her, man."

"Leave my mother out of this," he said.

"Pitiful, you can't talk with normal people."

They held a conversation in quiet, abrupt, but obscene Spanish with a lot of words that were abbreviations or dialects of what I knew. I just wanted my lunch back, to get rid of the taste of lye in my mouth. The lesser pirate left, and the chef looked at me. "Do you think it's possible for a man to change the way he speaks in a mere fortnight?" He spoke carefully, editing out the f-word that he apparently used like punctuation.

I looked him up and down; he was tall and lean, with straight, sharp shoulders. He stood with his arms crossed, one leg bent over the other as he leaned against the wall. Put him on the runway for Dolce & Gabbana, or Gucci, and he would make a slave of every fashion reporter on the planet. He was gorgeous. Exotic. Sexy.

And loco. "Uh—"

"You like what you see, chica?"

"I'd like it better if you would give me something to eat," I smarted off—realized what I'd said—and wished to die on the spot. Accidental double entendres were not lost on this man.

"Oh, I can feed you," he said, eyes smoldering as he untied his apron. "Sate all your needs."

"Hey!" a shout from the kitchen stopped him. "Tu madre!"

With imprecations about the lesser pirate's parenthood, the chef left. I stood for a second listening to the shouting in a mixture of Spanish and French, with a lot of z's and k's and what sounded like Shakespeare. It was a good thing I'd packed Pria Bars, I reasoned and decided to find my room.

From the air, this place had looked like a hollow box. Once inside, it was more like a maze. The building rambled. I'd started at one end and hadn't found the other yet. Parts of it were at least four stories tall, while some others were only two. Some sections of the roof were pitched, others flat. Gardens and fountains and archways and tiles followed each other in a series that was dizzying. It was a beautiful labyrinth, one that anticipated El Cid or Scheherazade strolling through any minute, but a labyrinth nevertheless.

My room was in one of the anchoring towers, wrapped with a spiral staircase. I was on the third floor, three wraps around the building. An archway at the landing sheltered two doors. A tag with my name was hung over the handle of one of them. I stepped inside. "Ohmigosh."

A thousand and one Arabian nights.

The far wall was glass, looking out to sea. A bed, bigger

than my dining room at home, followed the half-moon shape of the room. Its head was flat against the left wall, and its foot curved, mimicking the doors that lined the opposite wall. Mirrors—dozens of different sized, styled, framed, and positioned mirrors—covered the walls, like a thousand different changing portraits of me. They were the art.

I sank down on the bed, built on a low platform. It was firm, but covered with a duvet of the plushest down. The linens were well worn Frette in the palest tinges of ochre and salmon—colors from the final moments of sunset. Pillows and small rugs formed a seating area beside the window. The view was spectacular, and looked out at a small garden overhanging the dark blue sea.

One ornately carved table contained a full bar, stocked with jewel-toned glasses and table linens. I opened the wall of doors and found my luggage, my clothes already hanging, my shoes filled with cedar horns and lined up, my jewelry laid on a small table inside, my cosmetics bag set on a vanity that pulled out to the window.

This is what it's like to be rich, I thought, and opened another ornately carved table, this one serving as a nightstand. I found a five CD player, a DVD player, and a selection of about a hundred movies and records. I rolled over three times to get to the other side of the bed, and found an intriguing box beside a basket of—"Food!"

Picnics like this don't come around too often. Brie and wine, pomegranate jam and some kind of bread—still warm. A small pot filled with pepper-flecked chilled shrimp and another with couscous. I read off the note: "Turn upside down on a plate to serve."

Curious, I took the supplied heavy pottery plate, and turned the couscous dish upside down. Spices had been painted on the bottom of the dish, so the couscous came out, already presentation worthy.

I nibbled a little bit of it, ate all the shrimp, then wiped my fingers. The box beside my picnic basket was really the most fascinating piece in the room. It was inlaid with shells and metal and fabric, Haitian style. I turned the key.

This room was meant for passion, no question. And the contents of this little box provided all the lotions, potions and protections that anyone could want. I slid the drawer back and found another item, one that made me smile. I mean, I've stayed in hotels that provided "intimacy kits," but this was one step further.

Obviously this place was designed by a woman. Down to the last detail. She provided for the optimum in self-sufficiency in the form of curved crystal. I laughed as I cleaned up my picnic and went into the bathroom to wash my hands.

The sybarites who had planned the bedroom had doubled their intention in the bathroom. Mirrored ceiling. Tub big enough for two, with drink holders. Always a sign it's my kinda bathtub. The Middle Eastern theme continued here, but the tiles were brightly colored. My foot sank three inches into the bath mat. Commode, bidet, vanity with makeup lights, double sinks and a shower stall with strategically placed handholds, completed the room.

The candles were Diptyque, and the toiletries were Prada single-shots. A pair of aromatherapy sandals (Zanzibar's cinnamon) and a short, white silk robe were all provided in a straw basket with "It's Better in the Bahamas" stitched on the side.

I had died and gone to heaven. I looked at my watch. But before heaven became a reality, I needed to do some work: prep the clothes. I cleaned up a little, promised my exquisite room that I would be back, then headed downstairs to the main building to find my styling kit.

Color. I don't think I'd ever seen so much in one place. Texas is great—pretty in places, but never bright, never cobalt and fuschia and screaming orange and highway sign yellow. I walked down from my turret, through a flower-edged walkway, and into the courtyard garden. The building embraced these green trails perfumed with flowers and sprinkled with birds and butterflies and lizards and tiny green snakes. I stepped through the first doorway I found, and started following the hall. Rooms were on the left, huge and exquisitely decorated, or closed, the heavy double doors shielding their secrets.

After a little stumbling around, I found the soundstage. Even in this architectural fantasia, it had a light outside the door. It wasn't red; they weren't recording. "Um, excuse me," I said to the two black men working inside. "I'm the wardrobe stylist. Do you know where my suitcases were stored?"

"Ees dat debil girl," one of them said to the other. They both reached for pendants around their necks and watched me with inky eyes from sculpted chocolate faces.

"Dose clotes are in de workroom next to Oscar's room, mon."

"Who is Oscar?" I asked.

"He be de chef, mon."

Oh groovy. The taste of lye in my mouth; the rush as I remembered how gorgeous he was. "Where is the storeroom?"

They gave me directions and I walked further down the corridor until I found it. The door opened easily, soundlessly, and I turned on the light switch and saw another fantasy.

A stylists' fantasy.

The workroom was enormous, but divided into sections. The far wall was lined with bookshelves, filled with decades of fashion magazines and photo books. A fireplace (empty) took up a portion of one wall. My suitcases were lined against the other. A table, an ironing board, and a huge, antique pants presser took up some more space. I unpacked my steamer, filled it, fished through my bag of necessary objects for an outlet converter, and plugged everything in.

I'd brought rolling racks, but I wasn't going to need them. Seven were already provided, empty. Another, hung with clothes, took up space in the back.

With a Sharpie, I labeled a card for each girl's rack, just like a fashion show.

I've worked on quite a few music videos, but I've never been the brainchild behind a "look." It used to be that an artist hired a stylist right at the point when they were getting ready to jump into the big time—not before the first album even came out.

For instance, Faith Hill. She dressed herself in Early Nashville until "This Kiss," then suddenly she was everywhere, in designer clothes, looking like she'd arrived. If I remembered correctly, she did "arrive" shortly after that. Her stylist had a lot to do with that transition from hick to hipster, and now Faith was regularly listed as best-dressed.

And Britney Spears? Was she on the cover of *Vogue* before picking up Kurt & Bart, who created all the furor-causing clothes—or lack of—she's worn in recent years. Not hardly.

Styling a whole group of people, however, would be a little different. Not only did each girl's look need to be what she wanted and felt comfortable with, it needed to gel with the others. First I needed to get to know the girls a little. The rest would come. I was good with people; I couldn't do this job if I wasn't.

And when in doubt, there were templates aplenty: The Spice Girls had five images: Posh, Sporty, Scary, Ginger and Baby. (I didn't know that, I had to call my sister Ojeda's kidlets to find out.) Guy groups tended to have the baggy skater, a pierced goth, a chain wallet punk (especially if he was some other race) and the white bread, clean cut, you-can-take-him-home-to-Mother indie rocker. The idea was the same, girls or guys: Enough options so that every audience member felt included.

"First," I said, "music." I had brought my own MP3, but I

was curious what CDs were left here. Female artists out the wazoo. I picked Shakira, Laundry Service, and cranked it.

Head bopping and hips swaying to the country/tango blend, I pulled out my well-thumbed notes and started hanging clothes. I'd made a lot of decisions based on the proportions and measurements they'd given me. No photos. Apparently it was part of their publicity campaign. "All would be revealed" in a video/radio blitz that would take place three-and-a-half weeks from today. CDs would be in stores that day, and the girls would start touring at the end of the month.

Until my washing machine was fixed, the floor repaired and a new tenant in place, I would not be styling on the road. It was just too big of a mess to leave for six months. I needed to get another job. Or marry a plumber slash mechanic. "That's a chilling thought," I said and turned back to my notes.

Eladonna was a tall, normal sized black girl with exceptionally long legs. I'd brought her a lot of short skirts. I unpacked her bags, tagged the outfits and snapped Polaroids of the ensembles I'd already created.

Ka'Arih—someone would have to tell me how to pronounce that—had curly brown hair and brown eyes. She was about a size six, about 5'8". Curvy. She got lots of looks that played up her tiny waist and well-developed chest.

Rozima had dark hair and dark eyes. According to the notes she was about 5'7" and wore a size four. Normal proportions, so I picked up some normal clothes.

London was 5'10", a former runway model. Lindsay had rifled through some old *Vogues* and found a few snaps of her from a Chanel show. With those shots and her old comp card (also provided by Lindsay), I had a fairly good idea what would look good on her. Anything. Blonde hair, blue eyes, cheekbones you could ski down. She was my ace.

Jillyian was the lead singer, and according to the numbers,

she had Miss America's body with red hair and "black" eyes. I couldn't even imagine that. At any rate, I had gotten some fun things for her.

I was about to unpack my sewing machine, when it dawned on me to look around first. This was a well-stocked place. They probably had a serger just waiting for me. I set down my machine and started opening doors. More proof a woman had designed this place—storage for everything.

Costumes, in boxes. Wigs, all kinds and colors. Boots— most of them in . . . "Thigh-high lace-ups in size 13. Interesting," I said to myself. I kept looking. Store mannequins, dressmaking mannequins, ironing boards and spare steamers. A suitcase, bigger than my roll-on styling kit, beat up and buffeted by a thousand journeys and covered in stickers from exotic locations.

Curiosity took over.

Because I'm one of a million siblings, I looked over my shoulder so no one would catch me snooping, then opened the bag. Obviously it was a stylist's kit.

It was incredibly organized, filled with cosmetic bags, labeled, some laid on top of each other and others filed side to side. "Lingerie—evening." "Bras—nude." "Pantyhose—new" "Jewelry—Daytime" All the labels were printed on sticky paper and attached. I ferreted through until I found a "Notions" kit, then . . . "Aha!" I said. Then I immediately felt ashamed.

Womens' quality handbags often come with a little bag for storage, so dust and dirt don't wear out the bag. This stylist's hams were in similar bags, with "Pressing Ham" *embroidered*—for God's sake—on the front. Amazed and a little horrified at the amount of anal-retentiveness this kit revealed, I started putting stuff back.

How thoughtful for someone to leave a kit here. I guessed they must host a lot of photo shoots, video shoots and other fashion-y stuff. It was a perfect location. Whoever had put the kit together had done a great job. I tossed in left-handed scissors, every kind of tape known to man (carefully labeled, the end cut off and marked with a piece of ribbon). The notions kit had a thousand snaps, pins and buttons. I turned one over and saw a name that always strikes fear into my heart: Bespoke, T. Charles.

The button clattered to the floor.

Chapter Three

I was still standing, staring at the button, when the bookcase slid back. The crazed chef stood there, with his foot-long knife in the sash around his waist and a tray held above his head. I stared. *The bookcase moved?*

"I have come to apologize for my uncouth behavior and I hope that I didn't cause you any great distress with my," he swallowed, "outburst. Welcome to Ladeeva Castle."

"Thank you," I said and threw the button in the box, the box in the bag, zipped it and stuffed it in the closet.

"You will be pleased to note that I've been . . . challenged . . . to refrain from using a certain word."

I slammed the closet door and tried not to grin. His self-editing was so obvious that he was almost stuttering.

"I hope you aren't doing that on my account," I said. I hate intolerance. I think the motto should be, if you don't like what you see, don't look.

He coughed a little. "No. My mother."

"I see." A man who listens to his mother? A forty-something-year-old man who listens to his mother? A forty-something man who looked like *this*, who listened to his mother? Was that weird or wonderful, I didn't quite know.

"It is her desire," he said carefully, "for me to escort her on a fu-freakin' journey around the world. She fears that my choices in vocabulary might be offensive to those in her . . ."

He was choking.

". . . social strata."

"How long do you have before you go bon voyage?"

"Are you jesting with me?"

"No, not at all," I said with a smile. "Just being friendly."

"I have more than two weeks."

"Wow. Do you always believe in miracles?"

The chef lost his first battle with swearing right then and there. With a muttered promise to return, he left through the bookcase. I watched in amazement as it slid into view and he slid out. "This really *is* a castle," I said to myself. Last time I'd seen a moving bookcase had been in a black-and-white movie.

I looked back at the closet, where the button was hiding inside the kit. It was just a button. A button!

Tobin Charles Bespoke was a former client, the job had been horrific but profitable, and the mastermind and CEO behind it all, Thom Goodfeather, had given me a goal in my career: to avoid working for him. Goals are supposed to be stated in the positive, and I was positive I would not work for him again. I was convinced he was a very bad man, and the FBI agreed.

However, he also manufactured the most exquisite suits this side of Armani. So, I'd found a button in a stylist's kit. It proved the kit had been close to a great quality suit at one point. "It's just a button," I said out loud.

The button had nothing to do with me. Just a button. Thom Goodfeather wasn't going to come get me here when he knew my address in Dallas. "Don't be stupid," I said and set up the sewing machine. Then I unpacked all of the shoes, and started to tape the bottoms. It's a tedious job, trimming the edges so they don't show, and still covering the entire sole.

I was dancing to "Te Dejo Madrid," when the door opened. I turned down the music. "You're a vegetarian wench, eh?" Oscar was standing in the doorway this time, much more conventional.

"I'm not sure I'm any kind of *wench*," I said.

"We'll ask the judges at the end of the bout," he said and entered the room, carrying a tray. "Where shall I set this?"

My organized chaos had taken up all horizontal spaces, so I stacked some empty suitcases and indicated that platform.

He eyed it, bit back a few swear words, I'm sure, then set the tray down. "Are you going to eat now, or should I have called ahead and let you get that fifteen minutes of staring out of the way?"

The shrimp had been hours ago. "I'm starving."

"I thought you might be." He removed the cover and I almost whimpered. It looked like images from a *Gourmet* shoot. My mouth watered.

"A simple country lunch," he said. "Plaintain fritters, black-eyed pea salsa, mango, pineapple and coconut slaw and for dessert, a little key lime gelato."

I looked at the silver saucer filled with gelato. "It's yellow?"

He growled.

I stepped back.

"You, my uncouth lass, are as ignorant as a post! Key limes, contrary to what Luby's and others of that ilk do to food—though I hardly deign to call it food—that they claim is made with key limes, is a crime worthy of decapitation! Key limes are not green inside, anymore than blueberries are blue inside. Key limes are yellow! Yellow! A green pie is not key lime, it is an abomination wrought of food coloring and cartoon tastes! Key limes are yellow."

"Yellow," I said.

"Don't look at me that way, I am not a madman. I just cannot abide culinary ignorance, though in fact that is not culinary ignorance, that is just trailer park idiocy! Green," he muttered. "Split pea soup is green. Nothing is neon green like fake key lime pie except, perhaps, radiator fluid."

The fritters were uniformly round, the salsa was spiked with slivers of onion and tomato. "May I eat now?" I asked.

"Pardon me," he said, suddenly contrite. He pulled up a chair and placed the napkin in my lap as though it were a starred restaurant. "Would you care for wine?"

My fork was halfway to my mouth. "Wine?"

"Or beer, that would be better," he said. He went back to the door and picked up a picnic basket. Bottles protruded from it and he opened a Kalik for me.

I crunched into my first plantain fritter. It had the texture of fried bananas, but not as sweet. I groaned aloud, unable to help myself.

Embarrassed, I glanced up at the crazed man, and he was watching me, and . . . I don't think I'm overstating this, he was looking at me with lust. I almost choked on my food, his expression was so incendiary. We stared at each other a moment, then he leaned forward and dabbed at my lip. "Salsa," he said.

We locked gazes as Shakira sang about "cheap metaphors."

He turned around and walked out the door, pulling it closed behind him. I pressed the beer to my forehead, then my throat. The food was spicy, but I felt a bit melted for altogether a different reason.

And he listened to his mother.

"Dallas O'Connor?" a woman called as she opened the door.

I'd just finished my yellow, velvet-textured gelato and was

thinking about proposing to that nutcase named Oscar, just so he could cook for me. It had nothing to do with the breadth of his shoulders, his young Clint Eastwood features, his light olive skin and luminous eyes. The man was a cooking god.

I smiled at her. "Hi, I'm Dallas."

"Oh, thank God you're here. I'm Bette, Donny's assistant. When we heard how Mama Garcia just snapped on you, well, we weren't sure if you had stolen a boat and sailed to Alice Town or thrown yourself into the sea." Bette was short and round, with stringy hair and a harried expression. But her eyes were hypnotizing, silvery-blue and enormous. She couldn't be much past twenty-five. "Welcome to Ladeeva Castle. I'm so sorry you had a rough start. At least Oscar found you and fed you."

"Oscar, right." Just confirming. "What's his last name?"

"The chef? Oscar Izarra."

Ding. Latino. I should have known why I was inextricably, physically and emotionally attracted to him. Latino. Damn, damn, damn.

A friend of mine has a thing for Custo Barcelona. T-shirts, blouses, skirts, it doesn't matter. If it's Custo, she must have it. She's not a collector, because she doesn't keep them. She acquires a Custo piece, wears it for a while, then sells it. She's not into ownership, she just wants the experience of wearing each piece.

Since each garment is a copywritten piece of art, I can understand her compulsion.

I also have a friend who is a polka-dotted shoe freak. She buys every polka dotted shoe made. Asics to Zinotti, if it has spots, she's there. Also a compulsion, though she keeps all her pairs.

My habit is a little more complicated because it's not things, it's men. Latino men. Men with dark skin and names like Garcia, Alejandro, Ricardo . . . Izarra. The worst part is,

I don't even realize when I'm acting on the habit, it's so compulsive. Latin man? Must have him; instantly I desire to serve paella and dance the tango and quote Pablo Neruda.

Yeah, I know he wrote in Portuguese. Brazilian men respond to him beautifully.

I'm trying to get beyond my compulsion—one that's led me in and out of marriage, and more boyfriends than I can count with a straight face. Oscar Izarra was part of an addiction I was giving up. I sighed, sad and mournful already. That was a pool in which I dared not dip my toe. A great-looking, great-cooking, passionate, mother-listening pool. But the sign said "Do Not Enter, Dallas O'Connor. I Mean You." Latino men were big trouble for me.

"Oscar did find me," I said to Bette. "My lunch was amazing."

"You don't have to tell me," she said, patting a curvy hip, "I eat in his Miami place, Ziren, all the time. About midnight I get jonesing for his coconut *suspiros*."

Coconut kisses?

"Anyway," she said, "I just wanted to greet you. We have cocktails in about two hours, on the beach."

Pinch me! I nodded. "Great. I look forward to it."

"Did you get settled in okay?"

"This place is just magnificent. I've never—"

"The owner can go a little overboard," Bette said, "but her taste is excellent."

How can you overdose on Frette sheets or imported cassis?

She looked past me to the racks of clothes, and shuddered. "You are going to have your hands full, girl."

"Is there a problem?" I asked.

"Nope, you're here, FOP will be out of the recording studio soon, then it's going to be one, big, freakin' happy family." She smiled again, which just underscored her sarcasm, and left.

FOP—Fate of Paradise. I turned my chair and looked at the clothes. Eight outfits per girl had been the request. I'd brought three times that many, just for options. Being a wardrobe stylist is all about giving people options. I slipped my phone out of my handbag and dialed Lindsay.

"Artistic Alliance," she said smartly.

"How many stylists have they fired?" I asked.

"Dallas darling! How is the island? Have you met any fabulous dark men? Are you sipping something pastel with a parasol in it, under a palm tree, and just called to torture me? Personally, I'm at the Margarita Ranch sipping one of those lovely little concoctions with banana in it, in honor of you. So how is it?"

Lindsay has a way of deflecting ire. She starts off so jolly and gives you so many questions to respond to that you forget why you called. Not this time. "How many, Lindsay?"

"This is only my second darling, it's barely three o'clock."

"Stylists, not margaritas."

"What? Oh well, darling, I don't know anything as gauche as a number."

Which meant she did. I was silent, I even turned down Shakira.

"I mean, I only heard a teeny snippet here and there."

"Like?"

"Well, the girl who did that video, you know with all the stars singing that old song—"

"Yes?"

"They didn't like her."

"Who is 'they'?"

I could almost hear her shrug. "Whoever pays the bills."

"When did they decide they didn't like her?"

"Oh, well—"

"Lindsay."

"On the last day of prep. She'd been on the job ten days."

Groovy. "Anyone else?"

"Umm, well, who is it that picks the clothes for the Oscars? You know, the awesome one? Our fave?"

There are as many Oscar stylists as there are stars, but Lindsay and I agreed on one. "They fired her?" I sat up, suddenly a little unnerved.

"She didn't click with them, creatively, you know. It's nothing Dallas. Just artistic differences."

"How many, altogether, have had artistic differences with this group?" I said.

"Well . . ." I could almost see her gnawing her Fire Island glossed lip. "I've only heard about "—ty.""

"What did you say?"

"—ty."

"Twenty?" My head was light.

"Noooo."

"Thirty?" I reached for the empty beer bottle and placed it against my forehead.

"Uh, no."

"Forty?" I croaked.

"Yes."

"Oh God," I whimpered. "They've fired forty stylists?"

"Forty-two, to be exact."

Wouldn't want to *not* be exact.

Chapter Four

A t the cocktail hour, I stepped into the scene, which was a little unbelievable it was so stunning. Of course, I've heard people wax on about the Bahamas, but when I'd come down here for a fast three-day bikini shoot or a weekend bachelorette thing, I'd never really paid attention.

Now, I was paying attention.

The light was spectacular; it bathed everything in a glow that seemed healthy and sexy and full of life. The smells—the trees, the flowers, the sea and whatever was being grilled at the other end of the garden, made me want to strip and eat and dance, all at the same time. Everything was music: the tinkle of fountains, the soft laughter of men and women, the clink of expensive crystal and birdsong. Wonderful birdsong, punctuated with the scream of a peacock.

They are paying me to be here? I have the best job in the world.

Shoulders back, stomach and butt tucked, I walked down the stairs from the upper terrace of the garden, to the lower, where everyone else was. It was about twenty steps, then another twenty to the sugar-white beach. I looked over my shoulder, and saw how the sun turned the building to copper, and cast the palm trees' shadows on the walls and across the courtyard. I turned around and continued my descent.

I stopped on the lower terrace and accepted a mini bottle of champagne, with a straw. For a moment I watched the water. I've never been much into color; my wardrobe is largely black, my house mostly white. I've never painted, I've never bought something for its color. I'm a texture person, if I had to choose.

But the colors here, the vibrancy! I might move to the Bahamas, to Bimini, just to see this every day. I looked into the garden, the blooming flowers looked softer in the late light. About fifteen people moved around, laughing and talking.

I've never arrived, mid-job. The fact that so many stylists had worked on this project before me was disconcerting, but only a little. I know clothes, I know bodies, and I know how to sell a concept. This was different in that I was selling the girls, not their garments, but that should be the exciting part. Heaven knew I was sick of working on catalogues.

It's not an interview, I told myself as I hit the last step, you already got the job.

And I still had the Centurion.

"Hello, cherub," an angelic-looking man said to me as I stepped onto the velvet-green grass. "I'm Donny Pedretti, these young fillies' manager." His russet ringlets were the only angelic part of him, the rest was vying for sin in a big way. He was a medium size guy, but he projected height and breadth. His suit was Sean Jean and his shirt Brioni. He had nice (bare) feet, and wore a single ivory tusk on a chain around his throat. He could have been anywhere between late 20s and 50. His energy was great, he was timeless and hip. Tiny tinted glasses hid his eyes, but his smile was wide and a little wild. He kissed my hand.

Three girls ran to his side, giggling. One was light black, one was Hispanic, and one was some red-haired offspring of

South Sea islands that would have driven Gauguin mad with desire.

"Eladonna, Zima, and Jillyian, this is your new stylist."

"You're going to make us look like rock stars!" The redhead raised her glass and toasted us all, amidst shouts and cheers from the others.

"Thank you so much for coming," the Hispanic girl, Zima, said. "We're so happy to have you."

"So happy," Eladonna said.

"Thrilled," Jillyian said.

I smiled back at them as another redhead floated in. She carried herself like a cat, and had emerald green eyes and short red hair in a cut that screamed Paris and high-maintenance. "You are?" she said, offering me a limp hand to shake.

"Dallas O'Connor," I said.

"Dallas, that is just the coolest name," one of the band girls said.

"I knew this girl named—"

"I am Sascha," the catwoman said to me. "Donny vill not tell you, but I am best makeup in all bideo." She had Michelle Pfeiffer's cheekbones and Natasha & Boris's Russian accent. She shook my hand. "Smoke?"

"No, thank you."

"Pity. I need cigarette." She floated off, allowing me to admire the black flapper dress she wore, decorated with a thousand jet beads.

"This is London and Ka'Arih," Donny said of the two new girls who had joined us.

I almost choked on my drink. "'Carrie' is how you pronounce that?" I asked a curly haired brunette. Inside I was screaming Nooooo!

She nodded and smiled. "Ain't it cute? I mean, the way they spell it and everythin' at the record company?"

She was as sweet looking and sounding as kandy korn. When I thought I might not weep, I turned to London, one of the many models who'd adopted one name for the runway. She had been my failsafe.

London was bringing me down.

This mannequin-turned-chanteuse hadn't just changed careers, she'd upped her dress size three times. From a four to a ten, maybe an eight (but I was thinking ten). Her hair was a luminous golden sheet, her skin and eyes were clear and filled with health, and her backside would no more fit in lace-up Shelli Segal leather pants than—"How do you do," she said. "So pleased to meet you." But her eyes hadn't changed, they were still a haunting green, surrounded with two-inch long black lashes. True color lashes. Her hair was true colored too.

Her voice had the distinction of no accent; either growing up in California or attending fifteen schools in five years.

"Thank you, it's a pleasure to be here," I said.

"I'm Teddy," a man in black spandex said. "The dietician—"

"The exercise nazi!" one of the girls said.

"The sleep guru—"

"And our choreographer," Jillyian said, smiling up at him. She was probably in her early 20s, but she was realizing her power as a woman, it was obvious in the way she moved. I grinned and she winked at me. Teddy looked a little flustered as she ran her hand over his buzz cut. "He's the best, just the best." She continued to tease him, running her hand over his chest and his stomach. "He teaches us every single move to make, every way to twist and turn our bodies." As she spoke, she added some hip action. "He shows us how to bump and—"

"Drinks?" The lesser pirate thrust a tray into our midst. The sun was almost gone, and silent servants were lighting Moroccan lamps throughout the gardens. The wind shifted and I smelled gardenias and hyacinth and jasmine. "These are Negril Sunsets, with coconut cream, orange liqueur, orange juice, lime juice, and a dash of strawberry juice. Those garnished with orange are Orangeotangs, with orange, milk and pimento," he said.

"Pimento in a drink? Isn't that the red stuff in that poor-people's slimy cheese?" Jillyian snapped at him in a complete reversal of her other behavior.

Eladonna refused everything. "Coconut, milk, they're both bad for me."

"I can make you something else," he said.

"I really don't like rum," she confessed.

Donny took a Sunset and I did too.

Welcome to Paradise, for real.

Ka'Arih said she didn't drink hard stuff. "I'm just such a lightweight, alcohol goes straight to my head and makes me giddy." She giggled. "But I can take care of a six pack in the time it takes to get from my cousin's house to the border!"

Everyone laughed and toasted again.

"Well, to Dallas," Donny said.

"She's gonna make us rock stars!" Jillyian shouted, and all the girls joined in, then the crew that was scattered throughout the gardens picked it up until "rock stars" was a chant that sounded like it was alive on its own.

"See you at dinner," Ka'Arih said, and the five of them toddled off, Teddy leading the pack.

"Have y'all been here long?" I asked Donny, sipping my Sunset, the breeze playing with the fringe of the antique shawl tied around my hips.

"No, no, this little escape is only about five days old. I felt it would be more productive in the long run to get everyone here, convince them to turn off their cell phones, and get some work done." He flashed his dangerous smile. "Besides, that also leaves time for some fun, doesn't it, Dallas O'Connor?"

"Absolutely."

"Let me introduce you to the boys in the band," he said. "I

think you're really going to enjoy yourself. And get paid top dollar, it's not a bad deal, is it?"

"Not at all," I said with a smile.

Three men emerged from the shadows: a prep, a nerd and a stereotypical musician with long hair. They all just happened to be fairly young and decidedly good-looking. I was exchanging smiles with John, who was telling me he'd dropped out of Julliard, when a bell rang from the castle.

Sascha appeared out of the dusk and linked her arm through mine. "Come," she said in her husky-voiced heavy accent. "Dinner is good and Oscar is crazy. If we not sit now, he might throw knife. But at least he is not cursing tonight."

"Do you know him well?" I asked.

"Enough to know a man who cook like this, never does he need ask for blow job. Offers all the time," she said as we entered a dining room designed for the king of Africa.

A long table, set with china and crystal, red linens and zebra accents, awaited us in the center of the room. Each chair was a miniature carved wooden throne, crowned with a different creature. Two of the walls boasted walk-in fireplaces. Animal heads adorned the walls, and kilim rugs covered the floors. The centerpiece consisted of feathers, beads and blood red peonies, each the size of a child's head.

A waiter whisked dishes in and out of the room, and I found myself seated in a chair topped by a folkart-style carved mermaid. Donny was beside me, and the girls surrounded us. We'd barely sat down before Oscar appeared like a wraith at the foot of the table, the deep red of his chef's coat a perfect match to the flowers, the napkins and the rugs. This whole place was styled by a genius.

"Dinner tonight is either marlin steak with ginger sauce and yallo butter rice, followed by a salad of root vegetables, or wild mushroom ravioli with bonnet sauce. Dessert will be served in the drawing room, with coffee and liqueurs."

An army of waiters poured out of the kitchen and opened

wine, as others presented the dishes. I chose the marlin. Everyone was served. Oscar waited as the covers were removed, the bread was passed and we were poised. "Bon appetit," he said and vanished into the kitchen.

Mine was not the only exclamation at the artistry of the plate.

I come from a large family, and there were a few occasions in my life when the food was so stupendous, that silence fell. One was eating barbecued crab in Beaumont, Texas. One was the first year my granddaddy decided venison bacon would taste good in the Thanksgiving dressing. This was like those moments. Twenty people were immersed in their plates, the wonder of sensations running across their palates. I heard little moans of delight and a few comments about how good it was, but no one tried to converse.

Each bite was to be savored, and the wines were perfect accompaniment. I forgot about my erotic jungle gym of a bedroom. I forgot about my new-found adoration of Prada face care products. I even forgot about Oscar. We all ate slowly, trying to prolong the moment, but eventually, it was over.

Donny sat back, his eyes closed and his head leaning against the bear that ruled his chair.

"I'm going to have to get padded leg irons," I muttered as I sopped up the last of the rum-butter-ginger sauce on my plate. I know the rule; sopping is against it. My grandmama, were she dead, would be spinning in her grave (though not too fast, in case her skirt flared out inappropriately). But honestly, this food was worth a possible felony charge for kidnapping a chef.

"Oh!" Ka'Arih exclaimed. "Did you get the dungeon room?"

"There's a dungeon room?" I asked.

"Who knows what all is in here," Eladonna said. "Some people have more time and money than sense."

I made a little assent noise, but that was it. I know better than to brag on what I have. I'm from a big family. Someone else might want it. I looked down the table and saw John in deep conversation with Sascha. She looked at me and winked. I smiled and turned back to the girls.

"Fate of Paradise," I said, "what's with the name?"

They shrugged. "We just make the music," Zima said. "The marketing types make those decisions."

"Donny?" I said and turned to him.

"I don't work for the record company," he said. "I work for these angels." He smiled at them, and they smiled back, six beautiful people so pleased to be in their world. Donny coughed and turned back to me. "But research shows that groups with more than one name, but less than four, tend to sell thirty percent more records than groups with either four or more names, or just one name."

"So are the Beatles, *The* Beatles?" I asked.

He grinned. "I knew you would think of exceptions to the rule. This is current research. Today, the Beatles might be called O2b Beatles, or—"

The girls jumped in, throwing out suggestions so fast you couldn't tell who was who.

"Beatles JaRule."

"Backstreet Beatles."

"Beatles on Keys."

"P. Buddy Beatles."

"Destiny's Beatles."

The girls were giggling again. Donny refilled our glasses. "Fate of Paradise" is a name that links beauty images with the forbidden, which makes it more desirable to the average eighteen-to-twenty-three-year-old consumer."

"That's your market?" I asked them.

"Well, we're scheduled to take off most of our clothes and be shot by *Maxim* for the cover story," Eladonna said. "I hope it's because they're our market."

"Actually, research shows that a third of CDs are bought by those over forty years old, but they are inclined to buy what they like," Donny said.

"Ahh, so they're not influenced by massive advertising campaigns," I said.

"But teens buy twenty-two percent of all CDs," he said. "And even if their parents don't buy CDs for themselves, they'll buy for their kids."

I took a sip of wine and contemplated whether or not an 18 to 23-year-old should be considered a "kid." I said nothing.

"But honestly," Jillyian said, "I think our music is about the freedom women have today. Our songs are to reach out to her and tell her anything is possible—"

"Rock on—" Zima said.

"—And that any dream she has, she can make come true. You know, the past year has made almost everyone rethink, you know, why they're here—"

"That's so the truth—" Eladonna said.

"—and our message is to hang in there, do what you want—" London said.

"Don't put up with some guy's bullshit—" Eladonna said.

"But don't be uncaring—" Ka'Arih said.

"Or cold—" Eladonna said.

"That it can be about you, for a while, if you use that energy you get from whatever it is you do and turn it to help other people—"

I felt like I was watching a volleyball game, between Jillyian and the other girls' interjections. And everyone interacted, no one was silent. It was either well-rehearsed or these were in-sync females.

"And our songs aren't all about a guy—"

"That's so lame—"

"It's about chance—"

"About change—"

"About having fun—"

"About giving back—"

"I mean, we're all so lucky—"

"We're all Cinderellas in the end," Jillyian said.

"How did you all end up here?" I asked.

Donny leaned forward again, with another smile. He topped off everyone's glasses. "It was a contest."

"Fairest in the land!"

"Smallest feet!"

"Baddest ass dancers!"

They giggled.

"It was all of that, and so much more," Donny said. "The record company searched far and wide for talented musicians who could also write and dance and sing. We found Rozima in—"

"New Mexico," she said.

"Eladonna's from—"

"Chicago's where I stay. Or Madrid."

"But she was in pre-law in Georgetown, really," Jillyian said.

"Pre-law?" I asked.

Eladonna shrugged. "My parents are both serious type-A personalities. I'd shelved the whole music dream—"

"Then Nine Eleven—" Jillyian said.

"Yeah, that whole confusion made me think I had to try my dream, or I'd be sorry, whenever it came my time to leave this world, you know?" Eladonna said.

"How'd your parents react?" I asked.

"They were really cool. My mom had gone to med school with no family support, so while she didn't understand *musica* as a choice, she respected that I wanted to try."

"Eladonna's dad is some radical Republican," Ka'Arih said. "Bucks."

"What about you?" I asked her.

"I'm from North Dakota, but I lived in Virginia before that. I still sound southern, don't I?"

"You do," I said.

"But nothin' like you. You sound really southern."

"Born and bred," I said with a grin.

"I," Jillyian said, "had a very supportive family and the contest was being decided right down on Music Row, so I tried out."

"You're in Tennessee?" I asked.

"Grew up listenin' to Dolly Parton and Mary Chapin Carpenter and Shania Twain."

Good Lord, she was so young. I turned to Donny. "You didn't know these girls? You just stumbled on them as a manager?"

"Something like that," Donny said, rising. "Uh, ladies, Oscar has come out of the kitchen a few times, so we should head to the drawing room."

"He almost got Teddy in the butt yesterday with his knife," Ka'Arih said.

"Oscar really does throw knives?" I asked.

"Nothing actionable," Eladonna said. "Just artistic."

"He has a temper and I think he's a little crazy," Zima said.

"But he can cook!" Ka'Arih said.

"Damn straight," I said, surprised at how tipsy I felt once I was standing. We were the only ones left in the room. We walked through an empty double fireplace into an adjoining room.

Was I on a set in a Merchant Ivory film? This was a drawing room: damask covered walls, antique furniture and tapestries. Jillyian sat down at a pale-gold baby grand and began to move her fingers across the keys. Zima played drums, Eladonna played bass, Ka'Arih and London sang. I recognized the song as Blu Cantrell's, "Hit 'Em Up Style." The tune was groovy, and the lyrics were amusing. A girl goes shopping to pay her boyfriend back for cheating.

"Hey," Donny said, sitting down next to me, "the original

guitarist on that piece was named Dallas, too. Dallas and style in the same song, and now you're here to give my singers style."

"Karma," Sascha said, sitting down on my other side.

"Dallas is an unusual name," Teddy said. "Though, I met this girl in one of my strippercise classes named Aransas. That's a place in Texas, isn't it?"

"It is," I said. "Though I haven't heard it as a girl's name before."

The girls moved on to a Shawn Colvin piece, and Ka'Arih picked up a fiddle, while London sang and played harmonica.

"Named after city, this is common thing?" Sascha asked in her broad accent.

"I don't think so," John, the musician, said.

"Well, I don't know," Teddy said. "Paris Hilton."

"London, up there on stage," Donny said.

"And my siblings," I said, and started ticking them off my fingers. "Sherman, Houston, Beaumont, Augustina, Ojeda, Christi, and Mineola," I said.

They stared at me with open mouths.

"They . . . all your brothers and sisters?" Sascha asked. She blew smoke over her shoulder.

Teddy and John were laughing. "How did your parents keep you all straight?"

I shrugged. "They made up a code."

"What was it?"

"It really doesn't make a whole lot of sense unless you are from Texas," I said. "It's kind of lame, and seventies."

"C'mon," another musician said. "What's the code?"

I set down my glass. "So how 'bout d.a. ole Cowboys, man?"

Donny frowned. "That's the key?"

"Yeah. The first letter of each word stands for a child's name. S, H, B, D, A, O, C, M."

Donny frowned. "You're 'd'?"

"Yeah, I share a word with Augustina. But at least I'm not 'ole.'"

"What are the names again?"

So I went through them, half a map's worth of my siblings' names.

The girls changed to classical. "Are they going to play some of their own music?" I asked. "I haven't heard Jillyian sing live—but the demo was awesome."

"London sings when they are just playing around. Jillyian has to save her voice," Donny said. "Dessert should be here; I'll go see what's keeping Oscar."

Sascha stubbed out her cigarette. I'd seen her smoke five cigarettes. She never took more than two puffs, then she just let it burn down. "I go put on lipstick," she said, and left.

"Was it something I said?" I asked Teddy, the only remaining person.

"I guess they don't like performing for free," he said. "Either that, or like most bands, they can't play live, just in a studio."

Oscar, in civilian clothes (a Joseph A shirt and Diesel jeans), appeared. "Gateau De Patate and Coquimol are set up on the sideboard for dessert, and my sous-chef Palize will help you with coffee selections. We also brought in a remarkable coffee liqueur from Sangster's, in Jamaica. Enjoy."

At the mention of sweets, the five girls of Paradise raced to get in line.

I wandered over to Oscar. I'm just going to be polite, I argued with the part of my brain that flashed warning signals. "Dinner was delicious," I said to him.

"You are surprised?"

"That sauce, that steak," I said, ignoring his sarcasm. "I've never had marlin before. Is that the big fish with a spear-looking nose?"

"I'll teach you to catch it one day," he said with a smile. "If you are game, lass?"

Dallas. Bad Idea. I smiled and muttered something. Coffee. I needed something to counteract all the wine.

Palize, the lesser pirate, gave me a goblet of coffee liqueur.

Teddy offered me some cake from his plate, but I was perfectly content and refused him. "I shouldn't have any of this either," Teddy said. "Especially after dinner. Spiking my blood sugar isn't a great idea, but look at this." He shook his head in amazement as he cut into a heavy cake, covered in cream. "Amazing," he said. "You're a runner?" he asked.

I nodded.

"Morning or evening?"

I turned my attention to him. He was smiling at me, a big guy with abs so cut I could see the ridges through his Dri-weave shirt.

"Morning. I'm looking forward to hitting the beach."

"Wake me when you go," he said with a wink. "Make me do a few extra sprints."

Was it the alcohol or something else that made my pulse jag just a little.

The girls sat down and played a few Cole Porter songs, then Donny stood up. "I know the night is young, but it's time for the ladies of Paradise to get to bed, to *sleep*," he said with emphasis, glaring at them like a cross-dressed grandmother over the tiny colored rectangles of his glasses. "Dallas and Sascha will meet you on set. Come clean-faced and in workout togs."

He brushed aside any complaining. "Tomorrow night we can party, but you must look your best for the first day of the video."

Bette stood up. "The coffee bar will be in the soundstage area, and a full breakfast will be available in the dining room."

"I have to go," Teddy said. "Get my charges into bed. Will you be here later?" he asked me.

"I spent all last night clubbing in South Beach," I said. "I think I'll crash now and see you on set."

"Ciao bella," he said and coaxed the girls out of the room and off to bed.

"Now that the children are gone, the adults can play," Donny said to me. "More wine? Or some champagne?"

Sascha swooped in again. "I have scoop," she said to me. "Come, we go find peace."

"Later," I said to Donny and walked through the room with Sascha. She led me down a sconce-lined hallway and through a door. The warmth of the outdoors, the scents of night, and the sound of crickets surrounded us.

Sascha took my hand and guided me through the gardens; fountains and trees and tiled pools, until we were looking out over the water, in a little garden draped with white open flowers. "We missed it," she said as she sat down. "Two times I miss now."

"Miss what?" I asked, looking around. The moon was up, a chunky crescent.

"Those flowers" she said, pointing to a white morning glory. "They open in one minute as the sun vanishes. Moon-flowers they are called." As she spoke, she extracted a doobie from her bag. "You like?"

"I think I'm flying enough right now," I said. It's not that I haven't used grass, just not on a job. Or in the U.S. Truth be told, grass just made me horny and hungry and impossible to satisfy on either count.

"It makes me sleep like baby, but only after banging a boy like kettle," she said with a laugh as she inhaled and held it.

I chuckled. "Have you been here long?"

"I arrive after girls, two maybe three days ago."

"What's the deal with all the stylists?" I asked.

"What do you mean?" She handed me the joint "You are here," she said. "Beautiful island. Why not enjoy?"

I took a hit and handed it back.

"I just heard they'd been through a lot of stylists."

"Ahh, I know now. I see. Yes, has been a hard time to make everyone work together in States, so they came here to no distractions."

"So I'm the only stylist since y'all arrived on the island?" I refused another puff.

She looked at me as though my words didn't really make sense. "Aah . . ." Sascha shrugged her shoulders.

"Were you doing the styling *and* the makeup?" I asked. It was a common thing with clients who didn't know styling was a full-time job. The makeup artist would do both jobs until someone wised up, or the makeup artist protested. Or quit.

Sascha shrugged again—obviously she didn't want to complain.

"Y'all came here to get everything done at once?"

"Yes. Is final hour," she said on a long exhalation.

I stared out at the sand, the sea. "It's perfect here," I said.

"Tonight, do you want to sleep with John?"

"The musician?"

"Yes, very cute with blond hair and gray eyes."

"Why?"

"He would very much like to get to know you better, he said."

"Really, he said that?"

"No, but I see it in his eyes. My grandmother was gypsy, I have sixth sense."

"What about a dark man?" I asked.

"No, no. Better with John, to make beautiful blond babies."

"God, Sascha, you sound like my mother."

She laid a hand on my arm. "My God! My mother too! Always, it's Sascha why you no make babies, why there is no husband?"

"My mother cares less about the husband and more about keeping the gene pool well-peopled with O'Connors," I said.

"She doesn't want you to marry?"

"I think I'm too old for her to care."

"And your father?"

"He'd die, an illegitimate grandchild would just kill him."

"Your parents are happy?"

"Enough, I guess. They have a weird relationship. Co-dependents, do you know this word?"

"Two people who need each other so they can stay screwed up, da?"

I laughed. "Da, indeed."

"Well, I am stoked and now must find man who make me sleep like baby," she said and kissed my cheeks. "I see you in the morning."

"Should I wish you luck?" I said.

Sascha picked up the hem of her dress and pulled it off over her head. She had a flapper's figure, long and lean, small breasts, no hips and not much waist. Her jet bead necklace hung down to her black lace tanga panties. Both of her nipples were pierced. "With this, you think I need luck?" she asked. She smiled and turned down to the beach.

I laughed—not really.

I went back to the castle to find my room. I knew that my tower was on the opposite side of the island. How to get there, I didn't know. After wandering through the maze for a while, I bumped into Palize. He was showered and smelled sweet. He tried to hide the flowers he was carrying. "Where am I?" I asked.

"Where you are, or where you going?"

"Both," I said, laughing.

He pointed me through the gardens and the building. I thanked him and walked away. I turned around and called through the garden in Spanish, "Have a lovely evening."

"You too senorita."

I followed his directions and found myself at the foot of the stairs to my tower, or if I turned, I could take the path to the garden ledge that I had seen from my bedroom. You're drunk, Dallas. Go to bed.

It's a pity to waste that big bed, I told myself.

As though someone could read my mind, I heard my named called. I turned around and saw Donny. "Are you lost?" he asked.

"Not exactly."

"You never came back."

"I got lost."

He laughed as he walked down to me. His shirt was open a few more buttons and his glasses were on his head, holding back his hair. "It's a perfect night," he said as he stepped beside me.

I nodded.

"May I kiss you?" he asked as he slipped an arm around my waist.

I nodded.

Chapter Five

My alarm went off at 6 a.m. and I sat up, completely awake and fully energized. The bed was trashed and I shook my head ruefully as I slipped on my running shorts and bra top. My Air Rift Nikes were carefully laid on the floor of my closet and I slipped them on, then sneaked out the door. Donny's room was next to mine and I paused on the landing, wondering if I should continue the serious canoodling we'd began the night before, or go running.

He was cute, but that was last night. And let's not forget the small point that he's your boss, Dallas. I dashed down the stairs and inhaled the new day.

Sunrise was in a few minutes, and if I wanted to be by the water, I'd better move. I stretched, then started off slowly, through the gardens to the first archway, and out.

Pale golden light shot out across the water, turning it black and silver. The birds were in full conversational mode. I picked up the pace as I ran to the beach. I didn't know if there was a path or a trail. I'd just run along the water's edge.

I had days to discover this place.

"Good morning, lass," Oscar said as I jogged up to the

castle a half hour later. "I gather from the glow on your lovely face that your run was pleasant?"

"Spectacular," I said as I stopped. I stretched as I watched him. "What are you doing?"

"Shucking oysters," he said, and quick as that, he cracked open another to reveal its pearly interior and the gray jewel inside it. "Try one?"

"Only if I can have a Bloody Mary too," I joked, standing one-legged while I stretched my hamstring.

"That can be arranged, my lady." He held the oyster out to me. "Here, the freshest you'll ever have. While you were running, I was corralling these rascals."

I tossed back the oyster, slick and cool as it slid down my throat. Oscar handed me a Bloody Mary with a missing sip as I stretched my other hamstring.

"It was mine," he said, "so it's peppery."

I shrugged. I'm from Texas. I know hot.

I took a swig of the drink.

I *thought* I knew hot.

My eyes bulged. My face turned red. Oscar handed me another fresh oyster and I kept it in my mouth for just a second to cool off the fire. "You use a whole bottle of Tabasco?" I gasped.

"Erica's Pepper Sauce, from Saint Vincent," he said. "I like the blend better."

"I need water," I said, and raced past him to the castle.

"You're welcome," he shouted after me.

I burst into the kitchen and screamed as something flew into my face. I caught it—a wet wash towel—and glared at the thrower.

"Sorry, lady, I thought you was Bigshit."

"Water," I said, pointing to my mouth and fanning, in case the tears streaming down my face didn't tell the story.

Palize opened a bottle and handed it to me. I drained it in

one long gulp, and he handed me another. "Are you eating breakfast?" he asked.

I nodded. "But later. Call's at eight."

"Sure, lady," he said, already rigging his wet towel to fly at the door again.

I climbed the stairs, stretched my legs one last time, and entered my room. The maid had come and gone, and everything was neatly restored. I stripped and climbed into the shower.

In the middle of my second soaping, I thought I heard someone knocking on my door. I turned off the water and listened. Someone was knocking, but not on my door. And he wasn't trying to get my attention, he already had someone's.

Who was Donny having sex with, I wondered. I stood there listening, but didn't hear any voices. I turned the water back on, grinning.

Once clothed and relatively dry, I went to the workroom with a cup of coffee and a mission. I dug to the bottom of my kit and found the almost-disintegrated box I was looking for. I'd had it, and its contents, since I was eleven. However, until recently I hadn't used it.

My prized possession was a Ronco BeDazzler! It was a little plastic gizmo that looked like a Barbie sewing machine, but was really a stud-maker. Ralph Lauren, a few years ago, had a great print ad with a pair of studded jeans. Everyone I know sought those jeans: buyers, stylists, models, you name it.

The jeans weren't actually available. It was all about publicity. They were great jeans, but only Laeticia got to wear them. About that time, I remembered the BeDazzler! at my mother's, or rather, my grandmama's.

I had left work a few hours early and zoomed to East Texas, stopping in the town outside hers to brush my hair, make sure my shirt wasn't too cropped or too tight, my pants weren't too low or too tight, and my makeup was present and appropriate. My grandmama has "standards" and they aren't going to change, so it's just easier to please her and get whatever I want from her, than to argue about clothes and how they fit and hear the entire speech about "loose women."

Of which, FYI, I am one. According to her.

After we hugged, a strangely impersonal action (she loves me; she's just very . . . British. My father's side of the family is passionate Irish. My mother's are . . . restrained. Except for my actual mother.), and she discussed everyone in the family, dwelling on my brother Houston (the hotshot attorney), her favorite, over iced tea and cookies (each person is allowed two). Then I asked if I might look through her garage.

Some people organize things in file cabinets. My grandmama discovered huge plastic crates, and everything is in them and the crates are labeled. Eventually, I came across the box: Dallas, summer of 1975. I'd bought the BeDazzler! at a garage sale and had never actually used it, so it was still in the manufacturer's box.

Grandmama and I had a pleasant dinner about 5 p.m. at the Golden Corral. She chided me for not eating meat and I resolutely drained the salad bar of anything that could be perceived as nutritious, in order to make up for my almost manic inhalation of fried okra. I was back on the road home by seven, home by eleven. Elated by my find, I called another stylist friend of mine, and we ran to HyperMart (open all night), bought no-name, great-fitting jeans, and BeDazzled! the hours away. By the time we'd rhinestoned or studded everything in sight, the Z Café was open. We decked out in our new threads and dazzled Nick with our early morning panache.

After a huge delicious breakfast, complete with potato balls, we'd gone to our respective homes and beds.

Here and now I didn't have the Z Café, or my friend Patricia, but I put on a rockin' CD, Ishtar, from the collection. I was studding along, dancing along, and it was eight before I knew it. I consulted the schedule and headed off to the soundstage, where the first meeting of minds was going to take place.

"The song is about dreams," Donny said to me, and the girls jumped in.

"So we have the whole smoke machine atmosphere thing—"

"And the mermaid thing—"

"And the pirate thing, 'cuz you gotta search for your dreams like buried treasure—"

"And then we're all bein' ourselves, like just in jeans with no makeup and shit."

I looked over at Sascha. No makeup makeup was the hardest makeup to do.

"We're shooting the jeans segment this morning," Bette, voice of reason, said.

"No one's tried on clothes," I said.

"We're not shooting until ten."

"Can I go first?" Zima asked me. "That way I'll have more time to practice my solo."

"You did it the whole past two days!" Jillyian said. The princess was less perky this morning. I saw her glaring at Donny.

"I want it to be perfect," Zima said.

"Do you want them in the clothes I brought, or in their own clothes?" I asked Donny.

"The feel we're looking for is cozy, ordinary girls who made great choices to achieve extraordinary success," he said.

"What about a slumber party?" I said. Off the top of my head.

No one said anything. "I have footed pajamas, " Ka'Arih offered after a minute.

"Did you bring anything like that?" Donny asked me.

In my brain, I was cursing my astounding capacity to speak before I think. "Give me ten minutes," I said. "Girls, go get your jeans, your shirts and anything you could make into pjs."

"Maybe for makeup and hair they are in rollers and green face?" Sascha asked.

"Hold that thought," I said and raced back to the styling room. Ranting at myself didn't make it better as I looked through the clothes. I'd brought sexy clothes, nothing remotely slumber party-ish.

What's that song Pink sings? " . . . I'm my own worst enemy . . ." Was this some sort of self-sabotage?

I started in on the rack of left clothes. Jeans, T-shirts, a knockoff von Furstenberg dress, a pair of Chanel wrestling shoes—I'd seen them all over in Paris, replacing the Puma and/or bowling shoes look. I shook my head: they were a perfect example of a Fashion Victim.

Working in fashion, I see all kinds of people. A lot of models can't dress themselves (they never have to) and most stylists adore clothes, whether they can wear them or not. Then there are the other people, potential fashion victims.

A fashion victim is a person whose clothes wear her, instead of vice versa. A person who jumps at every trend written about, by every wannabe out there. A person who had no real soul for clothes, but who wants to be "in." A person with no personal sense of style. A person who wouldn't dare wear vintage, or a new designer, or something not in *In Style* this month, because she has no sense of self.

Fashion trumped those people.

A perfect example was the wrestling shoe fad, a shoe which out-uglyied even the earth shoe. If these wrestling shoes didn't have the Chanel logo, you couldn't sell them outside of Everything's A Dollar. At least someone had used the mile-long laces; they were gone.

I flipped through a few pair of men's trousers, and a sequined, breast-baring, crotch-slitted jumpsuit with cape. The box at the bottom held a few handbags, a pink satin pump, and a set of hair rollers. Nothing for my pajama party. I turned back to my supply.

Ka'Arih brought in footed flannel pajamas and a baby doll set in pink satin, edged with lace. "Are you comfortable in this?" I asked her about the sheer nightie.

She shrugged. "Just fix it so you can't see my nippies, I guess. See these little pigs?" she said, uninterrupted as she pointed to the design on the flannel pjs. "Eladonna should get these 'cuz she's always playing Pass the Pigs."

I looked at the pink pigs on the pjs, and continued my search through my bags. "Zima should be in a wife beater and boxers," I said, digging through my collection of men's patterned boxers. "London—"

"I have Victoria's Secret satin pajamas," London announced as she entered. "Long and short versions."

"Legs tan?" Sascha asked, trailing behind her, a ribbon of smoke still issuing from her lips. It almost sounded like a country, the way she said it: Lekstan

London hiked up her pant leg and Sascha made a disparaging noise. "Michael Kors, we fix that," she said. "But at least you are smooth."

Jillyian brought in a whole wardrobe of nightclothes. Most of them were designed so the wearer wouldn't get any sleep. "How sexy do you think this can be?" I asked them, though I knew I should ask Donny.

"We'll be wearing a lot less for that *Maxim* shoot," Eladonna said.

"And I think it's the spirit of the thing," Jillyian said. "If I'm dressed sexier than the others, that's the whole scheme. I'm like the diva. It's my job to be over the top."

"Just not as far over as L'il Kim," Eladonna said.

I grabbed a nightgown and robe for Jillyian. "Okay, then someone get Donny."

By the time we got started, it was almost noon. Behind schedule technically, but the energy was great—and that's the hardest thing to fake.

The clothes fit the girls' personalities: Ka'Arih in the pink baby doll wearing pink rollers, with strategic Band-Aids and cut up pantyhose for modesty's sake. Zima in boxers and tank with her hair in a ponytail; London in her satin shorts and long-sleeved pajama top with someone's sleeping mask acting as a headband for her long blond hair. Eladonna was the toughest to dress, but she ended up in a hockey jersey and multicolored toe socks.

Jillyian stole the show in a floor-length white satin nightgown and pelisse, trimmed with (fake) ermine, combined with pigtails and pig-headed slippers.

"You are very, very good," Donny said with a friendly kiss as he stood behind me and we watched the girls take their places. "You can style, too."

I laughed, and enjoyed the shivers up my spine. "Thanks for being in a place where creativity is appreciated," I said.

He put his arm around me. "Creativity is always appreciated." The cameraman began the countdown and I crept up to stand by Sascha. Thirty seconds of video meant shooting for hours. At the end, Donny (who was also directing) decided he wanted a pillow fight. The girls got into it, shrieking with laughter, and Donny called "cut" when they were all standing in the falling feathers, arms around each other, smiling.

"I love it when we make magic," I whispered. Sascha smiled in perfect agreement.

"Ladies and gentlemen, we deserve lunch!" Donny shouted.

"I'm so glad I don't have to clean up that mess," I said to Sascha.

"Thank God for maids," Sascha said as we walked into the dining area. "I wonder what is for lunch."

"Well, Oscar was cracking oysters," I said. "This morning."

"How was your evening?" Sascha asked.

"Well, not to tell tales, but Donny can certainly kiss. And yours?" I asked, turning to her.

She looked blankly at me. "I think I am a nicotine fit," she said and left for the gardens.

Apparently our budding friendship had parameters. Or she was dizzy from withdrawal.

The long dining room table had become a buffet, with smaller tables for dining by twos and threes scattered throughout the room. I sat down at a table, with my plate of fried conch and field greens salad, facing the view of bright blue sky and aquamarine waters.

"May I join you?" Eladonna asked, holding her tray and smiling.

"Please," I said. "I wanted to see the water."

"I hope we get a chance to get in it," she said as she sat down.

I looked at her tray. "Girl, don't you want to get some real food?" I asked. She was eating salad, no dressing, chicken breast—which hadn't even been on the buffet—and brown rice. "Or are you on a diet or something?"

"Food allergies," she said.

"I'm sorry, I had no idea. Last night—"

"Oscar's great about tweaking a dish for me. But this is easy." She leaned closer to me. "I have something I need to tell you before we go much further."

"Okay?" I said, looking at her encouragingly.

"My shoes, have you gotten them already?"

I nodded. Shoes had been an American purchase; feet larger than size nine got an adverse reaction in some Paris stores.

"I have one leg that is longer than the other; I make it up in my shoes. I add to the soles," Eladonna said.

"Okay."

"Can you help me?"

"I guess no one else knows?"

She shook her head and sat back. "You won't tell, will you?"

"I shouldn't need to, but if I do, I'll consult you first."

She shrugged. "Guess that's better than nothing."

"Is this a tête-à-tête?" Ka'Arih asked before sitting down.

"Not anymore," Eladonna teased. "Whatchyou eatin?"

Ka'Arih had gotten everything that was fried, everything that had a sauce, and everything that had sugar as an ingredient. "I like to eat," she said, and bit into her conch fritter. "And I just love fries. We'd always got 'em on Sunday if we were good in church."

"What kind of church?" I asked as I tucked into my own fried food.

"We're Northwestern Baptist Serpent Holders."

"What the hell is that?" Eladonna asked.

"We're a sect who believe in living on your own land and growing your own crops. We believe in being baptized by dunkin', and we believe that if you have faith you can handle serpents. And we believe in the enneagram."

Eladonna looked at me. "I'm Episcopalian."

"Lapsed Catholic," I said, then I turned to Ka'Arih. "What's the enneagram?"

Ka'Arih's mouth was full, so she motioned for me to give her a minute.

"It's something with nine," Eladonna said. "From the Greek root."

Ka'Arih swallowed and smiled at Eladonna. "Exactly right. The enneagrams are personality types, and there are basically nine, and basically everyone fits into one of the nine."

Teddy sat down with us, his plate as sparse as Eladonna's. "Did you say you handle snakes?"

"So what are you?" I asked Ka'Arih.

"What are the types? How did you make a religion out of that?" Eladonna asked.

"I'm number nine, the Peacemaker. We didn't make a religion out of it," she said, glancing around the table. "God revealed it to the people who were following his word and working on the land. At least that's what they tell me," she said with a smile. "Every organization, in order to do everything and meet everyone's needs, has to have all the nine types in it. That's how it will be successful. Like the band. Like Fate of Paradise."

"You need to count," Teddy said.

"There's only five people in the band, honey," Eladonna said.

"But that's not the whole organization," Ka'Arih said, covering her mouth with her hand as she chewed. "Add in Donny, and Sascha and Teddy and Dallas, and it's a perfect nine."

"You think the band will be successful because of that?" I asked her, interested for real now.

"We're all part of this?" Teddy asked.

Ka'Arih nodded as she took a bite of jerked chicken.

"In this failsafe success scheme, what type am I?" Eladonna asked.

Ka'Arih chuckled, "I think you're a six."

"What's a six?" I asked.

"A defender."

"I thought I'd gotten out of law," Eladonna said, pushing away her remaining chicken and rice. "What's that mean?"

"You get things done." Ka'Arih turned to Teddy. "You're a two, I think. A nurturer."

She turned to me, "I think you, Dallas, are a—"

Donny interrupted. "Ladies, we'd like to be in the studio during the heat of the day, and we'll do a photo shoot this early evening. Let's go!"

Both girls followed him like he was the Pied Piper.

Teddy stabbed his chicken. "A nurturer? I'm a nurturer?" he muttered.

I was left to wonder—what am I?

Chapter Six

About two o'clock, I headed down to the beach for a swim and a stretch. I was asleep on the sand when I sensed someone close by. I opened my eyes and looked around. Oscar was in the surf with an enormous rod. I watched as he threw something into the water from a bag over his shoulder.

Palize was standing about twenty feet beyond Oscar, with a similar long rod.

I sat up to watch. Oscar was wearing a shirt and knee-length shorts but I could see he had a lean build, corded with muscle. I watched the pole bend as Oscar caught fish after fish. His hand filled with catch, he came out of the water. I slipped on an embroidered Indian tunic top and stood up to pull on my miniskirt.

The smile he gave me made me giddy.

"Fair wench, what pursuits occupy you now?" I admired the lines in his face, his solid square jaw, the deep dimples and straight brows, as he linked the fish together and tossed them over his shoulder. His fishing rod was bamboo.

"I'm just hangin' out," I said.

"May I request your assistance?" He smelled like fish, and

his hands were mucky. He slipped into sandals and shouted something to Palize.

"Sure," I said. "Do I need a shower first?"

"No, you are as perfect as an egg. Come along."

An egg?

Our strides matched as we walked back to the castle. "What's your lure?" I asked while I pondered how to ask him what was perfect about an egg. But I didn't want to look like I was *fishing* for a compliment.

Even if I was.

"Tiny crabs," he said. "Groupers love them. But first we must ply their tastebuds with a *pintxos* of fray, so that they are hungry."

I didn't know what a pintxos was, or a fray. I guessed they were appetizer and bait, respectively.

"They're beautiful," I said, looking at the fish, who looked back at me with clean, clear eyes. "Like everything else around here, they are so colorful." The grouper were red and spotted. Photogenic fish, to be sure.

"Do you like to fish?"

"I don't know," I said. "It looks like a lot of work with that pole."

"Mashing," he said. "An old technique." We reached the kitchen door. Oscar turned to me, crossing his arms over his chest. "You must go sit in the garden."

"That's how I'm helping you?" I was confused.

"I'm not finished. Wait for about twenty minutes, then come in this door, okay?"

"Okay."

"And be wary, because Palize is one twisted mutha—" He swallowed. "In truth, my brother Palize and I prepare food around preparing each other for the grave. Thus far, the favor is mine, and I fear his retaliation may be less than circumspect. So watch your head."

"Okay," I said, with far less understanding and enthusiasm than before.

"Mama Garcia always shouts a warning, and we haven't hurt her yet."

"Y'all are just playing games. Right?" I asked, a little hesitant.

He smiled at me, and I felt all goofy again. "Twenty minutes," he said, and walked inside.

I wandered through the garden as I mentally categorized the clothes I had for a photo shoot. How I put them together depended on what Donny and the girls wanted to do for a backdrop, what image they wanted to project. I was ready; all the clothes were prepped. I checked my watch—a little pink Aqua G I'd picked up along the way—and saw my twenty minutes was up. What could he want with me in the kitchen? Face it, Dee, I told myself, pretty much anything he'd ask, you'd do.

Izarra, Dallas. No, no, no. My resolve at least acknowledged—though ignored—I went inside.

"It's Dallas O'Connor," I shouted before tentatively opening the door to the kitchen. No one was inside. It was just gleaming white tile and metal, with a butcher block table big enough to dissect a cow on. To my right, I saw steam.

"Hello?" I called as I moved toward the steam. It looked like KISS was about to step onto the counter—and I should know, I worked on the Lane Bryant/KISS runway show.

"Ahh, ees de debil girl," a rich voice said, and then Mama Garcia materialized out of it, like Gene Simmons, sans guitar and makeup.

"Uh, hi," I said. "Oscar asked me—"

"Oh he be working in his leetle kitchen," she said. "Back dere. But first, you must watch, chile, you must be careful. Dere be strong sperrids here." Today her dark eyes weren't unfriendly.

"Definitely some strong personalities," I said, "but lovely people."

"True-true, but t'ings ain't neber what dey seem," she said.

"Thanks for the tip," I said and escaped through one of the doors before she remembered I was the "face of Deat'."

Oscar had changed into whites, which contrasted with the pink and turquoise walls of the tiny kitchen. He turned to me with a smile. "Your timing is impeccable," he said, then his voice dropped, became husky. "Are you ready to do something you've never done, to experience the sublime?" His eyes glowed with passion, challenge. "Are you ready to trust me?" he asked.

What was the Blu Cantrell lyric? *Bangin, dancin, which way was he swingin'?* What was this man talking about? But I nodded. Why not? I was in the tropics; real life didn't apply here. It was the perfect setting. For anything.

"Taste this for me." He set down an oblong plate, with three puffs of white beneath star-shaped things, onto the small, pastel table.

"Is that fruit?" I asked.

"Star fruit."

"Oh, they come like that? I thought you cut them that way."

"I'm disappointed you'd think I'd resort to artifice, lass," he said. "I hold to three rules in my kitchen, and in my concoctions. One, everything must be fresh. Yesterday is too late. Two, everything must be local, with the obvious corollary that it must be in season. Three, the food will not be manipulated. Star fruit is fruit shaped like a star. I do not cut it. Nor do I tint anything."

"Oh," I said.

I'm profound at times.

"Are you able to assist me, lass? Or are you observing your fifteen minutes of—?"

"Well, are you going to give me a spoon?" I asked. "Or am I supposed to eat it with my hands?"

He handed the spoon to me, but then pulled it out of my reach. His voice dropped to a growl and his gaze burned into mine. "I need all of you for this, Dallas. I need you to express every sensation, every thought."

"Thought?" I choked out. My *mind* wasn't the most-engaged part of me right now.

"Food is for more than the belly, it is for the imagination. Thus, it is essential in this exercise that you tell me every impression as you receive it. Talk with your mouth open, I don't care, but tell me what you think." He gave me the spoon. "My hopes are hoisted on you."

I felt his gaze on me as I carved off a corner of the cloud puff. Thanks to thirty-some years of practice, and despite Oscar's fascinated observation, I found my mouth with the spoon. "Hot and cold," I said as fire took hold of my taste-buds. "Creamy and . . . mango? Pineapple?" My tongue swirled around the smooth texture . . . "Something that tastes like flan—and—" I inhaled air over the spicy peppers that sizzled on my tongue.

Oscar fed me another spoonful, watching me eat it. "Talk to me," he said in his seduction-slash-sampling voice.

"It tastes like . . . like Christmas morning, with a bite." I'd finished one of the clouds. "What is it?"

"A dessert I'm working on."

"That's . . . the spiciest dessert I've ever had."

"Exactly!" he said, his eyes burning with excitement. "There are four basic tastes: sweet, salty, bitter, and sour."

I nodded. He was educating me.

"A perfect food gives you the full range of taste, so you can experience it completely."

"Okay." Did he know I was clueless? I nodded.

"But it is a labor of Hercules to taste something that is really sweet, without the contrast of salty or bitter or sour to understand its sweetness."

"Okay."

"This dessert is very sweet, the ice cream, the flan, the fruit, but because of the pepper in the pineapple—"

"It tastes even sweeter," I said, understanding. "That's cool."

"Did you like it?"

I nodded. "I don't know if the others will like it—"

"Did I ask about them, or can you think without a committee? What about you?" He emphasized his point by touching my cheek, a soft touch that painted a line of heat down to my mouth. "Did you like it?"

"Yes. Is this something you've just created?"

"Yes." He stepped away and cleared the dishes, all three of them.

"How did we end up with you as our chef?" I asked. "You're imaginative, brilliant—"

He put the plates in the sink and looked over his shoulder at me. "Do you know who owns this place?"

"Sure," I lied. M. L. Diva. Whoever that really was.

"I'm her favorite chef. I needed a break, a chance to try some new things. She suggested I come here, and I decided to cook for your crew." He turned the water on to rinse the plates. "Unfortunately, for some of those mouths, I realize I could present ungarnished Campbell's soup out there and it wouldn't matter."

"Video crews are the worst," I said.

He turned back to me, drying his hands with a swipe of the towel. "I need palates," he said. "That's why I need you, Dallas." He reached across the counter and put his hand over mine. "You love food."

Okay, my heart sank. I admit it. Even though I'm giving up Latino boys, I had been willing to put off enforcing that resolution until after this shoot if Oscar was going to hang around.

He just wanted me because I eat.

"I don't eat meat," I said.

"You wouldn't try it?" His eyes were on my face, and I thought I could feel the throb of his pulse through his fingers on my hand. Maybe it was my own.

"I couldn't tell you if it was any good, because I don't know."

He sighed, dropped his head and moved his hand. "I should have known this wouldn't be perfect."

I got to my feet. "Just call me for your seafood and poultry needs."

"Is that enough for you?" he said and looked up with a sizzling glance.

I nodded. I felt a little dizzy, a little out of control. Were we talking about food? "How did you get the pepper in there, in the pineapple? I mean, I—"

"Pit-roasting the pineapple with black pepper." He leaned back into Oscar pose, his arms crossed, one leg bent across the other.

"How do you think that up?" I asked. "Roasting a pineapple?"

"I read," he said, as he put away the clean and dry dishes— when had he cleaned them? "I know these islands. I know their histories, their indigenous peoples, and how they ate. I was an anthropologist before I was a cook."

"I'd love to hear how that happened sometime," I said, in the lamest possible way to pick someone up. I was embarrassed for myself.

"Dallas," Bette stuck her head in the door. "Hi, Oscar. Excuse me. Dallas, Donny wants you on the terrace."

Thank God. He was saving me from my own compulsive nature.

Oscar and I said good-bye to each other and I followed Bette out of the kitchen. As we walked toward the sound stage I saw Ka'Arih, in stupefyingly bad jeans, standing in the garden, looking at the ground.

That's right, I reminded myself. I was here for clothing, not for hot haute cuisine and its creators.

The afternoon's photo shoot was actually rather easy; we were just photographing the girls from the back. In silhouette. No makeup, not much to do with hair, and I only had to worry about shape and texture. I pulled out all my twenty-first-century girdles and waist cinchers, and piled these twenty-somethings into the highest heels I could find. Then I added elements like a feather boa, a fringed vest, a burnt-out velvet shirt and a pair of jeans with lace inset legs for feel. Jillyian got to wear a hat. I clamped the clothes on them, making five of the curviest women around.

With moody smoke, murky lighting, and a lot of 'tude, it came off as super sexy.

This picture would be the back of the CD cover, and the songs would be listed around the edges. Unlike anything I'd seen, but very cool.

At four o'clock Donny whisked in and sent us to our rooms for a disco nap. I was resting on my bed when I noticed a rhythmic thump from the room next door. Donny's room. Curious despite myself, I sat up and listened. Who was he working over? Was it the same girl he'd had this morning, or was he a busier boy than that? They were trying to stay quiet, but the emotion of the moment was too much for the girl. The walls were thick, but the couple was loud. Getting louder. I grinned; this was the perfect place for romance. Or forget romance, for sex. Especially if his room looked like mine. I closed my eyes and lay my head back down.

She cried out, then her voice was smothered.

I sat up.

I recognized her voice from the demo tape: Jillyian?

Donny had a thing going with the sassy redhead?

Well, well. That could either be great or catastrophic, the leader of the band and the manager. I hoped for great, for everyone's sake.

When I woke up again it was dark outside and silent next door. Tonight's party had something to do with the phases of the moon, so I got up and looked out, but I couldn't see the moon from my room. Twenty minutes later I was cleaned up and changed for dinner.

I'd packed very little for this trip. A wardrobe of bikinis, a white linen shirt, a pair of capris, jeans, a miniskirt, accessories, and my gift from last Christmas: a Robert Cavalli weekender kit.

Most of the kits were snapped up before they ever hit retail, but a friend of mine at the *Dallas Morning News* got a prototype and gave it to me. It was the perfect escape wardrobe, and each combo was different. It had three shirts, three skirts, a sarong and a bikini. All in luscious silk, all in shades of bamboo and ivory and black. I'd packed it for "evening" and thought I'd be done. Overdressed, even. That was before Sascha showed up in beaded dresses and high-heeled slippers.

I might have to raid the left clothes rack downstairs at some point, but not tonight.

Denim mini, silk blouse, choker, and heels. I was ready. Sconces were lit tonight, and the air was still. A night bird sang in the distance, and I heard a trickle of music, but no voices.

In the dining room, a few hurricane lamps glowed on the table, but no one was around. The kitchen was spotless—which was odd. Did I miss dinner? Puzzled, I walked through to the little kitchen and found an open door. From here I could see a bonfire, with figures moving around it, on the beach.

"Hey," Oscar said, coming up behind me. "Where have you been?" His hands slipped around my waist. I smelled rum on his breath.

"I was asleep," I said. "I can't believe I almost missed this." I leaned back against him.

His hands tightened around me. "I would have come to get you," he murmured in my ear.

"Where is everyone?" I asked in a whisper. I couldn't care less.

"Down there," he said moving his lips over my neck. His breath on my skin gave me goose bumps. "Beach."

"Mmm . . . you came to get me?" I asked as my head fell forward, allowing him access to my nape.

"Mmm . . ." he kissed my ear, his hands massaged my waist. "No." He stepped away, back inside the kitchen. "I have to get back down there."

"Down there? What's going on?" I asked, flustered.

"Spillygatin'."

"Again I ask, what is it?"

"The Berry answer to a barbecue."

"Oh," I said. "Can I help carry anything?"

He paused for a second, and I felt those amber eyes sear through me. "Which child are you, Dallas? Not the only, or the eldest, so which one?"

"Why?" I snapped.

He just chuckled. "I don't have time for this, forget it. Go on down, I'll be there."

I turned around to leave and he called out again, "Just answer one thing, if you can, without fretting." I stayed facing away, but listening. "Do you hide from everyone, or is there something special about me that makes you so scared?"

"I'll see you down there, Oscar *Izarra*," I called, and took the path to the beach. No Latinos. Think, Dallas. Every time, it ends up in a fire—a conflagration, Oscar would say. Just keep away from that man. John is nice. Blond, but he can't help it.

Sascha met me halfway. "I was come to get you. Do you want—"

"Yes," I said.

She handed me something to smoke and something to drink. I sampled a little of both and exhaled from my gut.

"You vant to talk?" she asked.

I inhaled again and finished the glass of rum-spiked whatever it was. "No," I said. "I want to dance."

She kissed my cheek and led me toward the fire. "For dance, the beach is best," she said. Everyone I'd seen on the island was there, mixing in the darkness. Mama Garcia sat with three old men beside a shack that was decorated with hanging glass bottles and jars. One played a guitar, one an accordion, and one played what I swear was a screwdriver across a saw.

A giant iron pot sat among the red flames of the fire. Coolers filled with beer and wine served as tables for Thermos jugs. Sascha poured me more of whatever, and a soft, sexy music began—the guitarist playing alone. The girls in the band were fireflies, flitting around, laughing and flirting with the musicians and the island boys.

Oscar swooped up behind me, his hand on my belly over mine, his other extended, holding mine. "Just feel it," he said, as we bossa nova'd in the sugar sand. "It's the moon," Oscar whispered. "It pulls the tides in one's psyche and plans for him strife or joy."

"Is that Shakespeare or something?" I asked with a laugh.

"Alas, it was only a humble chef's spontaneous words," he said. "Mama calls it de *loa* moon."

He turned me in a pirouette, bringing me to face him, still moving in that hypnotic, sensual glide. "It's the moon that gives us strength. So we eat outside to honor it." He pulled me close, and I could feel the length of his body, the strength of it.

Have I mentioned he has a great body?

"What's a *loa?*"

"Mama practices *Obeah*," he said. "Ask her."

The song ended and someone called Oscar back to cooking. I stood in the sand, hearing the ocean, feeling the warmth of this man still against me.

The music changed mood, and Sascha grabbed me in a riotous dance with all the girls and Donny and the handsome black boys. Goombay, they called it. I'd never heard anything like it. The air was cooling off, but the sand still felt warm, and as we danced, we got hotter.

"Time for tasting," Oscar called. We turned to watch as he bent over the pot and held a spoon in his hand. I could see the steam rising from it. "Mama Garcia?"

"Ma-ma Ma-ma," we chanted as we gathered to watch Oscar feed her a bite.

After a moment of savoring it she said, "More Mello-Kreem. And more o'dat seasonin' pepper."

Oscar kissed her cheek and turned away from the fire.

We poured more drinks, and the Goombay played on.

"Dallas?" I heard him call me, minutes later, "Are you game, lass?"

"Dal-lus, Dal-lus, Dal-lus," my chanted name surrounded me. Someone pushed me forward, and I looked into Oscar's flame-licked eyes as I opened my mouth to taste. "What is it?" I asked.

Some of the fire faded from his eyes, "You have breadfruit, saltfish and basil in a coconut milk broth," he said. "No meat."

I ate what was on the spoon. "S'good."

"Spicy?"

"Not bad."

"Thanks." He turned away and I was jerked back into the

dance. Sascha offered me more rum, which I took, and more grass, which I also took. We danced until Oscar called us to eat. I received a wooden bowl and spoon, same as everyone else, and stood in line.

Eventually we all sat down with the steaming, delicious-smelling food. Oscar came and crouched down beside me. "Show me your dish, lass."

I pulled my bowl closer. "I'm not sure we're at that point in our relationship."

He grinned. "Come on Dallas, let me see your bowl."

"Why?"

"Dallas, you're four sheets to the wind, lass. If you eat meat, you'll blame me in your next sober moment, whatever week that will be. Just let me see."

"I can recognize meat," I said.

"I'm looking for a pig's tail," he said to me.

No argument. I handed him my bowl. He picked through it with a spoon and handed it back. "*Bon appetit*, lass."

"Is delicious," Sascha said, eating voraciously.

I looked at my food. Pig's tail was in this? I took another swig of rum and I dived into my dish. I couldn't see well, but it looked like chicken wings and fish, bananas, onions, and a thousand spices and herbs that I couldn't identify sober, much less now. The music stopped, and we all ate, the islanders speaking softly among themselves in a patois I couldn't make out.

Later, Ka'Arih played the fiddle while we listened, drinking Kalik, mellow with full stomachs. Oscar and Palize stamped out the fire, and the night grew cooler. Donny tucked a blanket around me and Sascha, and someone passed rich chocolatey brownies around. The music and the mood, the starlight and the warmth, blended into a dream of Paradise.

Chapter Seven

The next morning, the day was glorious, and remarkably I had no hangover, no carpet tongue, and I didn't remember doing anything stupid. Remember, being the operative word.

I was rolling out the racks when Sascha knocked on the door of the workroom. "Good morning," she said as we exchanged cheek kisses. "Have coffee?"

"I did," I said. Saint Oscar had presented me with what I thought was a cappuccino, but what turned out to be a mocha raspberry shot of energy almost as good as a run. Or sex. He'd been on his way out to the market for the day's food.

"Good," Sascha said. "So you show me clothes and we talk about hair and faces, da?"

"Sure," I said. "This is our diva." I stepped back to indicate a pair of jeans I'd made into a cross between Dolce & Gabbana and Bob Mackie. "With that iridescent tank and the Fake London blazer over it all."

"Jillyian?" Sascha said.

"Yes."

She pursed her lips and looked at the outfit. "Maybe I do braids, yes? And crystals on her face?"

"Braids?"

"No, no braids," she said. "Too Alicia." She squinted at the jeans. "I know. Bend hair, you know, like eighties."

"Crimping?"

"Yes, yes."

I shrugged. A little too Christina A., I thought. "I was thinking slicked back, a pompadour maybe. A little punk." I had one amazing earring for Jillyian, inspired by the Diane von Furstenberg fashion show, but it would only work with a retro look. I dug around in my kit and showed Sascha.

"Oh! Is brilliant. Her hair, it is thick. We see."

I nodded and moved on. "These are for Eladonna," I said, showing Sascha a denim and plaid flamenco skirt, to wear with ankle boots, a peasant-ish blouse and a stunning Valentino cummerbund.

"Very unusual. Madonna see this, she vill vant it."

The skirt was my own design. I was flattered by Sascha's comment.

"I make her hair smooth and blonde. Her makeup very . . . big. Earrings?"

I held up some hip-hop hoops and moved on. "And this is Zima." The shirt was fitted and crocheted, very delicate. I'd paired it with denim pinstriped pants and a flashy embroidered waistcoat.

"I braid her hair," Sascha said triumphantly.

"Perfect." And I had a hat that would be the exact finishing touch.

London had a denim duster, with fur collar and cuffs, which worked well to visually cut a few inches off either side of her waist and hips. With London's long blond hair in ringlets, it would be sensational. Beneath it, she'd have on black pants and lethally pointed pumps.

Ka'Arih got a Language grosgrain skirt, with a shrunken silver Lacoste shirt and a pale blue leather jacket I'd gotten in Paris straight from Galliano. I would have paid the four grand myself, but it was a size too small. "Crystal earrings," I said to Sascha, showing her a pair of shoulder dusters.

"I twist the back part up and sculpt her cheeks with bangs," she said.

"Sounds perfect."

Sascha stood up. "To work, then. I sit them in chair, send them to you in fifteen minutes."

"Deal," I said. I needed to resteam that peasant blouse.

I dug through my bag, looking for my pressing ham. My mother, when I was thirteen and she realized that I was embracing, not one, but all the Holly Homemaker traits, had bought me imported pressing tools.

"Imported pressing tools I left at home," I said to myself as I repacked my bag. My pressing ham, which is about the size of a small ham, but rounded and packed solid with beans or sawdust or something, was missing. It was really the only way to get an iron up into the folds of ruching. I sat back on my heels and looked around me. Mine was gone, but I'd seen one. Where?

With the Tobin Charles button. How many people had Thom Goodfeather and his minions in the Filipino Mafia actually killed? Or been responsible for their deaths? I'd probably never know. And I shouldn't worry about it. That was long ago—at least a year—and far away. Why was I thinking about it now?

I set up the iron and board and started opening closet doors. The extra styling kit was in the third closet. I grabbed the ham and set to work on the blouse.

I was finishing the last crease when they knocked on my door. "Soundstage! Five minutes!" I wheeled the rack with the clothes onto the stage, behind the curtain that was an on-set dressing room.

"What's the song y'all are doing today?" I asked Eladonna conversationally as I knelt to hem her skirt a little shorter in the front. "Please, could you stop moving?"

Eladonna froze. "It's about this woman who has always dated bad boys who broke her heart, and she wises up and meets this guy who's trash and tells him she's learned her lesson and don't need another class."

"Oh," I said through the four pins I held in my mouth while I basted the hem. "Cool. You're done."

Zima was next. "You look perfect, except for that vest," I said.

"We got this move like this, when we sing, *"Don't need no mo' o' yo class,"* she said, twisting the vest with every gesture. I rescued the garment. "Go on out there," I said. "Maybe you don't need it."

"Am I going to sparkle enough?"

She did look fairly sedate. I added jet cuffs that were almost as long as her forearms and pinned a jeweled pin on her brim. She smiled, pleased.

London breezed in. I spritzed her shoulders with adhesive and put the duster on her, sealing it to her skin. "I should let you dress me all the time," she said. "I really hate clothes."

"Are you going to be able to move?" I asked. She danced a little, and the jacket stayed in place. I straightened her pants legs, picked long blond hairs off her back, and sent her out.

Ka'Arih arrived, singing. *"Yo class, yo class, yo class. I don't need it, mm-hmm. Don't want it. Mm-hmm. Ah ah ah ah ahhha—"*

"Do I need to strap that skirt or something?" I asked.

"I'm in the back, since I'm a backup singer," she said, rehearsing her *"ah ah ahs"* again.

"What about those earrings?" I asked. "They gonna annoy you?"

She moved her head from side to side, then added a sliding

step and started singing again. "I think you're fine," I said, and shoved her out to the stage.

Jillyian was late, and when she arrived, I saw why. "Damn, Sascha got your hair up there."

"She kept talking about the Stray Cats," Jillyian said. "Is that mine?"

I looked from her to the relatively tame shirt. "Do you want more sparkle?"

She nodded. "I'm the rock-star diva!" She smiled with all the joy of a five-year-old; this girl was hard to resist.

"I have a top," I said, "but it's heavy and dangerous."

She winked at me. "Bring it on."

The sound people turned on some music and I froze. "Is this y'all?" I asked. I'd heard them, but not this song. It rocked.

Jillyian nodded, her eyes downcast. Pleased, but not arrogant.

"Damn," I said. "I'll be right back."

The top was literally Bob Mackie, borrowed from a Dallas makeup artist who sang in drag on the weekends as Cleo Glamora. He was slim, and the top had originally been Cher's. The makeup artist had bought it at auction, and paid a small ransom. I owed him my brother if anything happened to it.

And even a dashing, handsome O'Connor boy might not make up for such a disaster.

"You're going to be the stunning cat," I said, running back in. "This is you."

Jillyian looked at the bejeweled halter I held in both hands as she took off her tank and shorts. "It's awesome!"

"Turn around," I said, "Let's guide this over your hair."

The thing weighed about fifteen pounds, but once it was on her—"Girl," I said, "you are dazzling."

"Do I have pants?"

I laughed and brought out the Ronco'd pants, then helped

her into them, into the four-inch gladiator sandals also studded with stones, and moved her hair. The blazer was a no-go. "I'm a rock star!" she said, and started to move through the choreography.

"You sure look it," I said. I held the earring up, but it was too much. "Okay, you're good."

She grinned and scampered out, as comfortable in the shoes as she was in sneakers. I grabbed my on-set kit and followed her. Wait, I'd left the iron on. I dashed back to the workroom to turn it off, then ran back to the soundstage. On the way through the garden, I stopped and looked down. What I saw gave me an idea, but would Jillyian do it?

I picked it up anyway.

Inside, Teddy was doing the dance, reminding the girls of their movements without getting them sweaty. I picked up one of the down jackets in a chair by the door. The temperature was about fifty in here, to keep the girls cool under the lights. Teddy finished up and put the girls into position. Sascha was standing behind the cameraman.

"This is the first video?" I asked her.

She nodded.

"And everyone's name gets mentioned in the mix, right?" From what I'd heard, the debut album of most all of these girl groups did that—named the singers.

"Vhy? Yes."

I held up my find. "See?"

"What is with snake?"

"He's not poisonous," I said. "I'm thinking he'd make a rad earring."

"You Texans," she said. The light guys were still futzing, so I walked up to Jillyian. "Do snakes freak you?" I asked.

"I like 'em best on boots, but no, why?"

"When y'all are really ready to shoot, I'll come back out here," I said and ran back to the other side of the camera.

"In five, four, three—"

Fate of Paradise blasted us from all sides, and the five giggly girls became rock stars before our eyes, transformed by rhinestones and attention. I knew they were lip-synching, even though I could see their vocal cords moving. Beside me, Sascha hummed. It fit perfectly with the music. In fact, if her hum wasn't also smoke-scented, I would have never even noticed.

They had a sound that was going to rock the music world. "This is Jillyian?" I said to Sascha as the magical voice, a latter day Dusty Springfield, floated over us.

Without moving her gaze from the stage, Sascha nodded. "She is lead, yes?"

I was blown away. Jillyian was indeed the whole package. She could think, she could move, and, man, could she sing. Her voice was what was going to send this crew soaring above and beyond the competition. The lyrics of the song were fun, and the dance was complex and showed off each girl well. Their voices blended perfectly, but Jillyian's . . . "I want a copy of this CD," I said.

"This, we all get copy," Sascha said.

Sascha spent her time repairing stomach makeup, and I kept adjusting rhinestones for the maximum effect of sparkle. By the fourth take, I had the song memorized, especially the chorus. They'd sing the chorus three times and modify once to be the "bridge." Altogether, it was four scenes using the same music.

I slowed down the process, but made it cooler, because for every close-up, I inserted the snake's tail into Jillyian's earlobe. A live earring.

Ka'Arih, snake expert, suggested that Jillyian not dance with it. "Think about it, that lil ole snake, bouncing around. You don't wanna upset him, even if he isn't poisonous."

So I ran in and out of the set, inserting the snake into Jillyian's ear, and then taking it out. The effect was sooo amazing. And, as I suspected, Jillyian wasn't the least disturbed.

Lunch was called (per the union requirements of the video crew), and the girls stepped out of their clothes, put on robes, and sat down to scrambled egg whites with lobster and ackee. The crew got jerked fajitas.

Lunch wasn't on my schedule. I needed to repair pulled seams, strained snaps, and dangling stones. Real clothes weren't designed for an aerobic workout. I was in the middle of pressing the peasant blouse (again) when the bookcase slid back.

"Cinderella is hard at work? Or hardly working?" Oscar asked as he brought in a picnic basket.

I grinned. Was it possible to overdose on beauty? An island in the Caribbean, with this man, just might do it. Death by sensory overload. "Almost finished," I said.

"So are they, with lunch. Teddy is going to run them through another two takes, then, I understand, they are doing an ab workout before becoming . . . mermaids?"

"We're rocking along," I said. "Did you have any idea they were so good? I could listen to Jillyian sing all day long."

"They are quite talented," he said. "But it helps to have a good support team."

"Do you know what the enneagram is?" I asked as I finished hanging up Jillyian's jeans.

He paused on the way back to the bookcase. "Something with nine?"

I grinned. "Something."

"I must return to my kitchens before that misbegottten offspring of a handjob and a—" he caught himself. "We'll speak," he said, and turned toward the bookcase.

"Wait!" I called. "What's in my basket?"

Oscar's grin became lascivious. "Conch ceviche, breadfruit chips and passionfruit crème for dessert."

"That sounds divine," I said.

"Yes, and you can't ruin it by ignoring it," he said. "Time doesn't count." The bookcase slid shut.

I hung the clothes first, because I am a professional and I do respect the fabric. Then I bit into my ceviche—I fanned my mouth as I ran the clothes back to the set.

"Water," I said, half-running to the lunch table.

"With gas?" Sascha asked.

I shook my head. I wanted plain water. I don't like the bubbles.

She opened a bottle for me and I drank it all, in one long gulp. The ceviche had bite. Thank heavens for waterproof mascara, I thought, as I dabbed at my teared-up eyes. Wow.

We went back to work.

In the first take, London got her heel caught (don't ask me how) in the back of her denim duster and ripped right through it, from butt-height to the ground. The sound was like a scream, and everyone froze. She looked at the cut, and she burst out laughing. The girls started laughing, then the crew followed.

I was not laughing. I extricated her from the coat, left her in a towel, and ran back to my lair, pondering what to do about the coat. If I repaired it, it would still look ragged. Nothing to do except make the rip look deliberate. With a wince, I tore the jacket higher, now it was ripped from the neck to the hem. I clipped the length of it with rhinestone kilt pins. The deconstruction took three minutes, and we were back to work for several more hours. I need to check if her back had showed earlier, for consistency.

"Let's get some concert stills," Bette said before we changed the girls that afternoon. "Since everyone is dressed already, we can do it now. It's too late for the mermaids."

The lighting people had to reset the stage, Sascha had to retouch the makeup and I had to nitpick the clothes again. Nitpicking is a huge part of my job.

"We want them to look all gleamy, like they've been per-forming," Bette said.

"I should send outside to sweat a little," Sascha suggested, her voice heavy with sarcasm. She might be foreign, but she understood the subtleties of English.

"That might be a bit much," London said.

Teddy led the group in isometric ab exercises, and then Sascha spritzed them with John Frieda's Ocean Waves, which gave a sexy illusion of sweat, but didn't run or smell.

They looked very "Third Standing-O."

In less than an hour, we were done. I took the clothes, marked them carefully for the tour, and attached Polaroids of the girls gussied up. Then I straightened the room.

Tomorrow's mermaids would be an event.

I cleared off the left clothes, because I needed two racks for every mermaid costume. The clothes I folded and put into bags and on a shelf. The accessories and shoes I tossed into a big box and stuffed in an extra closet. Then I hauled out the supplies for tomorrow, including the mannequin so thoughtfully provided, and started to work.

Shakira was back on the CD player. I tangoed with one mermaid after another as I made their tails. Oscar came through the door, looked at me, set down a drink, and left.

"He doesn't understand about us," I said to the blonde mannequin and tangoed over to the drink. It was sweet and lime, the color of caramel. Yum. I hung up the blonde in exchange for a redhead who was tailless.

By the time the dinner hour rolled around, I was ready to drink and make merry. I took a quick cold shower, twisted my hair into a chignon, and decided to go for a Latin look at dinner: short skirt, long sleeves with deep V-neck, high heels, mascara, and serious lips. The silver ribbon around my throat with a jeweled pin was the final touch. It was kind of fun to dress up for dinner.

I traipsed downstairs, where the torches were lit already. Oscar winked at me as he handed me a mojito, and I walked down to the beachside gardens. The flowers were intoxicating, and the ocean's shades of jade green and deep blue were staggeringly beautiful.

Sascha reclined on a step in a black silk shirt that was unbuttoned to her waist, and wide-legged white pants. She and Coco herself could get away with that look. No one else on earth. Sascha's glass was filled with something blue.

"What are you drinking?" I asked.

"Nude Beach in Curacao," she said. "Vant taste?"

"I'm happy with my mojito," I said.

John wandered up to us. "I heard the mojito is the new Cosmopolitan," he said.

"I thought a kir royale was the new Cosmo," I said.

"I love kir," Sascha said. "Margarita is new mojito, da?"

Eladonna stepped up to us, and draped her arm over my shoulder. "Then you're saying the margarita is the new Cosmo?"

"What's the new kir?" Teddy asked, joining us.

"Should be this," Sascha said, holding her drink up. "Nude Beach in Curacao."

"I've got to get one of those," Eladonna said. John offered to go with her, and she grabbed Teddy too. I sat down beside Sascha, who was smoking her two puffs per cigarette.

"What is on your neck," I asked, peering closer. It sparkled and glimmered, but not like jewelry.

"You like? Is cheap, mendhi tattoo kit with glitter."

"It's very pretty."

"I was thinking, for mermaids you like this?"

"You are the super-genius. What colors do you have?"

"Blue, purple, green, and gold."

Teddy came back and threw himself at our feet in a very Hamlet movement. "He's not here yet," he announced.

"Who?" I asked.

"Guitar player for solo," Sascha said. "Zachariah Clarke. Clarke, with ee."

"He's flying in for the day?" I asked.

"You know him?" Teddy asked.

"No. Do you?" I asked Teddy. He shrugged.

"He was here, then he left for few days to do other gig," Sascha said.

Teddy rolled over on his chest, then propped his hands and kicked himself into a headstand.

Sascha and I looked at each other.

"I guess he's coming back for a few more," Teddy said from his upside down position. It was almost dark, we could barely see each other, except for the flickering torches.

"He is big shit. He stays in private suite," Sascha said. "He is very ugly though."

"Lass," Oscar said to me. "Another drink?"

I turned and squinted through the darkness to him. He didn't look like he had a glass.

"Ahh," Sascha said knowingly.

"Excuse me," I said and walked toward Oscar's voice. I could make out his whites in the darkness, a ghostly figure. "You have a drink for me?"

"I'm going for a sail tonight, lass. There's room for a crew of one."

"Are you Hispanic?" I asked, the mojito making me a little . . . abrupt.

He paused for a moment. "No."

"Your name is Izarra," I said, questioned really. "Isn't that—"

"It's an honorable old Basque name," he said in a voice that could have frozen the water. "When your relatives were being raped by Romans, mine were living in democratic villages perfecting the arts of cooking and whaling—"

"Os—"

"Your language, English, is an amalgamation of a dozen different conquerors that trace back to the Indo-Europeans who came from the steppes of Russia. My heritage boasts of a language distinct from any other, a lineage five thousand years old."

I. Had. No. Idea. I wasn't even sure where Basque was.

"I expected more from you, Ms. O'Connor. Surely not bigotry."

My mouth was still hanging open when he was long gone. I felt terrible. He'd so misunderstood. I stumbled back to Sascha. I should ask her if she knew about the Basque. I wasn't a bigot! Paranoid, yes. Racist, no.

"What do you vant to do with their hair?" Sascha asked me. Teddy was still upside down.

"You two should get into headstands," he said from the darkness by my feet. "It's so good for the psyche."

"I am in dress," Sascha said.

"You're in pants," I said.

She looked down. "My God! I am in pants! How did this happen?"

"You've been getting happy with ole ganja, without me?" Teddy said to her.

"Dallas is in skirt!" Sascha said. "I knew I saw skirt. Come," she said to me. "I will do headstand."

"Y'all go right ahead," I said, still reeling from Oscar's accusations. Bigot? Me?

"Is dark, Dallas," Sascha said, her head already on the ground. "Do headstand, come, come. No one will see your panties."

"Maybe she doesn't wear any," Teddy said as he sat up to guide Sascha through the moves.

He would never find out.

"Okay," he told her, "make your hands a triangle, with your head at the top, good. See your elbows?"

"Is dark, I can see nothing."

He tapped her elbow. "This is a shelf, so put your knee there first, now your other knee, then when you get your balance, lift each leg straight."

"Come on, Dallas," Sascha said, upside down. "Don't make me make fool by myself."

Teddy continued to coax her through, and Sascha shouted. "I am standing on head!"

It was loud enough that everyone looked and wanted to join in. Teddy ended up giving a class. In the torchlight I saw a forest of legs. Even London did it; her long skirt covered her face and bared her pink lacy undies.

I was the only person still on my feet. Ah, what the hell. My skirt was three inches long and wouldn't slide, not even with gravity. I bent over, balanced on my arms and legs, and kicked straight up.

"I have a joke," Ka'Arih said to us all, her voice sounding strange, probably from being upside-down. "We used to always tell jokes to get people to fall over. The last person left standing won."

"Okay," Zima said. "What's your joke?"

"There's a rabbi, a priest, and a rabbit," she started.

I didn't listen. I was too busy guilting. I had to march into the kitchen and set Oscar straight. I had to. Just as soon as dinner was over. He—

"I'll be damned," a voice said. A man's voice said. To my calves. A southern sticky-sweet voice, a whiskey-rubbed voice that could make a woman purr or buy any lame-ass excuse it claimed. A voice that had hemmed and hawed, hedged and apologized to me for an entire year. A voice I had once romantically nicknamed The Phantom. A voice that was now above me. Present. Here, in the flesh. Talking to my calves.

"Dallas O'Connor," the voice said. "I'd recognize these legs anywhere."

"Zac!" Jillyian screamed.

Perfect. The guitar player.

Chapter Eight

When I came out of my headstand and smoothed my hair—my skirt hadn't been, in any way, displaced—I saw a black-haired man. He wore head to toe black, a man with bad skin, white teeth, gorgeous bones, and guitar player fingernails. He was mobbed by the girls, then by Sascha, and greeted by the musicians and Donny.

The black haired man saw me watching, and smiled. "Hey, baby," he said in a voice that I've dreamed about on more than one hot and stormy night. "How are ya?"

The phantom, my FBI-working, guitar-playing, date-breaking, truth-hiding phantasm of a couldabeen boyfriend walked up to me and enveloped me in a hug.

"Well, Dallas," Donny said. "Guess you already know Zac Clarke."

Sascha held my arm as we ambled toward the castle. I could hear the sounds of a steel band as the notes drifted up to the building. "You said you did not know Zac," she said. "Why you lie?"

I fumbled. "Clarke," I said. "I didn't know his last name."

I didn't know his first name. In fact, Zac Clarke might not really *be* his name. Truth was fuzzy where The Phantom, by any name, was concerned.

"How many Zacs are guitarist from Music Row?" she asked. I knew Zac as an unnamed member of the FBI.

"I don't know," I said, speeding up my pace to reach the dining room faster and to end the conversation sooner.

"Where you know Zac from?" she asked.

A series of murders on a shoot in Washington state. "Just . . . around," I said. We'd met when he'd been undercover and I'd been in need of a friend.

"Ahh, he is ex-lover?"

"Uh, no, no, not really." A few kisses, caresses, and hot phone calls had evaporated into broken dates. Then he'd gone completely quiet—but after September eleventh, I wasn't surprised.

"You work on bideo with him before?" she asked.

"Yeah," I seized on it.

"You maybe do some hanky-panky in the sound room?" We were at the castle archway and she looked at me sideways. "You are terrible liar."

"Nothing happened," I protested.

"Ah, then maybe you get lucky here."

"I don't think so," I said. "You've known him long?"

She shrugged. "He is, mm, how do you say? Entrenchment in Nashville. Everywhere he plays. So, I work in bideo, I see him."

Maybe he didn't work for the FBI full time? Maybe—then why the hell didn't he tell me? Then again, he hadn't told me anything, except recently when he came up for air right before I went to Paris, he said he needed to see me. "Bad."

Whatever.

I took my mermaid-headed seat, and the waiters served a deliciously spicy pumpkin soup. Ginger beer was the only thing to put out the fire.

"Zac" was at the other end of the table. He was seated on a skunk-crowned chair. Appropriate.

Ka'Arih was explaining her enneagram stuff again, how every team needs these nine components. "We each serve a different purpose, a different capacity. Relationships are the strongest when each person needs something offered by what the other person has."

"So this could be some boyfriend test?" Zima asked, glancing down the table at the nerd musician. David, I think his name was. Did she have a crush?

"You want to test someone?" London asked.

"We can't all have millionaires willing to whisk us away if we get unhappy," Zima said, not unkindly.

London blushed. "He's not a millionaire. He's just comfortable."

"How many roses are in your room? And that's been since last week?"

"It fits," Ka'Arih said. "London's the Romantic."

London lifted the goblet to her lips. "Of course, romance is being on a island with a sexy boy who worships the ground you walk on." She smiled.

Eladonna gasped. "You're the one!" she said. "I wondered who he—"

"Ssh," London said. "It's not very romantic to kiss and tell."

"I'll be damned, the blonde's getting her some," Eladonna said. "You, Jillyian?"

The redhead looked at them coyly. "I'll never say. Except he's very, very big . . . hearted."

They all shrieked with giggles.

"What am I?" Zima asked Ka'Arih. "If everyone is different?"

"Well," Ka'Arih said as Palize and the waiters cleared our plates. "Would you rather go to a party or read a book?"

"I'd rather be in the studio."

Conversation ceased as tonight's dishes of butterflied lobster with almonds, or roasted pork in orange glaze, were placed before us. There were side servings of braised callaloo and mushrooms, *moros y christianos*, sauteed watermelon hearts and yam fries. The food was good, but I couldn't lose myself in it.

Oscar had the wrong impression; I had to set him straight. At dessert.

After we ate until we couldn't move, the plates were removed and dessert wine poured.

"Back to your questions," Ka'Arih said to Zima. "Studio or book, it's the same. You're an Observer."

Zima, beautiful Zima, looked as though she might cry.

Jillyian leaned over and put her hand over the other girl's. "That's why you can write such amazing lyrics, why you know what rhymes with 'incandescent' before we do. You're keeping track."

"We need you," Ka'Arih said. "It balances the rest of us."

"You're deep," London said. "You give us soul."

Zima looked at them all, her lips turning up a little in a smile.

"Not to mention you play kick-ass drums," Ka'Arih said.

Zima smiled, and looked down the table toward the nerd. David was a cute nerd, a Disney-styled nerd, with every little detail attended to. He even wore Vans. A cool nerd.

"Guess who's the Controller?" Jillyian asked them.

The girls answered in concert: "Donny!"

Donny, talking to Zac at the other end of the table, looked up when he heard his name. "What?"

Oscar came out with a silver salver. "Pick one," he commanded Sascha, then Zac, then Donny, then Teddy, then David, then Derek the third musician, the blond John, Bette, Jillyian, Eladonna, Zima, London, and lastly me. We'd chosen fortune cookies.

"You open these one at a time, ask the question and then

answer it." Oscar placed a hand on Sascha's back. "You first."

She cracked hers and read it: "*If you were to do anything besides what you do, what would it be?*" Sascha searched the ceiling for an answer, then threw the note over her shoulder and bit the cookie. "Would be porn star," she said in her sexy accent.

We all laughed.

Zac was next. "*If you could be a superhero, who would you be?*" "I'd be Spidey," he said, "Spiderman. Stan Lee had the right idea: hang around and watch the pretty girls change."

The table booed him, and Bette started to unbutton her blouse, telling him he could crawl in through her window anytime.

Oscar's face was impossible to read. This better not be dessert; I had to talk to him, up close and personal.

Donny was next. "*What is your biggest vice?*" he read. "Singers," he said amidst the hooting of the girls and the musicians.

"*Where would you go if you had one more month to live?*" Teddy read. "I'd go to Singapore," he said.

"Why?" Sascha asked.

"It's supposed to be breathtaking. And the women are supposed to be very, very . . . agile," he said with a comic wiggling of his eyebrows.

David was asked what he would do with a million dollars. "I'd buy my own studio," he said, "and I'd hire songwriters who could write whatever they wanted and it wouldn't matter what marketers said." He sent an anxious look toward Zima. She watched him with hero-worship. Eladonna and I exchanged a smile.

Derek was asked what supernatural thing he wished he could do, and his answer was fly.

John was asked if he could be anyone, who would he be.

He gave some athlete's name that I'd heard during the winter Olympics, but because I'd been on location I hadn't seen much coverage and I didn't know who the athlete was.

Bette's question was if she could be any animal what would it be. She answered a bear, so she could sleep through the winter.

Jillyian read her question, and her face paled. Her smile was shaky, but she read it aloud. *"If you had to reveal a big secret, how would you do it?"*

The table fell completely quiet and strangely serious. Why? I glanced around at the faces I'd gotten to know these past few days and felt a chill creep down my spine. I didn't know these people at all.

"I'd throw a giant party," she said, "then I'd write it in fortune cookies and pass them around!"

Everyone applauded and Oscar grinned.

Was there relief in their laughter, or was I just being a drama queen?

Eladonna was asked to name what her last meal would be. "This isn't fair to me," she said. "I can't eat half the stuff normal people eat," she said. "I can't do this one."

Zima pulled a question, *"What is your personal anthem, and why?"* and traded with Eladonna. She belted out "Survivor," by Destiny's Child as her anthem. We applauded her acapella take on Beyoncé.

Zima answered that she would like tamales, prime rib, Swiss steak and Brussels sprouts.

"What about dessert?" David asked.

"I don't like sweets," she said.

"She likes salty things," Jillyian said and my end of the table dissolved into giggles. "Especially to drink!"

Zima, bless her heart, didn't get it. David turned beet red, but looked more cheerful than he ever had.

London's question was what would you take to a desert island. I was surprised: she named books and CDs, flowers, bubble bath and her flute, nothing self-indulgent at all. I didn't even know she played the flute

It came my turn and I cracked open my cookie. "*Have you ever been hopelessly, madly in love?*"

I'd been prepared to tell stories on myself from childhood. This? I was blindsided. I glanced up and met Zac's black gaze. I looked away. Everyone waited for me to speak. "Sure," I said, as flip as anyone else. "At least once a week." Then I dared to look at Oscar—but all I saw was the swinging kitchen door as everyone laughed.

The party moved into the drawing room. I stood by one of the windows, looking out at the moon, waiting for my chance. Oscar announced dessert (Trés Leches cake or mango Napoleons), and I strolled over for some coffee. He handed me my cup, but he was looking over my shoulder. "Zac!" Oscar shouted. I turned around and saw the men embrace. "How are you?" Oscar asked him.

Well, well, well, and they talk about worlds colliding.

"Just comin' over to see my girl Dallas," Zac said. He smiled at me, but his eyes were full of warnings. "It's been a while since I've seen you in Nashville. When was that last time?"

Oscar was watching me with an expressionless face.

What the hell was Zac doing here? I'd been to Nashville, but certainly never with him. "You mean the dinner we were supposed to have, but you forgot to call?" I snapped.

"I ended up being in the studio late that night," he said.

"Sounds like you are on the hot end of a poker, my lad," Oscar said to him. "I'll go retrieve a fire extinguisher, because I think you are going to go up in flames."

"Zachariah Flambe," Palize said with a wicked laugh.

"I'll go with you," Zac said to Oscar. "Wait until the waters are friendlier."

Whatever.

I declined Teddy's invitation to walk along the beach, John's invitation to drink more, and Sascha's invitation to get stoned. My room, my haven, seemed like a good idea tonight. I escaped upstairs and ran myself a hot bath.

I was immersed, almost submersed, when I heard a knocking. Not Donny's sexual acrobatics again, but someone actually at my door. Who did I *want* to be at my door? Zac? Oscar?

"Dallas?" a female called.

"Come in," I said. One of the interesting things about this place was the total and complete lack of locks. "I'm in the tub."

I arranged a few bubbles a little better for modesty's sake, and waited until Ka'Arih opened the door. "I'm sorry to disturb you," she said, "but you've asked a few times what you think you are. In the enneagram."

"Okay," I said. "And the answer is?"

"Well," she twirled a finger in her hair. "Do you think you can change the world?"

"Uh, not the whole world," especially not tonight, "but maybe I can influence my little corner."

"When you cry, is it because you are mad or sad?"

"I cry at commercials and movies. When I get mad, I rant."

"I thought so," she said, looking at me. "You're a Perfectionist."

"Yuck, that doesn't sound fun."

"It's what you do, isn't it? Keep us all looking perfect?"

"Yes."

"Well, you probably extend that tendency to everything else. Your boyfriend has to be a certain thing or act a certain way that's considered by you to be "perfect." You probably have really high standards about taking care of stuff, taking care of yourself." She shrugged. "I just wanted to tell you so you didn't think I was keeping it a secret or something. God wants us all to know how we fit, so we can stop worryin' about that part and start workin' together."

The little prophet had stunned me.

"So goodnight," she said. "Sweet dreams."

I heard her slip out the door. "Sweet dreams," I said and sank beneath the water.

Zac was sitting opposite me, dressed in all black, and smoking.

I was squinting into the dawn, wet with sweat and still breathing heavy. He put the cigarette in his mouth and held out his hand.

"We need to talk," he said.

Good morning, Dallas.

Zac walked away and I walked to catch up. I hated this enforced spy behavior. Why couldn't he just speak to me at breakfast like a normal person? Or if he wanted to get me alone, come to my room? Why interrupt me at 6 a.m. in the middle of a run?

"What's going on?" I asked when I caught up with him.

"We're both working this job," he said.

"Yeah?"

"That's it."

"You wanted to tell me we were both working this job? You thought that was going to escape me?"

"We're both working it, but . . . things aren't what they seem," he said.

"You and Mama Garcia," I muttered.

"What about Mama Garcia?"

"She said the same thing to me," I said. "And I don't know what either of y'all are talking about."

"Baby—" he stopped and turned to face me. He grinned, the guitar player, and looked me up and down. "It's really good to see you. And you look really good. Sweat works for you."

"Uh-huh," I said. "Thanks."

Not buying. You see, I have this fundamental belief: people will do what they want to do. Correction, *male* people will do what they want to do. What my guitar player didn't realize, is that to my way of thinking, if he'd really wanted to spend any time with me in the last year, he would have made it happen. If it was something he really wanted, nothing would have stood in his way. Lesson? He wasn't really interested. I was just convenient at times.

Like now.

"May I be honest?" he asked.

"That would be a shock, but go for it, Zac Clarke. If that is your name."

"It is." He looked away and finished his cigarette, stubbed it out and then picked up the stub. He caught my expression of dismay. "How many times have you seen the assassin busted because the agent picked up his butts?" he asked. "And it's Zachariah Clarke, with an "e.""

"Okay." Fingers of heat from the newly risen sun touched my bare arms and shoulders.

"Like I said, it's great to see you. I mean, after so long. . . ." He tossed back his head, throwing black curls out of his eyes.

"Why are you here?" I asked.

"Business. I work in this industry."

"There isn't any cloak and dagger thing going on, then?"

He looked away. "I'm just following up on a phone call. No biggie."

"You came out here for a phone call?"

He focused those dark eyes on me. "When I heard Dallas O'Connor was here, yeah I did."

Really?

"I wanted to see you."

Really?

"On the other hand, timing is damned."

"How's that?"

He turned to me, and I noticed something new about him, even before he said the words.

"I got married."

Chapter Nine

The ring was bright and shiny gold, studded with a few diamonds. Altogether, it looked thought-out and planned, not just meeting someone on Tuesday and eloping on Thursday. I spoke instinctively; I was raised with Emily Post. "Congratulations. Best wishes to your bride."

"Baby, I—"

"Don't you think calling me baby is in bad taste?" I asked.

"No, I'm married, not dead. Besides, I knew you . . ." He tried again. "Baby, it all happened so fast. It was like this—"

I held up my hand to ward off his words. "Don't tell me. Just file it under 'classified' like everything else. Your name, your age, why you called me from all over the country and never made it to Dallas once. In a whole year! Why you sent me flowers and presents but never a personal note or even a freakin' e-mail! Just put it there, classified, and then I can close the file on The Phantom."

"Dallas," he said.

I walked toward the sunrise, away from the man. A quarter mile later, I looked back. He stood facing the sea, looking at his hand. His shoulders were slumped and he seemed exhausted and sad.

Guilt stabbed me; I really liked him. He was a nice person. How much gumption must it take to intrude on an old not-quite-girlfriend and tell her you were married? And he hadn't tried to get me into bed.

Nothing was a worse turnoff than a man who thought his marriage shouldn't interrupt his dating.

I looked back again, and Zac was gone. I took a deep breath and shot through the sand—I needed my escape today. I needed to run.

Sascha walked up as I stood sipping coffee from the crew's bar, watching Teddy lead the girls through a rehearsal for the next segment of the video. "You look so serious," she said, kissing me on both cheeks. I always thought Russians kissed three times. "Should be fun, shooting bideo of beautiful young girls singing! Come, is time to tan."

"Tan?"

"Without tan girls will look like ghosts."

"I'm confused," I said, looking around for a schedule. "What day is this?"

She chuckled. "Day after last night. You talk with Zac. Is all okay?"

I set down my coffee mug. "It's fine." I swallowed a little too hard. "He's married, Sascha."

"Ahh, that is why sad face! Oh, love is so brutal. In Russia we say mother Russia is like love, bakes you when is hot and freezes you when cold."

I grinned. "You really say that?"

She shrugged. "No. In new Russia, more likely to compare notes on the bond market, but maybe once they said that." She patted my shoulder. "You kiss Donny then, feel better."

"Donny," I said, dropping my voice to a whisper, "is otherwise engaged."

Sascha froze. "You mean?"

"He's spending a lot of time with Jillyian. Did you know that?"

Sascha's back was to me. "Jillyian? How do you know this thing?"

"We share a wall, and her voice is very recognizable. Anyway, no Donny, no Zac."

"How do you say in America?" she asked, turning around to me. "Their lose. Come, we tan the girls and you decide which other boy is going to be your Banda-air for rest of the shoot."

We marshaled the girls together in the spa, and passed out the fake tanning stuff. I like Clarin's mousse. Sascha explained why she always uses Estee Lauder. "When Soviet Union fell, I work for Estee Lauder in Red Square. I learn makeup there and I get paid. I tell you, for me, this was extraordinary."

"I always thought Russia would be so romantic," Ka'Arih, facedown on the table while Sascha rubbed her skin with an exfoliator, said. "All those long fur coats, and fur hats and little sleds—"

"Is nothing romantic about feet that are cold from September to May," Sascha said. "Turn over."

Ka'Arih, bless her heart, wasn't shy in the least. She sang as Sascha scraped her chest raw, then she bounced off the table and went to shower before coming back for the tanning.

"Since Estee give me this chance, ever since I am loyal to her," Sascha said.

"You sound like you have a personal relationship with her," I said. "Don't you have other products?"

"Yes, yes of course, but what I try first is the Estee Lauder. Always." Ka'Arih came back. Sascha poured a capful of Lauder's tanning cream onto a two-inch-wide sponge paintbrush and started at Ka'Arih's nape and stroked down, fast.

What was I supposed to be doing?

"Put on rubber gloves to do her front when I am done with back," Sascha said to me.

Oh, great. Me, the inexperienced one, got to maul the breasts of some underage enneagram-hooked singer. "So what's Sascha?" I said to Ka'Arih. "In the scheme, how does she fit?"

She didn't say anything.

"Is she asleep?" I asked.

Sascha nodded as she painted down the girl's legs. Then she took a flat stone, like from a riverbed, and smeared the "painted" cream everywhere else, into the creases of Ka'Arih's neck, into the backs of her knees and around her ankles. "Give it ten minutes," Sascha said, stripping off her gloves. "We go to other girl."

"And me?"

"After other back is done, will be ready for Ka'Arih's front."

The trick to fake tanning is to go light and even. Then reapply often to get the desired color. And it usually requires a friend, unless you are an octopus and can get to the small of your own back. Or unless you have Sascha's bizarre combination of tools—the sponge paintbrush, the round stone, and a piece of polyurethane that she used to "polish" extra color off.

By the time we were finished, we had five golden goddesses, each within a range that would be normal for her coloring. The final secret touch was Michael Kors's Leg Shine, a body slick. "Is the new lipstick," Sascha said. "Never will I be without it. Is so useful."

They all gleamed. Like rock stars.

The shoot, since it was truly outside and truly physical, was scheduled for the early evening—which gave the crew time to set up and the group time to . . . well, tan properly.

Unlike the other parts of the video, in the "Pirate" section, the clothes had to honestly fit. The girls were really climbing up (down?) the side of a ship. We were avoiding obvious pirate references—no one had an eye patch or a parrot—but Donny and the girls still wanted a pirate vibe.

The last few seasons' collections had been all about ethnic and romantic, so this part of the video was fairly easy to outfit. I gathered my options, steamed them, then loosely packed what I needed transported. The pirate "boys" were arriving at noon, from Miami, and their brings included dark pants, white and/or ruffled shirts and scarves. Jewelry, too.

I hadn't seen Oscar. Ka'Arih's words about being a perfectionist had stung almost as much as Oscar's accusation of racism.

Perfectionism was great in its place. I got paid a ton of money because I was a perfectionist. I always had funds for emergencies in my bank account, clothes for a party in my closet, and food for a sit-down dinner in the cabinet because I was a perfectionist. But to be a perfectionist with people? That didn't seem right. I wouldn't want someone who tried to make me "perfect." I wanted whoever I was, to be perfect for that person. I wanted it to fit.

Naturally.

I put on Air Rifts, shorts, sunscreen, a bikini top, and my sheer peasant blouse over it all. My hair was protected by a bandana, and I had on serious, although tiny, shades. I slung my tool necklace on and walked out of the workroom, only to pause in the hallway.

I heard a scream, a huge smack sound, and a shout.

From the kitchen.

I raced inside and found Oscar with his hands around Palize's throat. Palize held a knife, the haft of it against Oscar's back. They were surrounded by the fixings for forty lunch boxes—our names written on the sides—brown paper, and kraft rope.

The chefs' struggle resembled a dance, as they deliberately avoided tipping over any tables, upsetting any shelves or so much as bruising a lettuce leaf while trying to strangle and maim each other. I wasn't sure if I should scream or applaud.

It didn't look like play.

"You mouth-foaming imbecile," Oscar shouted as he moved Palize away from a wheeled cart with a dozen fruit salads in carved melon cups, slowly strangling him. "This time you've screwed up beyond comprehension."

"You're not my father," Palize spit back. He tried to kick Oscar's back leg. "He wouldn't treat me with such disrespect."

"Disrespect is what you've shown this kitchen!" Oscar underlined this point by throwing his back against the wall, to crush Palize's hand and make him drop the knife. "This is unforgivable."

"What are you going to do? Kick me to the curb in Miami?" Palize shrieked as the knife clattered to the floor. He pushed against Oscar's chest, but Oscar held him tight. "No one is goin' to work way out here for you, livin' like a nun!"

Palize was turning . . . purple. Not quite aubergine, and not red enough for plum. Just . . . purple.

"I would fire your ass, you little turd, but I want to keep you here, keep an eye on you," Oscar let the lesser pirate's throat go, with a push that sent the younger man reeling.

"I don't need your stinkin' permission to—" Palize swung at Oscar and Oscar punched him back, while dodging a pyramid of bread ready for slicing. They clinched again, though Palize didn't have the knife anymore, and the language had changed to something I'd never heard.

They were oblivious to me, to my shouts of "stop," to anything. Mama Garcia poked her head in and saw them, still fighting, both soaked in sweat. "Mama!" I cried, and gestured to the men. "They're gonna kill each other!"

"True-true. Ain't nuttin' to do, chile. Just let dem tire out or one to win. Happen all de time, dees two."

"Are those lunches ready?" Bette called from the dining room. "The Hummer leaves in—"

In the seconds before she opened the door, Oscar and Palize split apart, straightened their clothes, put the knife away, and returned to work. Their chests were heaving, but they were assembling foccacia sandwiches, fish wrapups, and fruit salads when Bette breezed in.

"Oh good," she said when she saw them. "Dallas?" she said to me. "Are you okay?" I had a vise grip on Mama Garcia's wrist. I dropped it.

"Fine," I said.

"Are you walking or riding?" Bette asked.

"Ri-riding," I said.

Oscar would finish rolling a wrap sandwich, and then Palize would add a touch of garnish, put it in the box and wrap the box in the same time that Oscar would make a sandwich. Their hands worked in complete concert. Bette left.

Oscar spoke to Palize, in Spanish. Threatened him with his life if Palize ever touched Oscar's knife again. Then he described what he'd do with the knife on Palize's body. Or rather, what would be left. It might have been horrible if it hadn't been so . . . culinary a description.

"Anything you need, Ms. O'Connor?" Oscar asked me.

"No," I said. This was obviously the wrong time to make peace. "What was that noise?"

"The crash or the bang?" he asked, still filling, folding, wrapping and slicing. He was insane, to be so calm after almost killing Palize. The more insane one was Palize, cooking with the maniac who'd just tried to kill him.

"The crash?" I said.

"The Bigshit dropped that pot on my head," Palize answered, pointing to a caldron-sized pot. He seemed oddly defiant and triumphant, despite the bruises around his throat.

Yikes. "The bang?" I asked.

"Mama Garcia shooting her air pistol to get us to stop fighting," Oscar said.

"I'm going now," I said, walking out the door.

"Nice ass!" Palize called after me in Spanish.

I heard Oscar promise Palize he was gonna die. I didn't think he was joking.

By three o'clock, we were fanning. The Bahamas were supposed to be cool during the summer, with highs of mid-eighties. Add in humidity of seventy percent, and another five degrees, and it might be today's truth. The ship we were on (can't be pirates without a ship) was anchored offshore, the sails dropped. It was from Bequia, I'd heard one of the sailors say.

The talent from Miami was uniformly dark and handsome—with many nationalities represented—Asian, Spanish, Brazilian, Argentinean, even a black Irishman.

Thank God they'd also imported a stylist to assist me. He was great, and had just moved to South Beach from . . . Texas. On the flight over he'd gotten to know all the extra boys, so it was easy for him to get them dressed in their ruffles and boots and on deck, on time, without damaging anything.

The girls were sweaty, and Sascha spent her time repairing melting makeup, while I tried to hide the cords that kept Fate of Paradise from falling off the side of the ship, yet still give the appearance they were actually pulling themselves up.

Fool the people, right?

"Why we aren't doing this in a nice climate-controlled studio, and a set, with the camera turned on its side, is completely beyond me," Teddy complained as he mopped his brow.

"Because it's such a pretty ship?" I asked. "Or because this is Donny's fantasy?" I wouldn't have guessed Donny got off on ships and heights from looking at his Prada suits, but once he put on shorts and well-worn climbing shoes, it became obvious.

Mostly Teddy, Sascha, and the ladies in the band realized this because we could all see his bubble-shaped tush; squats, horseback riding, and climbing produce that kind of firmness.

"Great motor, that boy," Eladonna said under her breath as I adjusted her shirt.

"Indeed he has," I said. "Your boots okay?"

She nodded. "You're the best."

Because of the humidity and their faux tans, I couldn't spray-tac the girls, so I put two of them in chokers, two in long earrings, and one in a hat. The ruffles were easier to deal with, though we lost a strip of color off London's shoulder thanks to doublestick tape. Sascha repaired it with makeup, and we were off.

In the finished product, the girls would be singing as they climbed up the side of a square-rigger. Cut to the "pirates" following them, starting up the end of the rope. Back to the girls, climbing faster. Now the boys fighting among themselves, until one falls into the water (we'd shoot that part later).

Cut to girls on deck, kicking the boys off. (Bungee cords.) Girls searching through the ship, with torches. (Fire and wood; that was fun.) Disarming boys with feminine charms. Boys slain.

Final shot: girls finding the treasure as the sun sets behind them.

We had two chances to get the ending right. The ladies nailed it both times. Then half the crew raced down to film the water scenes, including the stylist from Texas.

By dark, the video was done and we were on shore. The

ship was sailing away, we could see its white sails as the moon rose. It was a beautiful sight, one that produced shivers that had nothing to do with sunburn.

Bette passed out the lunches and beers, and we sat down to admire the stars while the Miami people took their lunches for the road. First a boat to Bimini—Donny was escorting them to Alice Town—then they'd catch a flight to Miami.

"Is good to work," Sascha said, leaning back.

"That's so true," I said, stretching my toes and leaning into her.

"Is even better to rest after work," Sascha said. We laughed.

"We're rock stars!" Jillyian, who'd turned out to be as nimble as a mountain goat, said, holding her bottle up.

"Rock stars!" we all echoed and clinked glass.

"This is so good," Zima said. "The food is always good, but this—"

"Always tastes better when you're starving," Teddy said.

"True-true," someone said, mimicking Mama Garcia.

"In fact," Teddy said, "I think we all earned a little present."

"Like what?" Jillyian asked, flirting with him.

"Like some of those brownies from last night. Those were the best—"

"They had some of the best," Sascha said.

"What do you mean?"

"Those were Oscar's famous Rasta brownies," Bette said. "They'd be as famous as his coconut suspiros—"

"If they weren't illegal," Ka'Arih said.

"There is that," Bette said with a laugh.

We all chuckled, so we didn't really hear her, but then Eladonna collapsed.

Choking.

Chapter Ten

The return ride was reckless. I was at the wheel of the Humvie while Teddy navigated and everyone else watched Eladonna. I apologized for every swerve and teeth-jarring bump, but I didn't slow down. I just prayed no one would jump in front of me.

Teddy had brought his cell phone, and called ahead to the castle.

Oscar and Mama Garcia met us outside. Oscar carried Eladonna into the drawing room while Mama issued orders to the island boys. "Ginger rum, I be needin' and some towels. Dat herbal poultice in my yallo-topped jar," she said as she settled beside Eladonna. "At da house."

"Do we know all her allergies?" I asked.

Mama nodded. "I got her whole medical file, faxed ober from da Main."

I would have asked when, but it seemed inconsequential.

"What was dis girl eatin'?" Mama asked.

"One of the lunches," London said. "Same as all of us. I believe hers was the wrap thing."

"Blue corn tortilla, fresh mahimahi, coriander, cilantro,

garlic, egg and oil in the mayonnaise, yucca and yam," Oscar recited as he knelt by Eladonna's feet.

"She choked—"

"Teddy got her breathing—"

"We can't wake her up—"

"She's allergic—"

"There's nothing in my kitchen that she's allergic to," Oscar said.

"Coconut?" I asked.

He didn't even look at me. "She doesn't like it, but she's not allergic to it." His glance was as sharp as the knife Palize had held. "And I didn't serve it to her."

As if by a miracle, Eladonna opened her eyes. "I'm gonna be sick," she said. Oscar produced a container, and we all backed up.

A few minutes later, she said she felt okay. Mama Garcia doused her with ginger rum. Eladonna acted like she was fine. The group dispersed, and Mama told some of the island boys to go get the stuff we'd left on the beach.

Oscar, white-faced, disappeared into the kitchen. I followed him. I passed the other kitchen guys, who worked silently in the kitchen, leaving as I entered.

"What do you want, Dallas?" Oscar asked, alone in the big steel and white room.

"I came to apologize," I said.

"For accusing me of poisoning a guest?"

"No."

"Then leave," he said, and started to sharpen a knife.

"No, I mean, I didn't ever think you poisoned the guest. I thought she ate something by accident maybe. How did y'all get her medical records so fast?"

Oscar turned to me. "It's my responsibility to keep you all healthy and satisfied, at least in the kitchen. To that end, I had anyone with medical complaints or food issues send me her records."

"That is so thoughtful."

"It's responsible," he said. "I don't often break trusts placed in me."

"I'm not racist," I blurted out.

He shrugged. "I guess I couldn't blame you if you were. Only in the last twenty years has being Irish not been a curse word in New York or Boston, Ms. O'Connor."

I think I preferred being called wench. I wasn't sure how to get the conversation back on track, but I opened my mouth to try, when Mama Garcia blew in.

Oscar looked at her. She looked at him, then me. "We wait," she said. "Only den we know."

"Two hours?" he asked.

"De maximum we wait," she said. "Where be dose oder loanch boxes?"

He looked at me.

"On the beach, I guess," I said. "Why?"

"She been poisoned," Mama said.

"But I thought you said—" I looked back and forth between them. "I don't understand."

"Jamaica poisonin'," Mama said. She looked out, as if she could see the sky through the walls. "Da storm be comin, dis is just de first." She left, telling Oscar she'd be back in two hours. That would be ten o'clock, according to my watch. Oscar didn't even wear one. He picked up his knife and continued to sharpen it.

"I, uh," I said, and backed toward the door. Suddenly he looked really dangerous and very angry. Hadn't everyone said he was crazy, including the employee he'd tried to kill earlier? The sound of the knife on stone was crawling inside my head. "I fall in love with Latinos too easily," I said, and backed through the door.

He didn't follow me, didn't shout a question, didn't even break his sharpening rhythm. I found myself in the torchlit hallway. Should I go up to my room? Two hours, I thought.

Something was going to happen in two hours. I walked toward the drawing room instead.

Paradise was spiked with snakes. Which ones were dangerous?

Ka'Arih and Eladonna had changed into shorts and T-shirts and were sitting on the floor, tossing things in the air. Eladonna looked fine.

"Dallas! We're playin' Pass the Pigs," Ka'Arih said. "Come on in!"

I needed a shot of Shakira. "I'm going to rinse the sweat off first," I said and went back into the hallway. I got the CD out of the workroom and went up to my room for a shower. I checked my voice mail, rinsed out my lingerie, and jumped around to *Ojas Asi*. I put on jeans, a shirt, and paused while brushing my hair. Where had the musicians been all day, especially Zac?

Downstairs, Ka'Arih was winning. Eladonna still looked fine. It was almost ten o'clock, and the other girls were coming in, refreshed. The clothes and bags from the beach had been left outside my workroom door, with an addition: an empty jar tied around the handle of one of the suitcases.

Weird.

Donny burst in from getting rid of the Miami day-workers. "What the hell is going on? I got a message saying that Eladonna collapsed and—" he stopped when he saw her. "You're fine," he said. "Thank God, I was so worried. I—"

Eladonna grinned weakly. "I don't feel so good, actually."

"You said you felt okay," Ka'Arih said, and reached across to check Eladonna's temperature.

I ran to the kitchen. Oscar stood with his back to me. "Whatever you anticipated, I think it's happening," I said.

He turned around. "Eladonna?"

"She doesn't feel good."

"Gastric lavage," he said, and walked into the hallway between the main kitchen, the fridge room, and the pastel kitchen. He took a bottle out of a doctor's bag. Mama Garcia came in.

"It be?"

"Dallas said Eladonna doesn't feel good," he said, and as he spoke he gathered a plastic bucket and towels.

"Time for cascatin'," Mama said.

The room I entered was different from the one I'd left. Eladonna was lying on the couch. Everyone was panicked. Oscar brushed them aside. Teddy got them grouped on one side of the room.

Mama Garcia and Oscar persuaded Eladonna to vomit her guts up; the mysterious cascatin'.

Soon the rest of us were standing in the hallway.

"I don't understand what happened," Ka'Arih said. "She said she was fine."

Sascha said she was going to the garden to wait. I stayed by the door. A half-hour later Donny opened the door. "It's okay. They say she's okay."

"Should you get a doctor?" Jillyian asked. "Medivac?"

"Mama Garcia probably knows what she's doing," I said. If it was something called Jamaica poisoning, it was closer to her backyard than anyone else's. Supposing the name did have something to do with Jamaica.

Donny nodded. "You can come back in," he said. "Oscar and I will help her to her room." Sascha went with them. Mama Garcia made me carry the barf bucket, and I followed her to the kitchen.

She turned on the water in the sink and we washed everything away.

"Is she going to be okay?" I asked.

"She gonna be okay," Mama said. "No one try to kill-kill, jes to make her sick."

"This was malicious, not an accident?"

"Jamaica poisonin' be a tricky t'ing."

"Is she going to be harmed, long-term?"

"No. She make it tru da night, she be fine." Mama turned to look at me then, her big black eyes sharp and angry. "Somebody tryin' to warn dis girl dat she in danger. Now who wanna do dat? A nice singer girl wi't pretty clot'es and good smile? You find sip-sip about dat, Miz Dallas O'Connor, servant o' deat'." She turned back to scrub the bucket. "You find dat out after a good night sleep. Go on, chile."

The night was cool and lovely, and it felt so strange because things were getting weird. It shouldn't be lovely if someone was trying to make Eladonna sick; those two things didn't gel. Did Mama Garcia think I was doing this? Who would hurt Eladonna? Send her a warning about what?

I was in my room when I heard a knock at the door. Zac? According to Donny, the musicians had spent the day in the studio "laying down" tracks for the next songs. I tiptoed across to the door, pausing to fluff my hair, rub my teeth, and gobble down an Altoid. He was married, and off limits, but I had a right to make him suffer a little. I tightened the sash of my robe and opened the collar, for just a hint of cleavage, and swallowed the Altoid.

Shakira was singing to her man, "*You are a song written by the hands of God.*"

Zac wasn't standing outside my door. A dripping wet, braided-hair, wild-eyed chef was. "Evenin', lass," he said.

"*Underneath your clothes,*" Shakira sang. I slammed on the pause.

"Take a gander," Oscar said, holding out his hand. "Do you see this?"

The light in my bedroom was romantic, suggestive—in fact, the whole room was. I pulled Oscar into the bathroom with its clinical light. I blinked at the thing in his hand. Had

I ever seen it before? It looked vaguely sexual, sort of like a flower, but—"Is it a vegetable?" I asked.

"It's a fruit, but in Jamaica they cook it with saltfish as a vegetable," he explained.

It looked a little like pear, but someone had cut it open. I could see olive-looking things inside. "Do you . . . want me to taste it?" I asked. Why else would he bring a vegetable to my room?

"Have you ever seen an ackee before?"

"No, is this an ackee?"

"Yes."

"Okay." I looked at the thing. "The significance is?"

"It's from Jamaica."

And?

"It's poisonous."

I jerked my hand back.

"Not to the touch, and only when it's unripe or rotten."

"How can you tell?" I asked.

"See this cut?" he said, and pointed to the uniform slices that had opened it. "Whoever did this had to cut it open. When it's ripe it opens; it knows when it's ready to eat, and it protects the eater until then. Naturally."

He was talking about vegetables; but my thoughts were quite different.

"This is what made Eladonna sick?" I asked, dragging myself to the here and now.

"I knew that under that lustrous golden mop you were a thinker. Yes. One of the islanders found this ackee, cut-open, minus an aril. The aril," he pointed, "is this white part; it's the poisonous part. There are usually three." There were only two now.

"Where did the islander find it?"

"Outside, beneath a tree. As if someone had plucked the aril and discarded the rest."

"Why did you bring it to me?"

"Mama Garcia said to. She said you could sip-sip—gossip around—and figure out who did this."

I laughed, short and sharp. "You believed her?"

"Mama knows people," he said thoughtfully. "She sees things other people don't."

"Who had access to the garden where this was found?" I asked.

"Everyone," he said. "Gardens aren't restricted."

The only person I'd seen in the garden, ever, had been Ka'Arih. But Palize had walked through once that I knew of, and Sascha and I'd been there a dozen times already. Anyone could have done it.

"What about the blade?" I said, and pointed to the cut. "Can you tell anything from the cut? Like, was it a chef's knife? And before you get offended," I talked on, "I'm just asking so you know whether or not a knife is missing."

"What—we'd find the knife and you'd know who did it?"

"Maybe."

He looked at the cut. "I need my glasses," he said.

"You wear glasses?" I couldn't imagine this sexy, long-haired pirate in a pair of horn-rims.

"I'm forty-six years old," Oscar said. "I do a lot of reading and wear glasses for that. Can you see?" He pushed the ackee into my face.

"Yes," I snapped. But I had to admit, not as well as I used to. The days of reading glasses weren't far away, especially with all the handwork I did. "Looks jagged to me."

"Serrated knife, you're thinking?"

"A person who can't cut? A person with shaky hands?" I handed it back. "Never mind. It was a stupid question. I don't know what I'm talking about." I walked out of the bathroom, and Oscar followed me.

"I have to get back to the kitchens," he said. "We can talk

about this in the morning." I looked up at him, and he glanced at me with a look of such electricity I was sure my hair was standing on end.

Did I dare ask him to come up and talk about it tonight? But before I could figure out what to say, he exited, leaving me holding the poison.

Chapter Eleven

Donny appeared to be pretty shaken up by the time everyone went to bed, even though Eladonna had woken up, and Mama pronounced her "fix-fix." By the time I woke up, though, Donny was back at his a.m. activities. I guessed his spirits had improved. I put on my shorts, tank, and shoes, then went out for my run. The day was going to be okay.

Mama Garcia had just freaked me out with her mystic-sounding talk. My mother has embraced fortune-telling in her advancing years, and the last time I'd been home in Austin she'd had a "Goddess Party" with live enzyme foods and a ritual that resembled a maypole, even though it was March. According to my ever-proper brother Houston, a "freak show" guest list had attended.

But when Mom got that faraway look in her pretty brown eyes and pronounced something, it had this strange way of being the truth. Mama Garcia gave off that same energy. I ran harder, leaving those eerie feelings behind me. The flowers were still orange and pink, red and purple, the water was still breathtaking in a million shades of blue and green. Everything was okay. I ran until I was empty and smiling.

At a breakfast of fresh fruit batidos (basically a Bahamian

virgin smoothie) and still-warm muffins, Donny announced we were jumping the schedule. The weather for tomorrow looked like it might storm, so we'd be shooting the mermaid part of the video today.

"Ready, Dallas?" he asked me.

I smiled and nodded. Thank God I'd gotten those tails done.

"*You* are the mermaid girl?" Teddy asked. "I've heard about you!"

Entirely by accident, I've become rather well known for my "mermaids." I don't know how, or why, but I did them once for a memorable catalog shoot, and I've been doing them ever since. Different each time, but mermaids. I had one whole portfolio just of mermaids. Like twenty-one different shoots.

This time, though, the costumes had to be at least partially submersible.

"I'm hot."

"This is sticky."

"Can I have something to drink?"

"Could we wear sunglasses?"

"I think I'm getting a rash."

"Kill them all," Sascha said to me as we listened to the myriad complaints of the mermaids on the seashore. At least no one had to go to the bathroom, which would have ruined everything.

"Take three," Donny shouted.

We ducked out of the picture, and the music of Fate of Paradise blasted us from all sides. The girls lip-synched along to their song while Sascha and I shared her tiny fan. It was hotter today than it had been since we'd arrived. I knew the girls were probably uncomfortable in those giant plastic tails, but this was the tough part of being a rock star.

Donny, in a complete change of mood from the sweet-natured boy who laughed and joked and wasn't above an afternoon hit, was playing commandant. No breaks, no resting, just get the damn thing done.

"Donny got a call from Bad Wolf," Teddy confided in us. "I overheard him talking. Somebody wants the video sooner."

"Who's Bad Wolf?" I asked.

"Big bad producer," Sascha said. "Record-company man."

"Sooner than what?" I asked.

"Before the music gets sent to the radio stations. I think TRL wants to premiere it," Teddy said. "But don't quote me."

Ooo. TRL was MTV's twenty-first-century answer to *American Bandstand*. A premiere on TRL meant a huge jump in sales, which corresponded to entering the *Billboard* charts at a higher number. Like number one.

You learn this stuff working on "bideo." "Wow," I said. "They've got it all goin' on."

"Bik time," Sascha said.

"But I thought Donny didn't work for the record company—?"

"Donny—" she started.

"Dallas!" Donny barked.

I raced over to him, my hands on my tool necklace so stuff didn't fly out and I didn't accidentally wound myself. "Yeah?" I said.

"Ka'Arih has to pee," he said.

"How many more takes are there?" I asked.

"Until we get it right!"

"What do you want me to do?" I asked.

"How long will it take her to get out of and back into the tail?"

Each tail was constructed of Saran Wrap, in green and blue and purple and pink, each sheet layered over and on top of each other so the final product was a shimmery, iridescent, form-fitting solid piece. The fins at the end were constructed of lamé and beading, a task that had taken me the entire flight from LA to NYC, when I was going to another job. (I've started keeping one set of three "mermaids" in my stock.)

I'd used the lower half of a mannequin to form each of the tails, and thankfully I'd used some different sized mannequins. London's I'd made here, using the dressmaker's model, maxed out.

Each girl had shimmied into the tail, then I'd wrapped it a few more times for a perfect fit. The only way out? Cut the tails, from hip to foot. This was a one-shot deal. And I'd told Donny that from the start, since he'd wanted mermaids no one else had done before.

"As I believe I mentioned," I said, "once the girls are out, it's over."

"What do you mean, over?"

"Over. The tail is ruined."

"You can't tape it or something? It's just plastic, right?"

"I have to pee!" Ka'Arih shouted.

"You want them to roll over on the sand, you intend to show every side of the tail," I said. "That means I can't patch it. We had this discussion."

"What should she do, then?" he asked.

"How much longer will it take?" I said.

"Dammit!" He stormed over to Ka'Arih. "If you all would actually do what we need you to, this will be over in less than a minute. Do you hear me?"

They nodded, all five.

"No more screw-ups, sing the right verse, roll at the correct time, don't start giggling, and don't get stuck. Just do it right for once!" He was bellowing; Donny had either lost it, or was coming into his own. I knew he'd gotten plenty of action, so he shouldn't be in a bad mood. Bad Wolf must translate into Big Trouble.

"Do we need makeup?" he shouted.

Sascha knelt at the camera's height and checked the girls, then powdered their shoulders in record time.

"Great!" Donny shouted. "Now shoot!"

Amazingly, they did it flawlessly. Sing, roll, sing, cut.

"Is it good?" I asked Donny.

He looked over at the cameraman, who gave him a thumbs-up. "Yes," he said. "Get 'em out of there."

I knelt by Ka'Arih first. "Just a second and you'll be free," I said, brandishing my X-acto blade.

"Don't push on my stomach, or I might—"

The image was in my head. "I'll be careful," I said, and cut. She ran into the water.

"Go far out!" Jillyian called to her.

"We don't wanna get caught in your stream," Eladonna added.

Ka'Arih disappeared into the water.

"Can we go?" Jillyian asked Donny.

They were all soaking wet with sweat.

"We're going to be in the studio the remainder of the day," London said.

"And probably night," Zima said.

"Please?" Jillyian asked.

Ka'Arih was playing in the water like a dolphin.

"Fine. Everyone can take a swim break," Donny said. "Don't ruin anything, and we can't stay out here for long."

"The sun," Sascha said from the depths of her big floppy hat. "Is very bad for skin."

I slathered on more sunscreen and pulled off my clothes before running into the water. "Oh God," I groaned, "This is paradise!" The water was cooler than a bath, so it felt refreshing, but it wasn't cold. "It's luscious," I said and beckoned Sascha. She ran in, wearing panties and the hat, squealing.

Everyone splashed in the surf. "Let's have chicken fights!"

Ka'Arih called. Jillyian climbed on Donny's back, and Sascha climbed onto Teddy's, and the two girls struggled to dethrone each other while we cheered them on, or sabotaged them. Jillyian won, tossing Sascha into the sea, and then the girls got into it, with a splash fight that drew almost everyone else.

Ka'Arih, the instigator, sat down next to me on the beach. Her hair was curly, even wet, and the glitter of her mendhi necklace accented her curves. "Why aren't you up there?" I asked as the girls climbed on Eladonna's and Zima's backs to chicken fight again.

"I'm the peacemaker, 'member?"

"I think you're the troublemaker," I said and pushed her.

She laughed and pushed back. "Really, Sascha and Jillyian are perfectly matched," she said. "Sascha's an adventurer. She'll do anything at least once. And Jillyian is an achiever. It's very important for her to project the right image, to be what people want to see."

"She is perfect for the lead singer, then," I said.

Ka'Arih looked over at me, with almost an expression of surprise on her face. "Right," she said. "She's perfect."

"You two ready to head back?" Donny asked, walking by us.

We got up and gathered our stuff, trickling back to the castle. We were halfway back when Zima screamed. Donny turned around and looked, swore, then took off running. I followed.

Sascha was lying on the sand, jerking around. Her eyes were rolled back in her head and white flecked her Communist red lips. Donny knelt by one side and grabbed her hands, and Teddy grabbed her feet. "Get out of here," he shouted to the rest of us. "Just go, don't let her know you saw."

I stood, watching my friend in the throes of an epileptic attack. I'd never been so helpless. "Her tongue," I said—I'd heard the danger of the victim swallowing her own tongue, or biting it; in fact it's the only thing I remembered about epilepsy.

Jillyian put her hand on my arm. "She's okay, they know what to do. C'mon."

We walked away.

Lunch was sandwiches, courtesy of a grouchy Palize. I took one look at his face and decided not to ask about Oscar. I was sitting in the garden, spraying clothes with a combo of water and lemon juice to give them a good worn look, when Oscar walked into the garden carrying his fishing pole and gorgeous catch. "They're very pretty," I said with a smile.

"They'd be so pleased," he said. "Being pretty is important to fish."

I sprayed him with the water. "Smart-ass."

"Aho!" he said. "You forbid me to swear, yet you twist your tongue around those nefarious words? That's worse than smoking in front of a man trying to kick the habit!"

"You deserve a little torture if you're going to be sarcastic," I said.

"I deserve a lot of torture," he said with a joyful laugh, and pulled me to him. There, in the garden beneath the palm trees, in the heat of the afternoon, when the lizards and the birds were still, he kissed me.

He tasted like sunshine. Like Coke with lemon. I was smiling when he pulled away.

"I didn't catch enough to feed everyone, unless we add some loaves and some God, but enough to experiment with. You going to want dinner?"

"Did you hear about Sascha?" I asked.

"Epilepsy, right?"

I nodded.

"Donny had already expressed there would be only four at

dinner, so it doesn't change my plans. Sascha's a big girl, she'll be fine."

"Of course," I said, folding my things up.

"Are you loose?" Oscar asked.

"How do you mean?" I asked with an arched brow.

He laughed again, and touched my brow. "You can lower that, lass. I wasn't asking as in easy virtue, but as in, do you want to talk to me while I cook?"

"I'd love to!" I was too enthusiastic. Izarra, Dallas. Remember?

But was my fear of his name because of what appeared to be a long, fruitless string of mistakes that had the common thread of men with Latino heritages, or because of some twisted perspective on perfectionism? My twisted perspective?

"Basque is Spain, right?" I asked.

Oscar picked up my basket and opened the door for us. "Basque is in Spain and in France," he said.

"How'd you get from there to here?"

"Cod," he answered.

"Oscar," Bette called to us. "I'm sorry, but—"

"Excuse me," he said, and left me.

I hung around for a while, but he didn't come back. I put the fish in the kitchen and took my stuff back to the dressing room. According to the schedule, tomorrow was a photo shoot—several different looks. I pulled clothes, steamed them, and walked into the kitchen on several pretexts.

No one knew where Oscar was.

Disgusted with myself, I took an offered Sahoco (sugar, rum and coconut) and went back to the beach. I swam, I frolicked, I watched the fish, I swam some more. At dark I went to my room, showered, ate my Pria bars, and went to bed.

Alone. On purpose.

* * *

Another perfect day in paradise, I thought as I scampered up the stairs after my run. Ten hours of sleep made me feel like a new woman, and I couldn't wait to get to work.

"Good morning, y'all," I said as I walked into the dining room.

"Where were you?" Eladonna asked, as she fanned her face.

"How did you get out of it?" London said. She was soaked with sweat.

"What are y'all talking about?"

"Teddy's class, the booty ballerina yoga," Jillyian said. "God, I'm dead."

"Even Donny took it," London said. "Where were you?"

"On the beach," I said. "What did he make y'all do?"

"Twist my body into a shape meant for a pretzel, not a human," London said. "I haven't seen my toes that closely since I was three."

"Did you suck on your toes?" Ka'Arih asked. "My mama said I sucked on my toes, not my thumb."

I looked at the schedule. "Are you telling me that we will not be shooting at ten?"

"Ask Bette," Zima said. "I can't move."

I poked my head into the kitchen, where all five of the cooks were rocking out to "Garbage," discussing what they'd like to do to Shirley, the lead singer. Oscar hadn't seen me, but at least I knew he was around. I checked in the drawing room for Bette, and the workroom, but I didn't find her.

Back in the dining room, everyone was gone.

Well, sooner or later they would need me. I returned to the workroom, cranked the music (Shakira, again), and composed the outfits.

Ka'Arih came in first. "Do you know who the photographer is?" she squealed. "It's Cattie Abramson, from Miami!"

Cattie's day rate was like $35K. She'd photographed the *Pirelli* catalog, *Sports Illustrated*, and virtually every celebrity and politician on the planet. "Damn," I said, impressed. I also felt a tremble of fear. Cattie was known for her absolute whiplash of a tongue and the unmerciful way she treated assistants and stylists. Damn.

I finished my coffee and got very focused.

The first "look" was Asian-inspired. London wore a Gaultier, chinese-ish black dress over wide-legged pants in a green, dragon-studded print. Sascha had ironed her hair straight and twisted some of it up. No chopsticks, though. Zima wore a black skirt, over-the-knee boots, and a Marc Jacobs–interpretation Chinese shirt (in peach) with an asymmetrical frog closing. Her hair was long, straight, and Sascha had given her fur-fake lashes, in fox.

Eladonna wore a red cheongsam. Her hair fell in ringlets and I'd managed to procure some antique Buddha earrings with garnets. (Garage sales of the old and rich can be so profitable.) Her own slingback pumps completed the outfit.

Jillyian, who really could look Asian if we wanted, was the least dressed. Seven jeans, a Dior denim patchwork camisole, and a Dior kimono. For fun, she wore red, platform, lace boots.

Ka'Arih was the star of this look. She'd never appeared more alluring. I put her in a sky blue clouds-and-mountains brocade fitted tunic, an antique (same garage sale) necklace with a blue tassel, and a pair of Carolina Herrera pants that were like second skin. Sascha had gone crazy with makeup and fingernails. But I really thought it was the blue that made Ka'Arih stand out so much.

Working with Cattie had us all nervous. She snorted coke while her assistants set everything up and endured her abuse in silent humiliation. Even Donny was a little quieter than usual. Sascha and I exchanged many, as my grandmama would say, "speaking" glances.

"What is with that thing," Cattie asked at about 11:45. "It's hanging. Is it supposed to be hanging?"

Sascha and I both tried to see what this expensive photographer was looking at.

"Makeup or clothes?" one of the assistants, a brow-beaten girl, asked.

"These aren't clothes," Cattie said with a snicker. "These are costumes!"

Sascha laid a hand on my arm, calming me. It was okay, I was calm.

"I mean, look at this shit." Cattie was standing by Zima, picking at her clothes.

I walked forward; models were used to being talked about like they weren't present, but these girls weren't accustomed to that disrespect, especially Zima. "Is there something you want me to fix?" I asked the woman. She was short, with thick glasses, a butch haircut, and the biggest square-cut diamond ring that I'd ever seen in my life. And I've styled some big gems before. "A problem?" I asked.

"Cattie!" the shout came from the back of the room. She turned around.

"Oscar! Love!" She wobbled across the room and fell into the arms of the man from Basque. They talked and laughed and we stood and waited. After ten minutes, Oscar led her away. The first assistant, Jane, looked at us, looked at her watch and then called lunch.

"Did we get what we needed?" I asked Donny. He handed me the Polaroids. I flipped through them, then asked the first assistant. Jane checked her rolls of film and nodded. Poor kid, I thought.

"C'mon, girls, let's change before lunch," I said. They trooped after me into the dressing room. "Back here in an hour," I said. "We need to try on for the next look." Call for the next look wasn't until 2 p.m. so I figured that should give me enough time to make sure things fit and matched.

The afternoon was an all-bronze vision. Basically easy, different necklines, different accessories, but the general rule of leather pants or skirt and top. Sascha had outdone herself, even adding some copper and bronze streaks to Zima's and London's hair.

Cattie, über photographer, was even less present. She criticized one of her assistants until the girl burst into tears. Cattie only wanted to listen to David Bowie and spent the whole time talking about Iman and David, what dear friends they were, blah, blah, blah.

By four o'clock we were at the last look: ethereal white dresses. The girls were lounging on white velvet sofas and it was all very dreamy. Two of them were in nightgowns, two in evening gowns, and Jillyian wore white leather pants and an angora halter sweater with $1,100 Jimmy Choo sandals and exquisite platinum jewelry that would have maxed out any of my cards, but that the Centurion handled with no problem.

The entire castle breathed a sound of relief as Cattie's seaplane took off, loaded with her gear and those poor people who worked for her, for $200 a day.

"I need drink," Sascha said. "She is big bitch, I hear this always but I never believe." She laughed. "Oho, now I believe."

"How could she talk about us like we weren't even alive?" Ka'Arih asked.

I glanced at London. Cattie had had some less than nice things to say about the former fashion model. "You okay?" I asked London.

"Just glad I quit," she said.

That night the girls played and we tangoed, drank, smoked, and laughed. I'd been here for a week, and I never wanted to leave.

*   *   *

I woke up earlier than usual, to peaceful silence. It was 5:45 and still dark, so I did some crunches and pushups before putting on my clothes and slipping on my Nikes.

The sun was just tinting the sky in coral and rose as I ran to the beach. I didn't think about anything; I didn't worry. I counted off the steps in sets of fifteen, my breathing even in my ears. The sand and sea streamed by, beyond the trees that were beginning to look familiar, decorated with empty bottles hung on colored string. The tide was out, revealing another twenty feet of beach. This place was as flat as a flitter. I ran on, edging closer to the surf.

Ahead of me, above the sand, the birds were circling. A stranded fish? Do fish get stranded, I wondered. I ran faster. I could just see a shape. The thing was large, whatever it was. I shouted to shoo away the birds.

Then I came to a screeching halt.

The thing, the white bloated thing, was . . . a body.

Chapter Twelve

I blinked, tried to reason with myself about dolphins, seaweed, anything, but when I opened my eyes, it was a human, it was a he, and it was still there. Dead, obviously, for quite a while.

Fish and water had done a number on him, but I did notice one thing: his hands were tied in front of him, and his hair was long and curly. His hands were *tied*. I looked away before I got sick.

Dead body. Zac being here. Tobin Charles button. Coincidences?

I looked back at the body. Who was he? Why did he wash up here? Why were his hands tied? What weird rope. Somehow, the rope looked familiar, felt familiar. I didn't want to turn my back to him, but I was less than halfway around the island. The tide was still going out, so he would be here for a while. I should tell someone about this. I should tell Zac. I should tell Donny.

"Don't, don't go anywhere," I said to the body, then turned around and headed toward the castle.

* * *

"Dallas! Good morning!" Bette called to me as I jogged into the gardens. "A good workout this morning?"

I nodded.

"Oscar has fixed a special this morning—sweet potato pancakes with some kind of rum syrup. You do eat pancakes, don't you?" The assistant looked over my perspiration-slicked body in Texas-flag running shorts and tank top. "You don't look like you've ever eaten pancakes."

I nodded again and started to do my cool-down stretches.

"See you in there," she said, and sailed through the doors to the dining room.

The sun was already warming, the flowers were already opening. All in all it was a beautiful day. I held my hamstring stretch for a count of sixty, then changed legs. A perfect day, with one imperfect glitch. How in the world was I going to tell anyone? Especially over breakfast?

I debated whether I should shower first, or just go make my announcement. I got up and walked into the dining room. The pack was at it, devouring lush fruit, fresh juices, and mountains of yallo-buttered pancakes, served family style. "Better grab somethin' before it's all gone," Ka'Arih said to me, her napkin coquettishly before her still-chewing mouth. "It's plumb delicious!"

"Good morning, my darling," Sascha said and reached over to buss my cheeks. It sounded like she said "darlink." "And your sleeping was good?"

I kissed her back and nodded.

"What's on the schedule today?" Zima asked, cutting her pancakes into little pieces.

How about picking up a body off the beach, I thought to myself. Instead of speaking I paced behind the chairs, shaking off the run.

"Dallas, please, must you parade back and forth without showering?" London asked. "I swear, being downwind of you is enough to put me off my pancakes."

That, I had a hard time believing.

"Well," I said, "I have something to tell y'all, and it's going to be kind of hard to stomach."

"Then please wait until after we finish," Teddy said. "This is deelish; I don't care about the carbs. Girls, we will be doing two training sessions this afternoon. Remind me."

They groaned.

"Dallas, some juice?" Bette asked.

I looked at the selections: fresh orange from a tree outside, fresh mango from Alice Town's market, fresh papaya from the garden, and packaged V8. Suddenly I felt a little queasy. I shook my head.

There was mostly silence, just the clanging of utensils against china while the group ate. Sascha didn't eat; she smoked her breakfast while drinking coffee. Donny breezed in, freshly shaved and showered, his dark curls damp still. Already he was immaculate in open-necked shirt and suit. "Good morning, cherubs," he said as he kissed cheeks down the table. "How is everyone?" He looked up at me. "A bit casual today, Dallas? Though it's not a bad look, all long-legged tan and sweaty. Might want to do something about—" he motioned to his eyes. "You look—"

"You've got raccoon eyes," Ka'Arih said, and giggled.

"There's a body on the beach," I blurted.

Silence. All eyes turned to me.

"A what?" Donny asked.

"A body, a dead body, on the beach. I found it while I was running."

London set down her knife and fork. "Ugh, this is not proper mealtime conversation."

"Is this the news you had?" Eladonna asked.

I nodded.

"A body? Really?" Donny asked. "That's fascinating."

"Especially for him," I said.

"Well, what did you do?" Teddy asked.

"What do you mean? It's a body. I found it on the beach."

"Did you move it, bring it—"

"We're talking a male. Older, bigger—" partially digested "— no, I didn't touch it."

"They can get way gross if they's left for a few days," Zima said.

"Thanks for that image," Eladonna said and pushed her plate away.

Donny, unperturbed, sat down beside Sascha. She moved away and crossed her legs and arms. "Where do I get a plate?" he asked.

"Palize!" Jillyian called.

The lesser pirate poked his head through the kitchen door. "Donny needs a plate."

"Get Dallas something," Teddy said.

"Get Dallas something," Jillyian repeated in her haughtiest tone.

"Dallas, you want a batido or somethin'?" Palize asked me.

"I think we should call the cops," I said hesitantly.

"Bring me a Bloody Mary," Donny said.

Palize vanished into the kitchen.

"Try it with the rum syrup," Bette said to Donny as he took her plate and covered it in orange-colored pancakes. "Or the pureed mandarins, that was so good."

"I thought those were a little sweet," Zima said.

"Mandarins are so tiny. What's the difference between them and clementines?" Jillyian asked.

"*Oh my darlin', oh my darlin', oh my darlin' Clementine, you are lost and gone forever, oh my darlin' Clementine,*" Ka'Arih sang.

"Isn't that the song about the meatball?" Zima asked.

"Who needs the cops?" Oscar asked, placing a batido in front of me, a warmed plate in front of Bette. "What's the problem?"

"Ask Dallas," Sascha said with a wink at me.

"Dallas has been out running," Ka'Arih added.

Oscar's look toward me was wicked. "Your casual attire is pardoned. You can wear shorts like that to my table at your will. For a batido, would you prefer banana or papaya?"

"You're so lucky you can eat bananas," Eladonna said. "They make me so sick. I didn't know anything was wrong until I ate this banana one day—"

"Papaya," I said.

Oscar threw his hands in the air. "I win! I guessed you would say that."

"There's a body on the beach," I said. "I think we should go get it, or go take a Polaroid, or something."

Oscar turned around. "A body?"

"Dead."

"Imagine that," he said. "Body assumes the form of an inanimate object, which could mean dead."

"Or just without animus," Eladonna said. "Like a body of water."

"Or a body of work," Bette said.

"Or a body shop," Ka'Arih said.

Eladonna shrugged. "Not exactly."

"This is a body, as in a corpse," I said. How could they be so blasé?

"Man or woman?" Oscar asked.

"Man."

"Been in the water long or—" he asked.

"Ewww! I thought the chef—" London started.

Oscar yanked me into the kitchens, and I caught the dish towel before it hit me in the face. Oscar shouted at Palize, threatening to cut out his tongue and feed it to his mother for the next Saints Day, with a side of eggplant. Palize flipped him off and turned back to cooking. The other cooks watched with inscrutable expressions.

Oscar lived in a weird, weird world.

"Will you do me a favor?" he asked me as he got a dry towel for my face.

"What?"

"Can you let these people eat their breakfast while it's hot? Do you think your dead person will wait?"

"Oscar—"

"Not to be rude, but if he's dead and lying on the beach, then he'll probably remain there, or do you fear his resurrection?"

"Don't blaspheme."

"You and my mother would love each other," he said. "Is another hour going to matter?"

"No, probably not."

"So you have time to go up, shower, and change into another one of those wonderful wacky outfits you wear, teeter down here on spindly heels, and then we'll go get him?"

I do not teeter. "We?" I said.

"I'll help you. I'll get some, I don't know, plastic bags or something. Blankets. I'll consult the stars to find out how to deal with a corpse."

"We could just take a picture," I said. "Show it to the cops."

"I guess so," he said, unenthusiastically. "In an hour, then."

"An hour," I said. "I think I'm going to shower."

He handed me my batido. "I think that's a good idea."

"Good." I turned to leave, then turned back to him. "Oscar? Have you seen Zac?"

He shook his head. "I think he left, or he's in the studio."

"Where's the studio?"

"The northwestern tower," he said. "The entire building is one grand studio; Castle Cay Studios. It's all soundproofed. They can do anything there, even make CDs."

"Thanks."

"If no one's there, it's locked."

I fled out of the kitchen, through the courtyard, and up to my room. A shower would give me time to decide what I was going to tell the cops when they arrived, when they started asking questions.

"*You are Dallas O'Connor? How many dead bodies have you discovered?*"

"*Today? Just one.*"

"*There are others? In fact, some would say you are Nancy Drew-like in your attraction to getting involved in mysteries.*"

"*Only a few others. And I'm not Nancy Drew, and I'm not in mysteries. I just have a bad tendency to be where bodies show up.*"

"*I see. Could you be a killer yourself, Ms. O'Connor?*"

"*I am not a killer.*"

"*Have you ever read Nancy Drew?*"

"*Not more than one. I couldn't understand a girl who would date Ned when the Hardy Boys were just a few doors down.*"

By the time my mental tirade had concluded I was standing in front of my closet door, looking in. I'd put on perfumed lotion, powder, deodorant—everything. We were going to be outside the rest of the day, shooting video of the girls lounging by the pool.

After we dealt with the body.

I slipped on a bikini and threw my long linen shirt and miniskirt over it, then added a wide-brimmed floppy hat and Gucci glasses. Some curved toe sandals from Turkey (gift from a model friend) and earrings. Of course, all of this was over SPF 30, which was over self-tanner.

I picked up my Polaroid camera from the workroom. "Are we ready?" I asked as I walked into the dining room.

"We're working outside today?" London said. "It's going to be hot."

"It is hot," Zima said as she came inside, gleaming with sweat.

"Donny," London pleaded. "Today? Why can't we shoot this evening?"

"You'll be half in the water, I believe," Donny said.

Bette, his brain, was already gone.

"I'm going to get the body," I said.

"The body? Oh, you mean that thing you found on the beach?" London asked.

"Donny, I think you should come since it's, well, this is all your story. Us being here," I said. "The police are going to have questions—"

"I don't think we have time to go see some imaginary—"

"Imaginary! You think I'm imagining a corpse?"

"Well—" Zima said. I looked from face to face. Eladonna shrugged. Ka'Arih looked pained, London avoided my gaze, and Donny gave me a sheepish grin. "We've all been very free, shall we say, with the recreation," Eladonna said. "It was probably just a bad trip or something."

"Hallucinations."

"Nothing to be ashamed of."

"I can't believe y'all," I said. "This man has been in the water, his hands were tied in front of him, his hair was all tangled around his face."

"Have you ever seen him before?" London asked.

"No. Of course not." I grimaced. "I didn't look that closely."

"Maybe a trespasser," Donny said. "LaDiva said she had to keep a close eye; those people would land on her beach and spend the day. A lot of people are looking for Atlantis."

We all stared at him.

"I'm not saying it's here," he said. "I just repeated what she told me. Apparently Bimini is one of the strongest contenders for being Atlantis."

"I thought we were in the Berry Islands," Ka'Arih asked.

"Bimini's the closest big island," London explained.

"We could be in Atlantis?" Zima asked. "That sounds like a song!"

"There was that movie about Atlantis," Jillyian said. "*Hearts in Atlantis* or something."

"That wasn't about Atlantis," Eladonna said. "Atlantis, the Disney thing, was about Atlantis."

I whistled, New York taxi caliber. "Atlantis be damned," I said. "There is a body on the beach. I don't think we should move it, probably not, but we could take pictures."

"Why wouldn't you move it?" Eladonna asked.

"Crime scene or something," I said. I should know this stuff by now, but I don't.

"If he washed up on shore, it's not a crime scene," Eladonna said.

"How do you know there was any crime, anyway?" Zima asked. "He could just be some dude on the beach."

"Well, his hands were tied," I said. "Doesn't that sound a little ominous?"

Donny looked at his watch. "I'm not going to get any work out of you until I go see this body, am I?"

"Not really," I said. "It's not a joke. I saw a body."

"When's call?" Eladonna asked.

Donny shrugged. "Ask Bette." He got to his feet.

"Oscar is going with us," I said.

"Come along, my beauties," Donny cajoled the girls. "It will be a pleasant little stroll. Just down the beach, right, Dallas?"

Down the beach, halfway around the island, I thought. But if I told them that, I'd be alone for sure. "Yeah," I said.

I pushed the kitchen door open cautiously and watched as a bucket of water poured over the blank space before me. Glad my shirt wasn't silk. Palize popped up. "Oh shit, lady, I didn't think you were here anymore! *Adonde* Oscar?"

"I thought he was here. We were going—"

"Oh, yeah, he said something about a phone and Mama Garcia."

"Thanks," I said and went back to the dining room.

"Come on," I said. "It will be a quick break; just walk with me. I'll take a photo and we can call the police when we get back."

"We're all coming," Donny said. "Lead on!"

Chapter Thirteen

I walked in the front while the girls attempted to write a song about living in Atlantis. Jillyian discussed mood, the big picture, Eladonna shot down anything not logical. Ka'Arih hummed. Zima threw out rhymes, and London tried to come up with words.

I've never been around songwriters before; it was painful.

"Atlantis. How about mantis?"

"You're going to write a song about a praying mantis?"

"Mantle?"

"The kind you wear, or the kind the chimney has?"

"Atlantis. Can we abbreviate it, or make it two syllables instead? Atln-tis?"

"Then who the hell is going to know what we're singing about?"

"Well, what are we singing about? What's so cool about living in Atlantis?"

"It's peaceful."

"It's beautiful."

"It's cheap—"

The girls all giggled.

"How much farther?" London asked Donny.

"I thought this was a tiny island! We must be halfway to Cuba!" Zima said.

"I'm getting a headache." Eladonna complained.

"My feet hurt!" London again.

I'd found the body about two miles from the castle, not much of a distance to run, but walking it at 10 a.m. was noticeably warm. This side of the island was protected from the breezes, sparsely treed, and bathed in sun. Oscar and Sascha had caught up with us and steadily walked to the front, to me.

"How long you been a runner?" Oscar asked as he stepped into stride beside me.

"About ten years."

"You run in school?" Sascha asked, on my other side.

"Track, but I wasn't great."

"So what happened?" Oscar asked. "What turned you from a mediocre and unenthused runner into SuperRunner?"

Sascha and I both chuckled. "I didn't suck in school," I said, "I just didn't have much focus. I got that later."

Later, when I'd been married to a Mexican who had grown up in the lap of luxury. Later, when we were living with his family, in their huge hacienda. I'd discovered running was the only way to get away from my mother-in-law, and my sisters-in-law, the only refuge from the constant questions about why I wasn't pregnant, why my husband didn't seem to be so happy, why I wouldn't conform to being a *señora* of the old school.

They were lovely people, in hindsight, all products of their upbringing and generation. I was just the wrong person to be in that place. I think it was on those runs through the groves, over the dirt paths, when I was learning about how to push my body and work with my mind, that I realized I didn't want to be where I was.

And when I left my marriage and started the process of

creating something from the wreckage, then running became my refuge. I didn't need money to do it, I didn't need permission or privilege, I could just run. Wherever, whenever. I gave Oscar and Sascha a somewhat depersonalized and condensed version.

"You got discipline now," Sascha said.

"You run every day?" Oscar asked.

"The only thing I do every day, I smoke," Sascha said.

"You take three puffs of every cigarette," I said to Sascha. "What is with that?"

She shrugged. "I get bored. I want a cigarette, I take one, two, puffs and then. . . ." She shrugged again. "It is boring. You suck, you inhale, you exhale, and every time the cigarette gets hotter and shorter and harder to hold—"

"Someone should give you a cigarette holder," Oscar said, stepping between us to throw an arm around her shoulders. "All the fun."

"The cigarettes, they make them too big." She stopped. "Where is this body? We walk and we walk. Where it is?"

Oscar glanced around. "Dallas, you're losing your entourage."

I looked back. The girls were slacking off. The sandals and flip-flops they'd chosen to wear weren't made for mile-long hikes. Donny was in deep conversation with Bette—probably scheduling, I thought—and Teddy stopped and started, doing some strange positions, then running to catch up. Was that yoga-boogie ballet?

Sascha turned her head, and the interlocking Cs on her glasses reminded me of something, but I didn't know what. The knowledge nibbled at my brain, but no luck.

"It's just a little farther." I said that, but I looked around.

"Did you do anything to mark the spot?" Oscar asked.

"The body marks the spot," I said. Trouble was, the whole island looked pretty much the same from any angle. Flat, with blue water, white sand, and a view of the castle. The view of the castle was the only thing that really differed, and I hadn't paid attention to it. The tide was coming in, but not far, not yet. I looked back at the castle. "It's a little farther."

We walked a little further. They didn't say anything, and I looked ahead of us. No body.

"How did you get to the States?" Oscar asked Sascha as we kept on.

"Boyfriend," she said.

"You followed him?"

"He gave me green card," she said. "I give him blow job." She shrugged, and we laughed. "Then, he tire of me, I tire of blow jobs, and we break up."

"Did you lose your green card?" Oscar asked.

"No, I make boyfriend, another boyfriend, in government. He pull strings and I am here, safe."

"Where in Russia are you from?" I asked.

"Vladivostock."

"Where did you meet an American?" Oscar asked.

"He was pilot, and got me ticket to England."

"And you flew from England?"

"No, I make new boyfriend. Maybe you know him, he work in New York," she said to Oscar. "He is chef."

"Really? And where would I find this rapscallion, lass?"

I stopped. We were three-quarters around the island. The body was behind us. We were walking on the water's edge. We hadn't seen it.

"Where is body?" Sascha asked me.

I sighed. This was weird. "It's gone."

"We're almost to where we started," Oscar said.

"I'm going back," I said.

"Sure, lass. Why not. Maybe we missed it," Oscar said as we turned around and headed back to the castle. I took off my shoes and walked in the surf, careful where I stepped. Then I looked up. "Birds," I said.

Oscar and Sascha were involved in a conversation about New York restaurants. He looked at me. "Birds?"

"I saw circling birds, before I saw the body."

He and Sascha stopped, and all three of us looked at the sky.

"I think your body, he get up and leave," Sascha said.

"I guess so," I said.

We met the girls on the way back. Oscar was still getting a chronology from Sascha, which consisted of associating with men in powerful places who had an appreciation of fellatio.

"Maybe you were running on the other side?" Eladonna suggested when we told them we hadn't found the body.

"Maybe he got to feeling better and walked away," London said.

"Maybe he was really a vampire and when the sun came, he exploded into a million pieces and those little gray flecks are really him," Ka'Arih said.

"Maybe the brutha who done him in came back to get him," Zima said.

"What makes you think he was done in?" I asked her.

She dropped her gaze and shrugged. "You said his hands were tied. Seemed . . . logical."

I'd thought the same thing.

"Unless it's some Atlantis thing," Jillyian said. "A death ritual."

"Yeah, to come back in another life," Ka'Arih said.

"Maybe you have too much fun last night," Sascha said to me. "You have hangover and see unclear."

"I wasn't hungover," I said. "I must have misjudged the height of the tide and he floated back out to sea." I looked at the clear water. You could see the sand on the bottom through it, and you could see the fish swimming. Surely I'd be able to see the body?

He couldn't have floated that far, could he?

"Well," London said. "I'll be back at the castle, should

your body desire some tea." Zima walked by me, patted my shoulder with sympathy, and joined London on the walk back. They were talking about Atlantis rhyming with romantic.

Donny looked around. "Well, maybe he'll float back tomorrow. Come along, ladies, we have a full day of work ahead. You're up for working, aren't you?" he said to me. "Not too disturbed by this little incident?"

How was I supposed to answer those two questions? "I'm fine."

"You're a brick." He patted me on the shoulder and walked away. Oscar stood beside me. I stared out at the sea.

"What did you see?"

"What? You believe me?"

"A lot of things wash up on these shores. Actually, most of the Bahamians are offspring of mutinied slaves who didn't know how to sail. When they took over the ship, they had to trust the winds. The Gulf Stream washed them up on the Caribbean islands. You never know what you'll find."

"I wonder where he was from," I said. "How he ended up dead, with his hands tied."

"Likely a tipsy cruiser whose friends don't even know he went overboard."

"With tied hands?"

"A kinky, tipsy cruiser?" Oscar suggested as we walked slowly back to the castle. "Did you ever read *Les Miserables*?"

"I saw it on Broadway."

"Well, in the book, Victor Hugo has these little croutons of story that are unrelated to anything. One of them is about a man falling off a cruise ship in the middle of the Atlantic."

"That's grim. What happens?"

"He shouts, he flounders, and he watches the ship fade into the distance."

I looked at Oscar. His Oakley shades had eerie red and green lenses. I couldn't see his eyes through the opaque glass, but I felt his gaze.

"And then what?" I asked.

"He realizes he's completely insignificant, completely alone."

Oh joy.

"Well," I said as we walked a little farther. "What do *you* think rhymes with Atlantis?"

I have quite a few friends who no longer drink, with the help of their 12-step program of choice. Several of them have shared with me, from time to time, how absolutely annoying it is to be at a party with a bunch of drunks. The drunks think they are hysterically funny, and that they are having the time of their lives, but to a sober person they are a bunch of idiots revisiting kindergarten.

This was my mind-set as I started the day. When I reached the haven of my workroom, not even Shakira could help me. I felt far more serious. More like Poe or Shelby Lynne. Sascha was in the spa, retanning our ladies of Paradise, and I was supposed to be getting their poolside lounging attire together.

I'd spent a fortune on bathing suits, and I hoped everything fit. The girls were supposed to be very Ibiza/Saint-Tropez rich bitches in this scene for the video. Which meant a black OMO Norma Kamali maillot, a Vivienne Tam bronze tankini, a white Armani one-piece, a sarong and top for Zima, who didn't feel comfortable too bare, and a dramatic tiger print Cavalli dress and Blahnik sandals for London, who flat refused to wear a bathing suit.

Enough quality gold jewelry to sink a ship, and serious sunglasses for everyone: Chanel bronze tinted for London; Armani black shades for Eladonna, to go with the maillot; gold wraparounds for Jillyian in the tankini; and Ka'Arih would get the . . . I flipped through my collection . . . hmmm . . . hologram aviators from Gucci. The girls all wore the highest, most fragile heels I could find at The Store and Forty-Five Ten, and the glitziest cocktail rings that didn't come in Cracker Jack boxes.

I sat back, my work done, and stared at the rack.

Zac was who I needed to talk to. Was he still in the studio? I slipped out of the door and down the corridor, through the garden, on my way to the music tower. I knocked on the door, heard nothing, then tried the handle. It didn't move, because it was actually locked, but the door wasn't closed, just pulled to. I pushed, and it floated open silently.

The place was quiet, but then I remembered the sound-proofing. A painting proved to be an elevator door, so I stepped inside and looked at the choices. Five floors, and a penthouse. I pushed Two, and the doors closed. When they opened again, I was facing the tinted glass window of a sound studio. "Hello?" I said as I walked in. "Anyone here?"

"Yeah," Palize said as he shouldered past me. He smelled like sweat. "What you doin'?"

I stepped back. "Is Zac around?"

"Oh no, lady, he left. He uh, had to get back to Miami. He worked all night and then had another gig."

"Why are you here?" I asked, curious. No one else was. "Where are John and David and Derek?"

"Oh, one of the girls left her sweater here and asked me to get it," he said as he held up a piece of black clothing. "I guess those other guys are sleeping. Are you going down?" He pushed the elevator button, and the doors opened.

"Sure," I said and we got in. The seconds it took to reach ground level seemed like minutes, and then we both walked out, neither of us mentioning that the door had technically been locked. I made sure to pull it tight. Now it was closed.

"See you," Palize said, and took off toward the beach.

That was a relief, because walking back to the building with him would have been strangely awkward; both of us busted. Then it occurred to me that he wasn't returning the sweater to whichever girl. He'd been lying.

Or he was going to give it to her later.

If he was lying, had he been lying about Zac, too? As I walked by the kitchen, I heard singing. I poked my head in, it was not any of the ladies from FOP. The room was filled with steam and Mama Garcia wailed on some Caribbean tune.

"Old conch is sweeter dan fresh conch
Old conch is sweeter dan fresh;
Especially when you add dose peas and rice
'Cuz to the old conch it make 'em taste so nice."

It sounded like a song from *The Little Mermaid*, and I found myself smiling as she sang and sang.

"What you do you
soak 'em soak 'em
wash 'em wash 'em
cook 'em cook 'em"

She gasped when she saw me, putting her hand to her breast. "Oh, chile, ya give me a fright! I t'ot you was a spirred. How you be?"

I smiled. "I'm fine, Mama. Are we having conch for lunch?"

"Oh, we be havin' conch, but for dinner, not lunch. Dose girls in dere bikinis say dey doan wan no loanch."

"Mama," I asked, "have you seen Zac? The musician?"

"He be gone-gone. Took a boat jus' dis mornin'. Called to Miami for rerecordin' or somet'in. Why, chile, you want to tell him somet'in'?" She looked at me with a spooky expression in her eyes.

Palize had told the truth. Damn. "No, no. I better get those girls into their bikinis," I said.

"Oscar be gone, too," she said. "Jus' for da day."

"Thanks," I said and I walked back to my dressing room. Should I call the cops on my own, just to be careful? I mean, I had seen a dead guy.

But where was he from?

Would I call police on Bimini? Miami? Nassau? And what would I say? I found a body, but I let it be washed back out to sea?

I opened my bag to slick my lips with gloss when it dawned on me. The body might wash back! When was tide? I needed to be at the beach at that time, to check. If it had washed up once, it would again.

And then I'd pull it out, despite the grossness, and call the cops.

Just as soon as I had the body.

The lighting guys had big fun as they tried to work with the sun and the girls. Sascha had slicked back Eladonna's hair into a braid, and I gave her enormous hoops. Ka'Arih's curls were tamed, and she wore a wide headband and a Versace pendant. Zima looked like she had no hair, just the von Furstenberg earring. London's golden tresses were ironed into a sheet, and she wore a multi-strand chain that went almost to her navel (like the slash in her dress). And Jillyian wore long chain earrings and a French twist. They tried to out-attitude each other with their snootiness but kept breaking into giggles.

Donny was sort of like me, a little tense, and tired of all the joking around. Finally he told the crew to come back in five, and drew the girls and the rest of us into the shade of a palm. "Ladies," he said, pulling off his glasses, the lines around his eyes a little sharper. "I know we're having fun, and it is so important to me that we do have fun, but you really need to focus. We need to get this done. We're *running out of time.*" He emphasized the last part.

Teddy looked at me, confused, and I shrugged. Maybe Donny knew they still had a lot of work to do in the studio, and that's what he meant by running out of time? We were all booked for another week. Though all it would take was a few days of bad weather and the schedule would be off.

"So, please, you wrote this song, you love this song, so give that to me. Let me see your passion."

"Restrained—" Sascha said.

"Restrained passion," Donny said. "You have all the elegance, all the class you need. Let us see that. Okay?"

They nodded solemnly and we all took our places, ready to work. I hadn't been able to use adhesive on the girls (tans, again) but they weren't moving much in these few seconds of video, just quietly singing the verse as the camera zoomed from one still, rich, snobby girl to the other.

It had a very static, Versace print campaign feel to it.

I peeked through the camera and saw the cameraman's angle was of the wide, tiled archway, the chaises, a corner of the bar, and the pool itself. Jillyian floated on a gold-toned inflated raft with Christoffle champagne flute in hand (ginger ale in the glass). Decadence. Spoiled. Overdone. Ennui. Style. Elegance.

The cascading flowers and boys in sarongs carrying drinks were the final touch.

Again, Donny hit the CD player and the song started. I watched the girls carefully, comparing them with the Polaroids I'd shot at the start.

The trick with film is consistency. If the collar is lopsided at the beginning and gets missed, then it's part of my job to make sure it stays lopsided so the whole scene looks as if it was shot at the same time—instead of looking as if it was filmed over a period of three days and added to, in some studio, later.

Necklaces are some of the biggest headaches when you're concerned about consistency, especially when the wearer is dancing. I personally think that is why chokers are so popular with musicians. Chokers don't move, unlike long pendants that constantly change places and rarely fall back into place naturally. Even double-stick tape doesn't hold them. The jewelry wasn't moving today, though.

Sascha and I ran in and out of the set during the few hours it took to shoot what would be 45 seconds of video. By the time the sun set, the girls needed to get in the pool to cool off, and we were all ready for a drink.

Mama Garcia had set trays with hibiscus wine and Cuba Bellas, a rum drink with grenadine and mint, out on a table outside Oscar's pastel kitchen. We all trooped straight from the shoot to pick up some beverage, then I gathered the bathing suits, the sunglasses, and shoes, and took them all back to the dressing room. The darkness in the room was severe after staring into sunlight all day long. I turned on the overhead light, and smiled.

The angel slash chef had a dinner prepared for me; there was a table set for one, and a hot box and a cooler where I guessed the food was. I stepped out of my shoes, draped the clothes over the rack, and read the note.

"*Beautiful—*" it began. I smiled. "*I won't be there until late tonight. If you get hungry, this is for you. No time limits—Your smile lights the world—O*"

My heart was pounding and my face was hot. He's a good guy, part of me reasoned. Even if he seems like he's trying to kill Palize. Mom would love him. Oh, she would. From his past to his braids to his vintage gab. Grandmama would loathe him, and Dad . . . I wondered what my father would think. He was the opposite of my mother. He was staid, old fashioned, gentlemanly. He opened doors for females, not because he didn't think they could open them themselves, but because he didn't think they should have to. My mother had probably been the first woman in Texas to burn her bra and buy "comfortable" shoes. My father still wore a tie to everything except a hog-killin'.

All I could imagine was that the sex had to have been great. How else could they be married forty years, live in two separate towns (Austin—Mom; College Station—Dad) and teach at rival schools, yet share eight children, nine grandchildren, and all major holidays? Well, I thought, there is the O'Connor charm. Wicked Irish. And my mother still had to-die-for legs and was the life of every party. They'd been happy; they just couldn't *stay* happy.

Could anyone, ever?

I set the note down and worked on the clothes. I rinsed the suits out in Woolite and hung them to dry. Then, curious, I wandered over to the food.

Curried crabs and dumplings, black-eyed pea salad, and Kalik beer. Gingerbread sweet potato pudding. The table he'd set looked like it was styled. A daisy-rimmed plate, an amber goblet, a cheerful checkered napkin, and all set on a butcher-paper placemat illustrated with a hand-drawn sun smiling as it came over a blue sea. Signed by "OI."

Oscar Izarra.

Ah, heck, he was so adorable.

I savored my food as I flipped through Polaroids. Before I got too much further, I needed to pull aside each girl and go through all her "on the road" options. First I had to match the clothes to each other, then I would show them to the girls, give them choices. The matching was going to take hours, and as I didn't feel like being with the others right now, now was a good time to do it. I sipped some more of the Kalik and started to make my lists.

And lists.

And more lists.

Styling is perceived to be so glamorous, and I guess that's because one works with PYTs (Pretty Young Things) and great clothes. In reality, it's a matter of carrying and list-making. I shuffled through the Polaroids and lined up five, then checked to see if there were clothes for each girl in them. Nope, two showed outfits for Zima. I looked through for a matching fifth, found it, then started over.

The hours and the silence stretched out. After I did what I could with Polaroids, I worked with the clothes themselves. As I planned the ensembles, I trimmed strings, tightened buttons, repaired studs and snaps, and applied spot remover. I was yawning for the fourth time when I looked at my watch. Midnight. I put the dishes in the basket, checked the bikinis, and turned the lights off before leaving.

My bed felt fantastic, and I promised myself I'd shower in the morning.

I can't say what woke me up, but it was sudden and strange. My heart was pounding as I sat up, looking around me. The room was fine. Still and empty, like my room should be. Had there been some noise outside? I got up, slid into my sandals, and threw on my embroidered Indian shirt, then opened my door. Donny and I were the only ones in this tower, as far as I knew. I heard no sound from his room.

What *had* I heard?

My sense of foreboding grew, even though things were quiet. Too quiet. Something had awakened me, something out of the ordinary. I'm used to sleeping through screaming fights, car crashes, and drunken confessions; I live on a cul de sac just off one of Dallas's main drags. If the wind is blowing the right direction, it sounds like the people who are drinking and smoking in Mike's Treehouse bar are really in my living room.

I opened the door and looked out. Because the staircase wrapped around the outside of the tower, I couldn't see much. I tugged at the hem of my shirt, wondered if I should get a robe, then heard another sound. Like a woman's voice—smothered. I ran down the stairs to the bottom, then looked over my shoulder toward the ledge garden—and my heart stopped.

Hanging from the branch of a tree, beneath the curve of the arch, swung a body. A lacy granny nightgown, draped with long blonde hair, fluttered in the wind.

Chapter Fourteen

"Help!" I shouted. "Help!"
I scrambled up the tree. I searched for the rope that held her. I reached down for her throat, felt for a pulse.

She had none.

Then I noticed something about her throat. It felt . . . strange. I tugged the body up, my suspicions confirmed by its weight. I was taking the pulse of a mannequin.

I heard laughter, smothered giggles, and I looked down.

Jillyian burst in from the courtyard garden, laughing her head off. The whole entourage followed.

"Oh! You should have seen your face!"

"White like sheet!" Sascha gasped out. "I think maybe you have heart attack."

"That makes two of us," I said as I dropped the mannequin, letting David catch her. The girls fell on each other, laughing so hard they couldn't stand. I accepted Teddy's hand to get out of the tree, though he wasn't much help since he couldn't stop looking at my legs. "You trying to kill me?" I asked them all.

"We knew you were disappointed you didn't find the body

on the beach, so we were giving you one," Ka'Arih said with a bright smile. They were all in nightclothes, all wide awake.

"How considerate," I said.

"You're not mad, are you?" Jillyian asked with wide-eyed innocence.

"No," I said. "Y'all got me good."

"Rock stars!" the girls said, congratulating each other on almost scaring me to death.

"Aren't practical jokes fun?" Ka'Arih asked.

I hate practical jokes. I'm not any good at them, even though, with my family, I should be. "My brother Houston would be quite impressed," I said. "My pulse is still racing. Congratulations."

"What's going on?" Donny called as he came toward us from the courtyard. He saw the mannequin lying on the ground. "Who's hurt?" He ran.

"It's a joke," I said, halting him in his steps. "You didn't know?"

He reached the mannequin. "How would I know? What, she was supposed to be dead?"

"It's just a joke," Zima said.

"Are you laughing, Dallas?" he asked.

"Is London laughing?" I asked. "Since the mannequin looks most like her."

"That's what happens when you are the one asleep," Teddy said. "Oh, Dallas, you should have seen your face."

They really didn't believe I'd seen the body on the beach. "I'll take the mannequin to the workroom," I said.

"Call's at five a.m., don't forget," Donny shouted to us.

The group dispersed, and I walked through the perfumed gardens until I came to the door. I slipped inside the palace and walked to the workroom. The mannequin was over my shoulder, her nightgown obscuring my vision. I turned the handle and fumbled for the light beside the door.

I froze when I heard a safety click off—inside the room.

"Cease and desist," a man said. "Take one more step and I'll give you a third eye in the center of your Neanderthal forehead."

"That would be a nice shot," I said. "I didn't mean to disturb you. In fact, I thought you were gone."

The bedside light clicked on, and I pushed the white nightgown away from my face. "Dallas?" Oscar Izarra was sitting up in bed, a white shirt open to his . . . navel. His chest was smooth. I didn't do any more looking.

"Sorry," I said and grabbed the door handle. "Wrong room." I backed me and my mannequin out the door, my face hot with embarrassment. I opened the next door, dumped the mannequin inside the workroom, and slammed the door shut.

Oscar stood at his doorway. "That's it? You disturb my peaceful sleep without even a by-your-leave? What were you doing with the artificial lass, anyway?"

"Someone hung her," I said. His shirt was a dress, and it did not hide his masculinity.

"A gallows sense of humor. I like it."

"I'm not surprised."

"Were you the discoverer of the body?"

"Ha, ha. Yes, I was."

"Did it scare you?" he asked. "Or did you feel a tremendous sense of satisfaction that there was another body to discover?" He was grinning.

"I have to say it scared me."

"Could there be truth in Mama Garcia's assertion that you are a sperrid?"

I shrugged. "Whatever. Good night."

I started walking down the hallway, but he stepped in front of me. "Is your heart still pounding?" He moved closer to me. "Are you scared to sleep alone?"

My heart was definitely pounding, but he'd changed its key.

"If you promise to stay, I won't even swear," he said.

"It doesn't bother me," I said, swallowing the taste of lye.

"It's not intended with disrespect," he said. "It's the culture in which I've labored for two decades; it's the way those of us who toil, day in and day out, over a hot stove, speak."

"Really, it's not a problem. I don't care."

"I don't believe you. When I swear, you always look like you have a bad taste in your mouth."

I laughed. "Ever heard of lye soap?" I told him about my grandmama. "And then, to make matters worse, when I went home to my mother's house, the blisters had just healed and I could taste something besides lye. Anyway, I was relating some experience to my mother, who is a complete hippie, university prof, Birkenstocks, the whole thing, and I . . . use the word. Well this liberated feminista bra-burning intellectual wigs out, reverts to her upbringing and I hear, "Young lady, I guess tasting lye for a week didn't teach you a thing."

"She washed your mouth out again?"

"Worse, she took me to visit a prison. I got to hear the women there speak for eight hours straight while I served up their meals and cleaned their commodes. For a week she made me visit." I shuddered. "I was so cured of that word by then, you can't imagine."

"Your mom sounds quite fearsome."

"Apparently yours is too," I said.

He took a step closer, and eased me against the wall. Casually, he placed his hands on either side of my shoulders. He wasn't touching me, but I was trembling anyway. "I can't believe I'm talking about my mother, while I'm standing with a fetching blonde in the moonlight."

I laughed, a soft breathy sound as he moved his head close to mine. I felt his breath on my cheek and throat. I was reminded suddenly that he, too, wasn't wearing anything but a white shirt. He smelled like soap, like fresh bread and spices. And he was hot, with a heat I could feel all the way through both our clothes. He inhaled my scent, then touched my cheek with his face. "I have to get up in one hour," he said.

"Sorry to disturb you," I whispered.

"You'll be very sorry," he said, and dropped a kiss on my breastbone. "Someday."

His door clicked shut. I was standing outside it, my head swimming.

And oh so awake.

I went back into the styling room, jammed the bookcase so it couldn't slide open, and put my headphones on. Brooks and Dunn were about my speed right now, so I slipped into some sweat shorts, cranked the music and continued my matching and coordinating. Clothes were wonderful to lose oneself in.

I was going through the left clothes when I saw the Chanel wrestling shoes.

My blood turned cold. I reached for them with a trembling hand and saw a confirmation. They had no laces.

When I closed my eyes, I saw the body on the beach, hands tied by logo'd ropes. Not ropes, laces. Interlocking Cs were Chanel, and they had been so out of place I hadn't recognized them. Chanel and shoelaces didn't go together for me. Whoever had trussed the body up had been here, been in this room.

Either it happened before the group arrived. . . .

Or someone on this island was a killer or an accomplice.

I looked at the shoes. Would they tell me who it was?

"You worked for Chanel, didn't you?"

Admittedly it wasn't subtle, but it was as good as I could do through a mouthful of pins while hemming London's skirt. She sat filing her nails (yesterday's French manicure had been replaced with rosy pink) in a bustier and stockings.

"Lagerfeld," she said. "Gaultier, de La Renta, Blass, Alaia, Betsy Johnson." She sighed. "I did it all."

"Do you miss the runway?" I asked.

She looked at me. "For some girls it's genetic. They never have to diet, never have to worry about their bodies. They don't even grow cellulite." She shrugged as she filed another nail. "I was hungry for about thirteen years. Dizzy. I didn't have energy for anything." She fixed her jade green eyes on me. "I almost wrecked my voice with bulimia and drugs."

I was hemming her evening gown fast, thinking faster. There was a connection between the wrestling shoes and whoever had tied the body's hands. What it was, I couldn't imagine. I wasn't even sure why I was asking questions of the girls. Except something was hinky; they were being too casual. Yesterday's Atlantis-obsessive talk had been an effort at distraction.

They were hiding something. So I had to ask questions. (Don't ask me why; I felt bad that I'd let someone's body float back to sea.) "Is there anything of Chanel that you really loved?" I asked London.

"Of Chanel? Well, I have some vintage stuff. Nineteen sixties. I have some early eighties accessories, from the Lagerfeld years, but most of the clothes are completely impractical for my life."

"I would never have guessed you thought something was impractical," I said.

"It's like python boots. I have a blonde pair. Where in New York am I supposed to wear them? Surely not walking! Chanel is the same. Great for ladies lunching and taking cabs, but—" she set down the file—"I blew all my money. I'm as poor and reaching as any one of those girls who won this contest. We all sink or swim on this CD."

The blue satin evening gown was ready, and I poured her
into it. "Are you being shot from the front or the back?" I
asked. The gown had been for London at size four, not size
eight, so either the front or back was going to be sacrificed.

"The front."

"Okay," I said, straining to bring the back together. There
was just too much girl.

She hummed as I rigged the back, checking her front in the
mirror. She had a lovely, husky, sexy voice. She was a lady
who could sing the blues. "What do you think of Teddy?"
she asked. "Isn't he cute?"

"He is cute," I said as I laced her up with cording through
the hooks and eyes. There was a two-inch gap across her
back, but the front looked smooth and perfect. Rather than
taping her breasts up, we'd taped hers down. More like a
French noblewoman that way, and less like Dolly Parton.

"He's also a shallow prick," she said. "He's so hung up on
BMI and calories and nutrition. This is music, it's supposed
to be about what's in our hearts and our talent, not about
whether or not we're size four! It's about being real, instead
of a flat Barbie doll."

I wondered if that was the underlying reason London had
gotten out of modeling; she wanted to be real. A rock star
who was "real."

Oscar wasn't the only one who lived in a strange world.

In the mirror, a stunning woman with blonde ringlets and
an aquamarine necklace stared back at me.

"I like who I am, what I look like," London said, meeting
my gaze. "I don't think there's something wrong with me. I
believe a woman can have breasts and hips and eat cake once
a month. I don't think that should diminish me in someone's
eyes. Do you?"

"Not at all," I said.

"Maybe I'm a lesbian," she said. "Have you ever kissed a
woman, Dallas?"

"Are you asking me to kiss me, or just asking?"

She looked away. "Just asking. I like men."

"Me, too. Now go sing, and don't get messed up."

As she was walking out the door, I gambled. "London, I was in Paris and I got these great shoes but they kill my feet. Would you be interested?"

"What size?" she asked.

"Ten quad-A."

"Heavens no! My feet are nine and a half B. What kind of shoes?" she asked.

"You know, some of those flats that look like—"

"Ugh. I wear heels; even my tennis shoes have heels."

"Great. Send whoever's finished in." With the grace of a duchess, London gathered her skirt and swooshed out the door.

Zima looked dazzling from the neck up when she came in from Sascha. My job was to make her dazzling from the neck down. Her gown was bronze taffeta, and her necklace was citrine with brown diamond drops in an antique gold setting. I adjusted the portrait collar of the dress, and stepped back. "Do you know how to walk in this thing?"

Zima shook her head.

"In an evening gown, you kick the skirt away from you." At least that was runway style. "But I think you are sitting most of the time."

"Yeah, that's what they said. Dallas—"

"Yes?"

"I'm sorry about last night. We didn't really think you would wig so bad."

I grinned. "No problem. I'm used to practical jokes."

"Do I have shoes?"

"What size?"

"Little, like eight."

I pulled slippers out, and she slid into them, humming beneath her breath.

"Do you like Chanel?" I asked her.

She looked blank. "Is that a musician?"

I grinned. "You're beautiful. Go on."

"You ready for me?" Eladonna asked from the doorway ten minutes later.

"Come on in, Mademoiselle," I said in a faux French accent. "I 'ave your finest creation right 'ere. You will be radiant in zis purple."

"I dig purple!" she said.

I smiled.

"Are you going to offer me the shoes?" she asked as I was lacing the back of her dress.

"The shoes?"

"Yeah, London said you were trying to give away some quad tens. Flats."

"Are your feet tens?"

"No, but if you want I can buy them from you. My little cousin, she'd totally love to have a pair of shoes from Paris, and she walks to school."

"Where does she live?"

"In D.C., but in one of those enclaves where the poor and uncultured are kept out, except to cut the grass."

"Yeah, maybe," I said, turning her to face me. I hung antique amethyst earrings from her ears and admired the confection of curls and braids and twists Sascha had made from her hair. "Here are your shoes," I said, handing her a pair of doctored pumps. "They're waiting."

"Good. Zima and I are in a Pass the Pigs championship, and I may be winning."

"Pass the Pigs?"

She smiled. "We played it while waiting for profs, in school. You toss these pigs like dice—" she waved her hand. "Maybe we can play at the party tonight."

"I didn't hear about a party."

"Oh, wait, it's tomorrow. Donny thinks we'll have the visual stuff wrapped up and we'll get rid of the video guys and be able to concentrate on music the last week. Plus there's a hurricane on the way."

She swayed out of the room on that note.

Chapter Fifteen

"Do you eat Mexican jumping beans?" I asked Ka'Arih, who was incapable of standing still.

"No, but I love Jelly Bellies," she said. "The marshmallow is my favorite. Toasted marshmallow. It reminds me of the harvest festival, when we all gather around and burn leaves and eat over the fire."

"Is that part of your religion?" I asked. Ka'Arih's dress was red and very cantankerous. The dresses were all period costumes, from different periods (don't ask me, I'm not a historian). Hers had a bustle, which required padding and a special corset. It still smelled musty from the theater's storage room.

"Toasted marshmallows?"

"No, the harvest festival."

She sang as she shifted her weight from foot to foot. I was about to stick her with a pin, just to get her attention, when she spoke. "You know, it's weird. I think that food that Eladonna ate, I think it was supposed to be Jillyian's."

I looked over her shoulder into the mirror and met her gaze. "What do you mean?"

"I heard y'all talkin about Jamaica poisonin', just as a scare. I think someone was trying to scare Jillyian, not Eladonna."

"Why?"

She smiled a bright, sweet smile. "I have no idea. I just remember the girls passing the lunch boxes, and we got them confused in the dark and all, and at the last minute Jillyian and Eladonna traded again. Jillyian said Eladonna had hers."

I started to button the hundred or so hooks and eyes up her back. "Hers?"

"In the dark it was hard to read the names, you know? Eladonna and Jillyian are both long. They couldn't decide, and everyone was feeling pretty reckless—" She hummed again. I reached the top and turned her around. Jewelry would be gilding the lily, but I put some small drops in her ears. "Just so you don't feel left out," I said.

She stood while I buckled her shoes on (size eight-and-a-half). I didn't even know how to ask about Chanel. "Don't tell anyone I said anything, okay?" she said. "I was just thinkin' out loud. I shouldn't have been listenin' to Mama Garcia when she was talkin' to you and Oscar anyway."

"Where were you when you heard us?"

"Uh," she said and looked away, "I was in the garden."

"Just standing there?" I asked.

"No, no, I was walking through. To my room." She smiled again, but Ka'Arih sucked as a liar. My little sister Augustina got the same tightness across her forehead when she lied. Augustina was in nun school. "You won't tell, will you?"

"Nah," I said. "You have a deal."

She danced out the door and closed it behind her with a smile.

Eladonna ate Jillyian's food?

I was putting lotion on my hands when the bookcase clanked. "God's teeth!" I heard Oscar shout. And then he said a lot of words that would greatly displease his mother and convince Palize that his boss had no self-control.

I ran to unwedge the door, but he was gone.

I waited a half-hour, alone, for Jillyian. Not that I wasn't busy; I hanged and folded, prepped and listed, photographed and cataloged, and finally opened the door to see what was going on.

Bette was the first person I tracked down. "Have you seen Jillyian?"

"She's in makeup, I think."

I walked into the makeup room, off the soundstage, but no one was there, not even Sascha.

In the drawing room, the damask draperies had been replaced with velvet and the soft Aubusson with a vibrant Persian. A man was bringing cages in, and the girls were nowhere. "Has anyone seen Jillyian?" I asked.

"She was having words with someone. You're talking about the little redhead, right?" one of the prop people said.

"A redhead, right. Where was she?"

"In the garden, the courtyard thing. By a fountain."

Great directions. I shielded my eyes in the courtyard as I looked for a missing diva-in-training. *No aquí.* I went back to the dressing room, and she was there, facing away from me. "Sorry," she said in a congested voice.

"No problem," I said. "You're the client." I pulled a radiant teal dress off the rack. "Let's get you into this."

She nodded, still not turning around, and pulled her shirt off, then her pants. She was skinny enough she didn't need the corset, but the dress wouldn't fit properly without it. I handed it to her, and watched as she fought her tears and tried to put it on.

"You want to talk about it?" I asked.

"He just has no right!" she snapped. "We're sleeping together, we're not in love!"

Poor Donny.

"Why does one have to be the other? Why does he have to be so hateful?" She was crying again, and dressing would have to wait.

"C'mere," I said, and pulled her down on the chairs. "Let it out."

She hugged me and sobbed, and I patted her shoulder and commiserated.

"He's not anything that special," she said. "He's kind of slimy. He said he loved me and I should have wondered then, but . . ." She sniffled. "He just makes me mad."

Her face was blotched and her eyes were swollen. She'd wrecked her makeup and hair, but she was calming down. "He might be more special than you think," I said, defending Donny just the littlest bit. "And he thinks you're wonderful, which makes him have good taste at least, right?"

She gave me a watery smile.

"I'm going to get some tea bags for your face and round up Sascha to redo your makeup. Meanwhile, I'll send Oscar in with a little chocolate. You just rest here for a few minutes and I'll be right back."

Kitchen first. Palize was waiting behind the door to trip me, and I jumped over his foot and ducked Oscar's flying pan. "I need tea bags—chamomile, I think, or green. I need a little pick-me-up drink and something with sugar or chocolate," I said. "And I need you to tell me where Sascha is."

Oscar nodded and proceeded to gather the items for me. Palize stood at my back, chopping something. I took my basket and turned to him. "If you ever try to hurt me again, even by accident, I'll break your leg and send it to your mama." I said. In Spanish.

Once Jillyian was medicated with chocolate (a few endorphins should fix her right up), I set off in search of Sascha. No one had seen her; Donny was on a conference call in another wing. I began to fear she'd had another attack. I had run out of options and was walking toward the studio when I heard her shout. She was coming up from the beach?

"Where the hell have you been?" I asked. "I've been looking for you for hours." Exaggerating, yeah.

"I take break. I did my job!" she said, immediately defensive. Couldn't blame her.

"Sorry," I said. "Jillyian messed up her makeup and needs a redo."

"I thought was practicing already?" she said as we race-walked back to the dressing room. "That is why I take break."

"She—I," I shrugged. "Anyway, she's ready for you."

A half hour later, Sascha and I followed Jillyian as she glided down the hallway. The combination of antique furnishings and retrofitted woman was a little dizzying—like we'd time-traveled for a second or something.

Those fears were quelled when I stepped onto the set where, amidst the antiques culled from other countries, and Oscar's lovingly constructed tea tray, there were enough people and technical gear to host a small concert. Birds squawked in their cages, the island help muttered in their lingo, and the film crew cursed at each other, at the electrical capacity of the castle, and at their respective agents and unions.

"The girls aren't going to pick up these birds, are they?" I asked around.

"We might let one of the girls take this cockatiel out of the cage and hold it."

"You cannot let it shit on the dress," I said to the bird wrangler.

"Lady, I can't promise you when Kiki has to let it go or not. We can always clean it up."

"The dresses are on loan; we can't clean it up enough."

"I'm just going by my orders, lady. They want someone to pick up the bird. Talk to your director, not me."

The director was shipped in from Miami, with his own crew. One of the most annoying things about video is the hierarchy. Everyone has his or her job, and that is it. No picking up the slack for a colleague, no pitching in. And no complaining above someone else's head.

The director probably wouldn't even speak to a lowly stylist.

Donny came in a few minutes later, and he looked harassed. "Donny," I said, getting in line before the other complainants, "the girls can't hold the birds. It's too unpredictable."

"What?"

"Bird doo," I said.

"We pay you to clean it up, don't we?" He was being snotty, haughty, and I realized it was probably a trickle-down. He'd been chewed, so he was ready to chew on someone else.

"If it happens on one of those dresses, it's going to cost you five grand," I said, naming a number to cover the cost of a replacement. God, I'd have to find a seamstress, and—

"Fine. Zima takes a bird out of the cage and lets it fly free," he said and turned away from me. "Next?"

The bird wrangler smiled smugly, and I shrugged. If Donny paid, why should I care? I began to run through my mental Rolodex of *modistas* who could tackle a period dress for under five grand, including material.

"Are we ready?" Donny asked. He cued the director, who cued the guy who cued the music, and we were off. The girls lip-synched their way through the verse, once, only goofing at the end when Eladonna stood on the inside hem of her own dress and almost fell into the tea tray.

It was a cut, and Sascha and I ducked in. She powdered them, and I checked their appearances against the Polaroids

I'd shot. A fluffing of one's cleavage, a minimizing of London's, and then we were off set and gearing up for the second take.

"Blondie," the director said, pointing to London. "This time you should try opening the cage. You're standing closer."

"I can't turn around," she said.

"You can't—" The director swore and turned to Donny. "What the hell is this, she can't turn around?"

Donny spoke to London. "Trade places with Zima."

The girls traded places. Everything was cued, and then we filmed.

¶ The song, the video, was going great. At the bridge, Zima opened the cage to let the bird fly free. Symbolic of kicking a boyfriend to the curb, according to the lyrics.

Instead, she screamed. She jumped back into a Louis Quinze table. The table held a vase, which turned over. The vase dumped water and flowers down Eladonna's back. She shrieked and jumped up. Jillyian screamed and tried to scoot away, but London stomped on her dress.

Jillyian fell into Eladonna, London fell on them both.

The three of them overturned the sofa.

Oscar's tea tray was airborne, as was the cockatiel. We ducked pineapple and cream cheese finger-sandwich missiles, and the indiscriminate droppings of the bird. Chaos, women screaming, men shouting, and birds, dozens of them, squawking.

In the middle, Zima cowered, her eyes big and round and fixed on whatever was in the cage.

A single gunshot silenced everyone.

"What the hell is going on?" Oscar bellowed.

Then the bird aimed, fired, and nailed the navy jacket the chef was wearing. Oscar lifted his gun. The bird wrangler jumped over to his side. "Don't! You brute!" he shouted at Oscar. "Stanley," he called the bird. "Stanley, come here right away. You've been a very bad boy!"

"Retrieve that flying bag of feathers immediately, "Oscar said, "or he will be the centerpiece of my dining table."

As though the birds all understood, they set off a racket. Oscar fired again, in the air. Everyone except me cowered on the floor. He was firing caps, not bullets. I don't think anyone else knew that.

The girls helped each other up, but one was missing. Eladonna lay on the ground. The sofa, a carved wooden thing, had fallen on her. People started to gather, to help her up. I walked over to Zima. "What happened?" I asked.

She pointed to the cage. I looked inside.

A crude doll made of a corn cob and bits of green cloth, with a Sharpie-drawn face and human hair, stared back at me malevolently. A giant pin pierced its middle, holding a note in place. "Be Weare," it said. *Beware*? I looked over my shoulder where the guys were lifting Eladonna's limp body onto the righted sofa. I looked back at the doll and shivered. It had dark curly hair.

Chapter Sixteen

"Take her to de tamarind tree," Mama Garcia said when Oscar brought her into the room. "Quick, like now, is the only t'ing to fix off dat bad magic."

"What happened?" Donny asked. "And don't give me this shit about voodoo!"

Eladonna appeared to be sleeping. She wasn't running a fever, and she didn't appear wounded anywhere. She just wouldn't wake up. Zima hadn't cried, but she looked like she was trying desperately not to. Ka'Arih held Eladonna's hand and spoke to her in a soft voice. She had been doing that since they'd laid Eladonna down on the couch, three hours ago.

The bird men had cleared out, the video guys too, especially the rude director. Donny's hair was standing almost on end he was so frazzled, and Jillyian watched everything, twisting a handkerchief. London had been the one to show grief; and she hadn't stopped crying yet.

Oscar was tight-lipped as he ordered people around, especially Palize, who'd kept everyone supplied with coffee and sandwiches while we watched Eladonna. Sascha kept track of Eladonna's blood pressure and pulse.

It was a Snow White thing. Eladonna looked like she was just asleep. Just impossible to awake.

"She needs an MRI," Teddy said. "There could be damage, brain damage, oh God—"

"When she is touching de tree, den be okay to take out dem pins," Mama Garcia said to me. "First, her must touch de tree."

Somehow I'd become the keeper of the doll.

"It can't be because of that corn cob voodoo," Donny reasoned with Mama Garcia. "The sofa must have caught her in the middle and . . ." He threw his hands up in the air. "I'm not a damned doctor!" He'd called Bimini, but their emergency people were already out helping a sinking boat.

"Trus me, Mista Pedretti," Mama Garcia said. "Dis girl, she is go'wn be fine if you take her to dat tree. Butchu betta go now, before dat storm come."

"Will you go with us, Mama?" I asked.

"Sure, chile, I wouldn't send you alone."

A strange group trekked across the island. Behind the castle a twist of trees crowded together, adorned with bottles and ribbons. We moved silently closer while the guys carried a makeshift stretcher. I followed Mama Garcia, the doll in my hands.

"You have de face of Deat', so it won't hurt you," she'd said.

Zima and Ka'Arih held hands as they walked. London followed, with Teddy. Sascha walked beside the stretcher, with Jillyian on the other side.

It was the first night of the new moon. Mama Garcia had forbidden "electric torches," so we carried the real thing—all in all, it felt like a scene from a movie that would star Johnny Depp and require costumes.

Voodoo dolls? It would be laughable if Eladonna wasn't convincing us. I didn't believe in the stuff, but if it was real, did it need my vote of confidence? Nope. I kept walking. Softly, a voice rose ahead of me, singing a hymn. I blinked back tears as I walked. Eladonna would be all right, surely?

The next question was, who had done this and why? Beware of what? It was beginning to *sound* like a Nancy Drew story. What had Eladonna done? What did she know? Had she seen something?

Did she know something about the dead, washed-ashore guy and . . . and what? His hands had been tied, by someone who had access to this castle, but I hadn't seen any wounds on him. I mean, I only suspected he'd been killed. Had Eladonna seen him be killed, and the killer was coming after her?

It didn't make any sense; none.

When we reached the shore, the wind had shifted.

"Storm blowin' in," Mama Garcia said.

"It wasn't on the news," Donny protested. "A perfectly clear week, that was the forecast."

"You take a look at dat sky, and you tell me," she said. "Here, set that chile down by dis tree. It is de only good fix-fix for *voudon.*"

The guys set down the stretcher. London took Eladonna's hand and held it.

"Now, we all have to pray," Mama Garcia said. "London, you touch her hand to dat tree. Dallas, when her eyes flutter, like d'ere about to open, you take out dat long needle from de doll."

I nodded, apprehension streaking down my spine.

Mama Garcia started singing, a melodious, sensuous song whose language I didn't know. Ka'Arih continued to sing her hymn in a low, now-minor key. London placed Eladonna's hand on the tree.

The singing continued as we all watched.

"This is nonsense," Donny muttered.

Mama Garcia sent him a look, and I wondered if the face of death had traveled from me to him. Eladonna's eyelids began to flutter. My hands were shaky as I pulled on the pin, then yanked it out.

Eladonna's body spasmed. Her eyes stayed closed.

"She sleep still?" Sascha whispered. "Is magic gone?"

Mama Garcia opened a bag she'd brought with her and tied a small parcel around Eladonna's long neck. Beside me, Palize shivered. Maybe he really believed this stuff, being from these islands. Was he from these islands? I didn't know.

"This will protect her, so when she wake up, she be fine," Mama said.

Lightning flashed in the distance and we all hurried toward the castle. By the time we reached the garden, rain fell in sheets, the wind splayed the palms, and it sounded as though demons howled in the night.

Inside, the power had gone out. Oscar went to start the backup generator, and Mama Garcia lit candles.

"What do I do with this?" I asked her, the doll and pin still in my hands.

"We gotta bury dat doll, tomorrow, by de tree. Dose pins? I doan know who dey belong to, but dat be da person who did dis to Eladonna. Someone wish her bad juju."

"Is that her hair?" I asked, pointing at the doll.

"It is. Always burn your nail clippings and hair, chile. If not, someone could do da same t'ing to you."

I nodded and let her finish with the candles. Palize and Oscar fried some conch and grilled sweet yams for a snack, and we huddled, waiting for the storm, watching Eladonna.

About 2 a.m. the storm arrived, and Eladonna awoke. "Where am I?" she asked. "What's going on?"

"We're all watching the storm," Donny said. "How do you feel?"

She sat up and rubbed her stomach. "Hungry."

*   *   *

After Oscar fed Eladonna some chicken and rice, we all went up to sleep. I still had the doll, though it creeped me out. "I don't believe in this stuff," I said to myself, just for the noise of it. After ten minutes of pacing my room, I decided to tuck the doll in on the opposite side of the bed and see if that helped me feel better.

I crawled in on my side of the bed. Now I felt calmer.

We were lying exactly the same, flat on our backs, arms over the coverlet.

My eyes closed watching her painted face.

In the morning, the doll was gone.

Donny was up to his usual games, his morning sex with Jillyian. I swore and jumped out of bed. I don't sleep that soundly; who had come into my room, and why steal the doll? I threw on my robe and slippers and went to Donny's door. I knocked, loudly.

The man was impressive, I had to admit. He just kept at it, so I knocked on the door harder. Nothing, except Jillyian was getting louder. Finally I just banged on the door, but then I noticed something. Either Donny had lovemaking down to an art, or this was an exact repeat of noise from another day. "Donny?" I said to the edge of the door. Then I tried the handle. It opened.

I'd walked in on my sister Ojeda once. When my parents were downstairs watching election returns and arguing, she'd sneaked her no-good boyfriend into the room we shared. I was supposed to be somewhere else—I don't remember. But it was a strange, embarrassing experience for me. She didn't care, and I don't think he did, either.

Now they had three children and had been married for fifteen years.

I was braced myself, but it was for no reason.

No one was in Donny's room.

No one was having sex.

It was just a Walkman playing a track I'd heard before, through portable Bose speakers. Aimed at my wall. What men will do for their reputations. I closed the door behind me, struck by the thought: where was Donny if he wasn't banging his girlfriend/lead singer at 6 a.m.? I closed my own door and stared at the bed.

Why take the doll? Was there something about it that would give away the creator? I thought as I dressed. Anyone had access to corn cobs. Cloth, too, because the workroom was unlocked. Hair? That was a grisly thought, but it didn't really have to be Eladonna's, it could just be dark. A brush lying around the makeup table would be easy to clean and pocket. Sharpies? They were everywhere—used on labels, used on cards, used by everyone for everything. *Beware.* Who would misspell beware?

Anyone who wanted to confuse everyone else. It was so obviously contrived.

Why? What had Eladonna done? Or who was stalking her?

I walked down the stairs in my shorts and halted halfway. The rain had stopped, but the blue skies and warm breezes were a thing of the past. The sky was gray, and the air felt like oatmeal. Altogether, not my definition of paradise.

My run took place on the other half of the island, past the trees with tied bottles swinging in the wind, and back to the castle.

No one was at breakfast. The crews were packing in hopes of getting out before the weather got worse. Bette had taped a Sharpie-written note to the coffeepot. *One-shot shoot at 9 a.m.*

I fixed some coffee and hustled to the dressing room. I had steaming to do.

Today's look was educational. Class costumes.

Sascha knocked, then poked her head in. "Good morning," she said. "Sleep good?"

"Yeah, and you?"

She came in, makeup and hair perfect, but her hands were shaking. "I dream bad all night long. Worse than government, dreams with dead women and long teet'. You have this in your country? People who drink the blood and don't die?"

"Vampire is the word I think you are searching for."

"Yes, yes, vampires, but girl vampires that eat the baby."

"That's dreadful, Sascha! I don't know about those kind of vampires." Truth be told, I wasn't much up on vampire lore past Count Chocula. "Well, don't tell your dreams before breakfast," I said, pulling some clothes off the rack.

"Vhy not?"

"They'll come true."

"I eat already."

"Great, then we're safe."

"What do you dream about?" she asked me.

Chanel shoelaces and voodoo dolls and banging that ends up being a body hanging from a tree, in a blue dress. "Clothes," I said with a smile.

"The clothes are broken? Roo-een?" Sascha asked carefully.

I hadn't even thought about the dresses from yesterday. Were they ruined? I'd gathered them all and hung them, but between the water stains, the stomping and the tearing, Fate of Paradise was buying five period evening dresses. I needed to call Lindsay to have her fax Donny the invoice for those before this job was even over. Five thousand per dress? I should have said seven.

"I don't know," I said, stepping toward the rack. "Okay, now, school clothes."

"This will be boring," Sascha said. "Professor makeup? I know no professor who wear makeup."

I showed her the graduate outfit I had, three different private-school uniforms including the ever-popular Catholic schoolgirl kilt, and one Baby-Phat student.

"Who in vhat?" she asked.

"London was going to be hip-hop," I said. With her size it was better to go for the deliberate laugh than to dress her up as a schoolgirl and let her be laughed at. And the Phat jacket was the exact color of London's eyes. "Eladonna . . . she was going to be the graduate in cap and gown."

"What happen to her?" Sascha said, lighting a cigarette. "Vhy Zima scream over little doll? Why think Eladonna, anyway? Vas in green, not purple."

I froze in front of the rack. Sascha was right! I'd assumed Eladonna, everyone had, because she wasn't getting up. But dark curly hair could apply to several of the girls. And Eladonna's dress had been purple, royal purple. Had someone stolen the doll so I wouldn't realize that? That was a lot of risk for very little profit.

But then who would be telling Jillyian—*Jillyian* in teal green—beware? I was back to the same old questions. Why? Who? "How do you think the person got the doll in the cage?" I asked as I hemmed the skirt of one plaid uniform.

Sascha laughed. "Everyone in and out all day? Is not problem." Her accent seemed thicker today. "Valk by and stuff in cage in one minute. No problem."

Why? I asked myself as I bit off the thread. I turned back to Sascha. "I'm putting London in a hat."

"No other hats?"

I shook my head.

"Today we shoot very fast," Sascha said. "Girls will be here in ten minutes."

I turned on the steamer and the iron after she left. Mama Garcia caught me as I was finishing the last outfit.

"How are you, Mama Garcia?" I asked, as I hung the clothes on the rack, each with a bag of accessories.

"I be fine, chile, and you?"

I nodded. "Good, thank you."

"And dat doll?"

She must have seen the reaction on my face.

"Dat doll is gone? You lose it?"

"It was snatched from my bedroom during the night," I said. "Someone must have sneaked into my room and taken it."

"Ohh," Mama Garcia drew the syllable out into a commentary on all the evils that could befall. "Dat bad, dat. Very bad."

"Mama, do you think it was of Eladonna, or someone else?"

"Whatchu mean, chile? You t'ink someone else in danger?"

"I don't know how voodoo works. Is a doll like that, is it for only one person or could it be for two?"

"*Voudon* is not dat doll. Dat doll was a bad Hollywood idea of *voudon*. No island mon would do dat."

"A white person did that?" I asked. "One of us?"

She nodded.

"But you acted like we had to get her to the tree, that the magic was real. I—"

"Jes' because it woan done right, don' mean it won' work. You rile up dem *loa*, t'ink to make mock-mock of d'em . . ." she shook her head. "Dangerous magic."

"You gave Eladonna some . . . some . . ." I searched for a word. "Protection, right? That little pouch she is wearing around her neck?"

"*Juju* isn't strong enough," Mama Garcia said. "No, it be your problem now."

"What? Getting the doll back? I'm going to look, I just haven't—"

"No, chile, you are responsible for Eladonna now. Her blood be on yo' head and hands. You her protector."

I stared at Mama Garcia, speechless.

"You come 'ere wearing de face of Deat'. How funny it be if you be Deat?"

"But, Mama, what if it was really supposed to be Jillyian?"

Mama's eyes got big. "Den you have two souls on yo' watch."

Chapter Seventeen

At 9:15 a.m., the music of Fate of Paradise blasted through the classroom set on the soundstage, and the five girls did their parts flawlessly. By ten the video guys were loaded up, and by 10:30 the sky was black, wind shrieking and trees bending.

Delicious smells filled the dining room, and we all wandered in there, a little bit lost in this dark place. "Whoa," Teddy said when he saw the table. "Are we making a sacrifice?"

The table had been set already, adorned with red candles and a plethora of rooster feathers and Mardi Gras beads in black and red.

"It's for boosting the *loa*," Ka'Arih said. "I helped Mama Garcia."

"What's the *loa*?" Donny asked.

"Like the local gods or something," Eladonna said. She seemed recovered; no one had referenced yesterday's weirdness.

Mama Garcia appeared at the swinging doors. "Glad you all here," she said. "De storm be comin', so if everyone will stay in dese two rooms," she said pointing to the drawing room and the dining room, "we'll be jes' fine."

"What are you cooking?" London asked. "It smells heavenly."

"We cookin' for da next few days, in case de power go out," she said. "Bonefish stew, conch, yams, shreemp, you be fine-fine."

"What are we supposed to do?" Jillyian asked, looking around. "Is the storm going to be bad?"

Outside, thunder crashed.

Mama Garcia smiled. "'Urricane Grizelda go'wn to be a beetch," she said. "Ladeeva, she got some games in dere, jes' for days like dis. Go'wn, I gotta cook."

We trotted into the drawing room. Shutters had been hung on the outside windows, and the curtains drawn, and for a moment it felt like a cold stony castle instead of a Moroccan pleasure palace. Personally, I wanted to go to my room. If I got cut off, I'd light candles and run a hot bath. One of these people was a little deranged—faking voodoo and then stealing a doll out of my bed.

Though that involved only the opening of one little door, it was the principle of the thing.

"We can try centers with different games," Ka'Arih suggested. "When we teach the kids at summer church school, that's what we do. We set up a bunch of little tables and rotate half the group every ten minutes or so, to another little table. Everyone mixes and mingles and no one gets bored."

Jillyian sat down at the piano and ran her fingers across the keys.

I sat down with Teddy, who said, "Jillyian, if you want to sing and play until the storm is over, Dallas and I will be delighted to listen."

She jerked her hands off the keys like they'd turned to flames. "Uh, I think I'll save myself for the studio." She got up and wandered to the window.

"Come on," I said, "we won't be critical."

"We promise," Teddy said.

"Do you still have headache?" Sascha demanded of her. Jillyian looked at Sascha and nodded. "I do," she said. "Oh," Teddy said, "I guess it's the barometric pressure. Do you want any aspirin?"

Jillyian was lying, I'd swear to it. And Sascha was helping her. I stood up. "Well, if there's not going to be an impromptu performance, I'll go work on clothes. At least until the lights go out." They laughed halfheartedly at me, and I escaped.

Someone, several someones, was lying. And if they were all in that room, their rooms were open. If I had "two souls" on my conscience, then I had no problem looking behind a few doors and snooping through some drawers. I was, after all, a big sister. I knew how to spy.

The problem with my program was that I didn't know where anyone else was staying. Oscar was next door to the workroom, and Donny was next door to me, but I was clueless about everyone else. "Let the adventure begin," I muttered to myself. I wandered over to the bookcase in my workroom, and looked for the catch to open it. I figured it was on a passage that fed directly into the kitchen, since it always admitted Oscar.

In the movies there was always a panel you had to press for the secret doorway to open. I moved books, magazines, I pushed and I pressed all around the bookcase, and it didn't budge.

"He stood against it," I said to myself, and positioned my back against the wall.

A click. A whir. I jumped forward in time to see the panel slide back into a groove, then slip out of the way while bringing another compartment with it. A person-sized slot. Here goes, I thought, and stepped inside.

The door was as fast as a Mercedes convertible top, and it moved back into place.

Like opening a matchbox, I slid out into the kitchen. From where I stood, I could see Palize, Oscar, Mama Garcia, and three island boys, all hard at work. Next to me was the freezer, then the short hallway that led to Oscar's pastel kitchen. I was about to step back inside and return to my room when I saw a replica space across from me. Another secret passageway? I glanced at the cooks—they hadn't turned around—then I jumped across into the other box.

These sliding boxes apparently were operated by weight—some form of dumbwaiter? I slid to a stop in the dining room. In the far corner, Donny and Jillyian were having a quiet but angry discussion. He was berating her, looming over her, and she stood with her head bent and arms folded. She didn't look like she was going to cry; she looked like she was going to shout. To my right, inside the compartment, I saw a switch. I pressed it and disappeared behind another wall.

Now I was in the drawing room, or rather, behind a tapestry in the drawing room. The remaining seven people were grouped around a table, tossing things into the air. "They're makin' bacon!" Ka'Arih shouted, and Eladonna complained that she'd lost another round. The pig game? Again, I reached for a switch and went behind another wall.

I ended up in a hallway I'd never been in before. Stairs led up, and I took them. At the top I saw four rooms. What's behind door number one, I asked myself and tried the knob. Silent, easy opening. "Wow."

It was a purple palace.

The bed was about six feet off the ground, closer to the frescoed ceiling of silver stars on lavender clouds than to the Carrara marble floor. As in my room, the linens were exquisite. Fresh flowers filled every vase and jar in the room—about twenty of them. The smell of roses and gardenias was almost overwhelming. Whose room? I opened an armoire door (French country, bleached to a silver wood) and looked at the clothes. Comme des Garcons, Sigerson, Katyone Adeli. Size ten.

London's room.

I slipped into the bathroom, done in all-white tile with lavender touches. A footed tub, a vanity with silver implements. What the hell was I looking for? I walked back into the bedroom and asked myself what I hoped to find. Proof that London had done the voodoo doll?

Think about it, Dallas. She is not about to touch an old corn cob. It's not going to happen. And the shoe does not fit. Just in case, I opened the armoire and looked at her shoes. She wasn't kidding about her tennis shoes having heels; they were the cutest little Barneys' Dove Nuotano Gli Squali pumps, in blue and white—and size nine-and-a-half.

I left her room for the next.

Where London's had been like ice, this room was fire. Screaming yellow and orange linens, layered on top of each other. The bed was low to the ground with a headboard of cloth that became a half-canopy, thanks to monofilament strung from the ceiling. The rug was a kilim, and incense burned before a low table set with a variety of statues. An altar?

Was this the voodoo person?

I looked around the vanity, the closet, and concluded I was in quiet Zima's room. Corn cobs didn't seem like her, either, but wasn't it said that still waters run deep? With this in mind, I looked through her bathroom trash.

The girl had used four condoms since the maid had been in.

With extracurricular activities like that, she didn't have time to make a doll and plant it in the birdcage. I glanced at some music she had on her nightstand. It wasn't a piece I had heard, but she was obviously writing it for the group, with the indications of who comes in when. I looked at the notes,

and wondered about my ability to read. My mother had fore-
told that menopause and glasses were going to come for me
soon, unless I had a child. I squinted at the note, and it said,
"S comes in."

S? It had to be a misshapen J?

I set the paper down and continued my prowl.

The next room was empty, and the fourth was filled with
bizarre hooks on the ceiling and Velcro straps close to the
bed. This goes with the size-thirteen platform heels, I thought,
and went back downstairs.

About this time, I figured it would probably be a good idea
to check in somewhere. I still heard rain outside, but I wasn't
sure where I was inside the building. The wall I'd come out of
was closed, and I had no idea how to open it. With a shrug, I
took a left, now walking down the hall that ran at right an-
gles beneath the stairs.

I found a set of stairs that went down.

What the hey, I took them.

Four more doors.

The first room was carved from rock, with a real cave-
woman feel to it. The bed was set in front of a fireplace and
covered in a fur throw. There were no signs of habitation.
The next room was cold and filled with wine. A cellar.
Beyond that was a closet, a huge storage room with costumes
and wigs. If I had a chance, I'd come back and see what
looked familiar. The fourth room was locked. Back up the
stairs.

I took the hallway and found another set of stairs. These
were going up. One door on one landing. I walked into the
room and felt my jaw drop.

An aquarium took up one twelve-foot wall. The bed was a
hammock, and the opposite wall was an unobscured view of
the water. The linens were shades of blue and green. Stop
gawking, and start searching, I groused to myself, and won-

dered where the closet was. I went into the bathroom and found it—a whole room with a massage table in the middle. Ka'Arih's stuff, including a box, labeled "Willie."

The box rattled at me. Rattled like a reptile.

Oooh boy. I backed up.

Her trash was gone and I didn't see any Sharpies lying around, though I did find her passport.

Carrie Wilson, Route 8, Sheep's Hill, ND.

She wasn't kidding.

I went up another flight of stairs to another door. There was a theme here. Fire, Water, this should be Earth. I was right. A huge tree grew through the floor, in the middle of the room. Since it was the third floor, I had no idea how they pulled that off, but I stayed focused and looked through the items on the bronze and marble vanity (no Sharpies, no sign of corn) and through the closet, made of wood and bronze, decorated with leaves. It was Eladonna's room, and the only intriguing thing was all the women's underwear. Two distinctly different sizes and styles.

Some of these belonged to London or . . . Bette? Mama Garcia? A cross-dressing Oscar?

The bathroom was clean, of course, but filled with signs of two women, two different complexions, two different tastes. Well, well. I dashed up the stairs to the next room. The door was plated with gold and locked, really locked, like five times. Okay, maybe not here.

I took the stairs up to the final floor. I was obviously in another one of the towers. The room was round, with a walkway along an all-glass wall, similar to a lighthouse. I watched the storm for a minute; rain outside lashed the windows, and beyond I could see the white of the surf. Mostly it was black. I turned around.

This place was a nest.

Three steps down was the room, per se. A bed, covered in a white satin duvet. A nightstand of bronze twigs. I opened the drawer (I had *no* idea where the bathroom or the closet could possibly be) and saw another Passport. Jillyian's, I guessed.

The photo was terrible, and suggested she wasn't a real redhead. The name, however, made me sick and dizzy.

Jilly Anne Pedretti.

Chapter Eighteen

I was sitting at the sewing machine when the bookcase opened. Oscar walked in, a basket in his hands. The lights flickered, but held. "How are you?" he asked stiffly.

"Fine," I said.

"You don't look fine."

"Can't be a fashion plate every day," I said.

"You got a call, a Lindsay in Dallas?"

"I wonder why she didn't call my cell," I said as I watched him unpack my care kit.

"If your phone is like most cell phones, it doesn't work when the wind is seventy miles per hour."

"Is that the wind speed?" I asked.

"Dallas, are you okay?"

"What do you mean?"

"You're bringing to mind a Stepford wife. Monotone voice and glazed eye."

"Fine," I repeated.

"You didn't show for lunch, and no one knew where you were, I mean, you weren't here—"

"My room," I lied.

"Well, I figured that. I hoped you weren't in the storm."

"Are there other secret passageways?" I asked.

He poured me a glass of beer. "Dozens. Ladeeva saw too many Scooby Doos or something, and riddled the place with them."

"Is there another way to get into my room?"

"Not that I know of. The towers are pretty inviolate. They are designed for privacy." He prepared a plate for me. "Why?"

"Someone came into my room last night and took that voodoo doll."

Oscar set down the plate. "Came into your room?"

I nodded.

"While you were there?"

I nodded again. "I was asleep."

"And you didn't think to mention this little soupçon of information, until just this moment?"

"Remember your mother," I warned.

"Damn my mother, and she'd agree! You were invaded and you didn't tell me?"

"It was morning and . . . I . . ." I thought I heard Donny banging either his wife—in which case I need to get to confession ASAP, because I don't know if necking is adultery—or his sister, which is beyond words . . . and I went next door to learn that it was all a setup and . . . ?

"Dallas? Wench, you have the weirdest expression on your face."

"Having a *Flowers in the Attic* moment," I said, and sat down to my lunch.

"Are you scared?"

"Not for me," I said.

"For whom?" he asked.

I looked at the man. He was tall, taller than me, about 6'3". He was lean, but loaded with muscle. He had a raging temper and a propensity toward violence. I didn't know much about him except that he was proud, he was 46, he was thoughtful, and he was Latino, and seemed to have a balanced relationship with his mother.

He kissed like sunshine; he laughed with the joy of a child, and he was intuitive. But I didn't really know him. He could be a killer. I dropped my gaze. "Thanks for bringing me my food," I said and smiled. I took a sip of my drink. "What is this?" I coughed a little, as it went down the wrong pipe.

"Ginger beer and rum, it's a Dark and Stormy."

"Appropriate," I muttered.

"What are you trying to tell me?" he asked.

I sipped some more of the beer. "Thank you," I said. "I appreciate you taking care of me."

"Ahh, my service is complete, and I am dismissed," he said with a sarcastic bow and walked to the bookshelf.

I took two steps after him, reached for his waist. He turned around. I stopped, six inches away. "Was there something else you required?" he asked.

I wanted to ask him to hold me, to just assure me that the insanity of everything I was thinking was, of course, wrong. He looked at my mouth; I felt woozy just seeing the expression of want on his sharp-lined face. "I wish I could get you to live the way you eat, Dallas," he murmured as he bent to kiss me.

I pulled back. "What do you mean by that?"

Oscar touched my face. "Passionately, with abandon."

"Just because I haven't slept with you doesn't mean I'm not passionate."

"It has nothing to do with the physical act of consummation. It's an attitude. You're ambivalent."

"I am not."

"You are. About everything. You have one foot in, one foot out. You're waiting for the sky to fall, even with me. Why?"

Part of me was pissed, offended. Why had this idiot ruined a perfectly wonderful moment, and precluded a potentially wonderful evening? However, another side of me, a deeper, more elemental part, was intrigued. Oscar was pushing me, testing me. He wanted me to think, to know what I was doing.

"What thrills you, Dallas? Clothes? Booze? Boys? Girls?" He leaned closer. "What makes your pulse race? What gets you off?"

"Are any of those answers your business?" I could have pulled off being offended a little better, if I hadn't sounded like a sex hotline, with heavy breathing and a low voice.

"Don't get defensive. I just want to get inside you."

My turn to make a rude noise.

"Yeah, God's bones, girl, I do want to be into your body, but also in your head."

"If you think there's nothing but ambivalence in me, then why?"

"No, that's what I've seen. I think there's more. I won't be inane discussing icebergs and their tips, but you get the gist."

I stepped and looked into his carved face. "Look, if you want to fool around, let's do it. There's certainly chemistry between us, and the island is a great environment."

"Direct, aren't you?"

"Why not?"

"You really don't get it, do you? I don't want just your body in my bed. I don't need to have sex with a beautiful woman to validate myself. I'm not twenty-two. Time is too valuable to spend it half-assed, or halfhearted."

"I won't waste your time, then," I snapped.

"Dallas," his hand closed around my wrist. "What I want is to make love with you."

Saints preserve us. Me, preserve me. My heart was beating like a jackhammer and I couldn't look away from his eyes.

"I want us to both want to," he said. "I want it to be encompassing, mind and body. I want it to be real. I want it to last."

I might faint. "You have a strange method of seduction."

"No, I'm trying to slip into the only door I've found in you," he said, not gripping my wrist anymore, but caressing it. His voice dropped, and he moved closer to me, surrounding me with the smells of bread and spices, and man. "I'm going to make you a promise," he said to me, his breath on my ear sending shivers down my spine. "I'm going to cook for you." He kissed the edge of my jaw. "Every sauce will be made anticipating tasting you. Each fruit and vegetable will be selected, perfect and ripe, ready to . . . pluck."

True-true, if he weren't holding on to me, I would be falling down.

He turned my face to look into my eyes. "When you're ready, look at me and I'll know it. We're that connected."

We were that connected, on a completely internal, visceral level. But he didn't need to know I felt the same way.

"It won't matter when or where. I'll finally get to see the real Dallas O'Connor. Until then," he said, releasing my wrist, "*Bon appetit.*"

I watched him slide away in the bookshelf. I drained the drink still in my hand, and stared at the bookcase. Other rooms, Dallas. Think. Focus.

Three other guests' rooms I hadn't invaded, and I should. Teddy, Palize . . . and Oscar.

I ate the home-baked johnnybread and left my shark quiche. What part of his seduction was that? And what kind of woman was I to listen to his words, revel in his food, and break into his room?

Sascha, I thought, I hadn't looked in her room, either. But why would I? She was the makeup artist and possibly the most innocent person here.

Except there had been that lie I suspected her and Jillyian of working on. The headache that had so conveniently kept

Jillyian from playing for us. She could just be shy, I told myself. A likely story.

I wandered into the kitchen and asked Mama Garcia where a phone was. She was sitting, smoking a cigar with a distinctive umber band. That's right, we were Cohiba-close to Cuba. I went across the hall, and she was right, there was an English red phone booth down aways.

Lindsay answered on the fourth ring. "Artistic Alliance."

"Lindsay, it's Dallas."

"My God, darling! Are you okay? We've been listening to the weather and feared—"

"I'm fine, I'm fine," I said. "It's storming, but it's not bad."

"Well, thank you for calling to check in and let us know. Would you like me to call your Mum or Dad, just to fill them in?"

"Uh, might be a good idea." My parents have eight children, and I'm well into the 35–44 age range, but they still worry. "Yeah, do that, just so they aren't calling and not getting my cell phone and . . ."

"Sending out the National Guard?"

That wouldn't be my parents, that would be my brother Houston, who was a worrywart with two secretaries at his beck and call to follow up on his every little concern. "Right."

"Well?" Lindsay prompted, about to hang up.

"Hey, check something for me."

"Sure, love, what?"

"Were any of those other stylists here, I mean here on the island?"

"Why?"

"You are as bad as my seven-year-old niece," I said. "Can you just do what I ask instead of asking why?"

"Dallas, when you start asking odd questions it's because something's happened. Everyone's alive on your island, right?"

"Right, of course."

"Then why—?"

"I, uh, there's a stylist's kit here," I said. "All left-handed stuff. I just wondered if someone misplaced it."

Silence. "Hello?" I said.

"In the decade I've been in this business," Lindsay began. Her English accent gets stronger when she gets riled. Her "ben" had become "bean." "I've run across quite a few establishments that provided excellent resources for those whose kits are lacking."

"It could be a substitute kit," I said, though a lefty would bring her own kit; and left-handed scissors, etc. would be worthless to anyone else, so it would be as useless as a back-up kit. "But just in case . . ."

"How many stylists do you know who go about *misplacing* their kits?"

"Okay, okay," I said. "I just thought since you were there, you could do me this little favor—"

"Dallas, darling, I love you, I've done you a thousand favors, and will continue to do so. But I am not going to call every agency in the United States of bloody America to find out who lost a styling kit because you are eye deep in some strange circumstances or whatever!"

"I wasn't suggesting you call agencies," I snapped. "I was thinking airlines."

"Oh. Well. I'll get right on it. Am I just supposed to recognize the stylist's name?"

I was about to hang up, to apologize and just quit. Why was I gnawing on this? I didn't know. I was looking for a corn cob or a . . . name. Wait. "Lindsay, can you hold?"

She sighed. "For you, darling, anything."

Sarcasm *and* English accent. Bad signs. "I'll be right back." I said.

I dropped the phone, ran to the styling room and tore open the third closet's door. The bag was there, the extra kit.

I looked for a tag, none. I opened the kit and started feeling through the pockets that lined the side. My fingers brushed a Polaroid. I pulled it out.

The corpse, when he was still alive, grinned at the camera with his arms around Ka'Arih and London. Zima and Jillyian were crouched at the bottom, with Donny between them. Eladonna was standing in the back. Had Teddy taken the photo? I flipped it over, then turned back to the picture and looked at the bottom. A smidgen of a shoe—a yellow-and-white shoe.

The photo had been taken by the wearer of the Chanel wrestling shoes!

Chapter Nineteen

Every last one of these people had lied? I stuffed the photo back and picked up one of the bags, this one filled with fake breasts. It was monogrammed on the front: GNR

I ran out of the room and grabbed the phone. Of course, Lindsay had put me on hold. I listened to the classical music station in far away Dallas while my mind raced. They'd all seen the dead guy. Somebody had laced his hands together, either before or after he died. Someone here, because the shoes were here.

The line cut out. I hung up and called again, but then got Lindsay's voice mail.

"Lindsay, look on the charter flights for two or three days before I took this job. You want a man with long, dark hair, a ton of luggage, and the initials GNR. Do you have the Centurion information? I bet he flew that way. Maybe Amex can help? I—"

My time ran out. I tried to call back, but the line was dead. I tried again, but I couldn't even get a dial tone. The phone was out. Was the storm worse? This is beginning to feel like a bad movie, I thought as I hung up the receiver.

Was someone in this place a killer?

* * *

I was walking across the hall when Sascha came out of the dining room. "Dallas! You have been so quiet all day!"

My smile was pathetic, I admit.

"Come, come, we decide to have party tonight. Masquerade, da?"

"Masquerade?"

"Ladeeva has costumes, and lights will go out anyway, so why not drink and smoke and bang and make bad weather go away?" Her Natasha accent was extremely strong today.

"Why not?" I asked rhetorically.

"Good! Come, we go to storage room," she said, tugging on my arm.

I resisted. Maybe they'd killed the other stylist. Maybe this was how? I wasn't going to be next. "Are you sure? I think we should ask Mama Garcia," I said.

Sascha held up some keys and jingled them. "Her idea!"

Great. She was in on it, too? Was there no one I could trust?

"Come, come!" Sascha said and dragged me into the drawing room. "Dallas will help!" she announced to the pig gamers. "Let's go!"

Led by Mama Garcia, we journeyed through the warren of halls to a huge room. Inside, mannequins were adorned in either diva costumes or S&M attire. They were kept in huge plastic bags, but it was easy to "shop" for what you wanted, because they were displayed like a museum collection. Mama insisted we'd have more fun if she handed out the costumes and then no one would know what the others were going to be.

My first masquerade (with killers) that wasn't gay, and I couldn't even pick my own clothes. That bit. Mama handed me a plastic bag and then closed the door.

"You want?" Sascha asked, holding up a joint. She'd been waiting outside the door for me. My nerves felt stretched as guitar strings, only the noise I would make was going to be a painful shriek instead of music. Two days ago, I wouldn't have thought anything of Sascha's waiting; I would have laughed and had fun. Why not, I asked myself. It's storming to hell outside, there's nowhere to go, nowhere to run. They aren't going to kill you if you just keep your mouth shut. Get stoned, sleep with Oscar, and then it will all be over and you can go home and berate yourself for stepping away from your ideal of perfect behavior, or *whatever.*

But what about the stylist, what about the laces? And Donny with Jillyian? If she was his wife, why were they pretending otherwise, and if she was his sister ... Ewww! Maybe cousin by marriage or something. . . . There's nothing to do, no one to call, no choice, I reasoned with myself. Just get through. It will be over soon.

I took one of Sascha's cigarettes with a sense of resignation. I didn't have to worry about hating myself in the morning; I hated myself now.

"Why did I think this wasn't going to be gay?" I muttered as I stood on the staircase and looked down at the partyers.

Porno Scarlet O'Hara, a.k.a. Sascha, standing next to me, replied in an excellent drawl. "They ain't gay, shughar, they is festive."

The more I learned about the mysterious woman who owned this place, the more I was drawn to her. A dark fascination, like watching a car wreck. I shook my head at Sascha's appearance. "I know men in Dallas who couldn't look as good as that," I said. "You have drag queen down to an art."

"Is Bourgeois Coup de Théâtre mascara, and Maybelline cake liner," she said in Natasha-ese. "In Moscova, I am best makeup for boys playing girls."

I straightened my fur hat. While Sascha looked like a southern belle, minus thirty feet of skirt and at least a foot of bodice, I was some stripper's interpretation of a Czar. "Das Vadanya," I said.

"Vhat is that?"

"Russian, right?"

She laughed. "You speak Russian like I speak Chinese."

I had a feeling that was not a compliment.

One of the uh, not-gay men, looked up and I realized that it was . . . Donny?

"He should have left off the glasses," I muttered. "Kinda wrecks the overall impression." And since I wasn't altogether sure what kind of man he was anymore—weird, was my best guess—I wasn't sure if I was repulsed or attracted by his leather pants and vest ensemble. A straight Village Person. He couldn't really walk; I think he'd hooked his leather straps up wrong.

"Hey, comrade," a man crooned into my ear.

I spun around and burst out laughing. "What the hell are you?" a hairy, muscular Cher asked me. When did he get back?

"I like the feather headress," I said through giggles.

"'Half-Breed' was always my favorite song," Zac said in an injured tone. The effect of a breechcloth and suede bra top was disconcerting—and the makeup was downright strange.

"Should shave," Sascha said, "before applying foundation."

"I just wanted Indian warpaint, but the guys—" he gestured to the boys in the band, "— persuaded me otherwise."

"Where's E! now?" I said. "This is unbelievable."

"An intriguing way to forget a hurricane," Zac slash Cher answered.

"Vhat is under your skirt?" Sascha asked, teasing him.

"If you show me yours, darlin'," Zac said in his sinful voice, "I'll show you mine."

"Excuse me," I muttered and slipped through the crowd. Another reject from the Village People stood by himself, glaring at the group. He was smoking a joint, and between his black glasses, short black hair, clean shaven face, and leather vest, I just couldn't figure out who he was.

"Hey, sexy," he said in a Spanish accent. "Dance with me."

Music was playing over the loudspeaker—Diana Ross, or was it Donna Summer? I always get them confused. He grabbed me around the waist and began to move with me, grinding his groin against mine. I pulled back and pushed him away.

He grabbed my butt, and I dug my nails into his earlobe. "Let me go."

"If you want to know about the body, about the lies, meet me in the kitchen," he said in a low, fast whisper.

"Palize?"

"No, no, not the kitchen," he said. "Your room."

"You know my room?"

"First night, remember?"

He did know my room. "Tell me now," I said.

"Am I interrupting?" Oscar asked. I turned around, guilty appearing if not feeling. Maybe feeling, too. Palize knew something? Was I hallucinating?

"Hi," I said.

Oscar wasn't looking at me; he was glaring at Palize. "Touch a woman here again and I will cut your fingers off and stuff them down your throat," he said in guttural Spanish.

Since Palize wore glasses, I couldn't see his eyes, but he gave Oscar the finger, then hastened back to the kitchen. Oscar looked me up and down. "May I take your coat?"

Everyone else looked ridiculous. Not Oscar. He wasn't in chef-wear, he was in a Texas tuxedo (jeans, white shirt, and black jacket) and looked good enough to attack.

"I may be a little chilly," I said.

"All the better," he muttered. Slowly, he held out his hand

and I reluctantly unbuttoned my Communist red jacket to reveal a bustier worn over black pin-striped hose and thigh-
high boots. My ears burned under the flaps of my woolly hat.

"Way to go, comrade," Cher said.

"Great tights," Porno Scarlet said.

"Interesting epaulets," Oscar said.

They were on my bare shoulders, attached to my red top
by nude mesh. The fringe tickled.

The shouts and applause I received were unexpected. The
electricity was still working, so the lights were on, but low.
Jillyian was in a Cleopatra gown, three inches long, with a
serpent attached to her breast. Eladonna was a Pilgrim in hot
pants and thigh-high boots. London had Marie Antoinette's
panniers, but her gown ended mid-thigh, and her blond wig
stood another foot taller. Zima was a gangster, but her shirt
consisted of wide suspenders and double-stick tape. She had
a black tie knotted around her throat, and a matching fe-
dora. Ka'Arih was a huntress; and if you combined her outfit
and Zac's, they would amount to only one-and-a-half-yards
of fawn-colored suede.

All the guys who wanted to be dressed as men were in
Village People leather combo variations. John, the cute blond,
had on lederhosen and a permanent blush. The rest were in
drag.

"If the floodwaters come," I said, "we all have to stay inside."

Sascha guided me to the punch bowl. It smelled like rum,
looked like rum and poured like rum. But it had something
else, too. "What is that?" I asked, sniffing. Coconut? Chili
peppers? I sipped a little, and then I felt the bite.

I poured Sascha a glass, too. It tasted so good, we had several cupfuls.

Part of me knew I wanted to be blind, in every sense. Did
Palize really know something?

Part of me wondered if they, whoever "they" were, were

encouraging my not seeing by keeping me stoned and drunk. "Is pathetic excuse," I said to myself. Or I addressed myself, but spoke out loud in Natasha-ese.

"You sound like perfect Russian speaking English," Sascha said. "Now you are ready for party!"

"You still sound like the perfect Russian speaking English," I said.

"Whhhy, thahnk you," she said in her amazing Georgia-peachery.

"You are velcome," I said. Giggling, we walked back toward the group. People were mingling in a definite R-rated way.

"Howdy, cheffy," Sascha said, coming up behind Oscar. As he turned, she grabbed him and kissed him. Hard. Oscar turned the tables on her, and my toes curled inside my boots watching them kiss. I discovered another glass was in my hand, and I drained it.

"Holy Mother a Gawd," Sascha said in her Scarlet when Oscar let her up for a breath. "I'm gonna take you home to the range, young man!"

"Ride and rope," I said in Russian-ese.

"Don't start what you can't finish," he told her with a wink. Then he finished her glass and went to get her another one.

"I think that is for you, not me," she said to me in her normal accent. "Oh, but his kisses—"

"Don't," I said. I knew he'd been talking to me; he knew I knew. The lights flickered, and everyone ooed, but they stayed on. "How long do hurricanes last?" I asked.

"Is this a freak show or what?" Teddy asked me. I turned around. He was in black workout gear and a lot of cologne. His expression was alarmed and completely sober.

"When did you get here?" I asked him.

"About ten minutes ago. I was—"

"No, on the island."

"A few hours before you, I guess. Why?"

"Think, Teddy. Do you know a stylist with the initials GNR?"

He frowned. "Why?"

"Do you?"

"No, I don't know. I'm terrible with names."

Did I dare show him the picture? "Was there any other stylist here before me? Have they mentioned anyone?"

"Hey!" Teddy shouted, looking over my shoulder. "Leave her alone!"

I turned around. Palize was trying to kiss London's bountiful 18th-century cleavage, and her look of total horror wasn't discouraging him. Teddy picked Palize up by the collar and tossed him. The sous-chef landed on the ground, his sunglasses half off his face, and the room got quiet.

"He just wouldn't get his grimy hands off of me," London said with outrage. "He's the *help*!"

Palize ripped the glasses off and looked at us. "You think you are safe, you rich whiteys. Your day is coming!" He ran out of the room. There was mumbling, but everyone was too messed up to pursue anything. I saw Donny glaring at Jilly-ian, and the look she sent him was hateful. Maybe they were married, about to divorce?

Then why would he help her get ahead? Unless he was taking a piece of the action? I walked over to the punch bowl and refilled my glass with the peppery sweet stuff. I turned around and watched the group.

Donny, in all his leather gear, was being fake- (I think) whipped by Bette, who was doing a Victor/Victoria thing. Eladonna watched very carefully. Bette, I realized. Bette and Eladonna. They wouldn't kill a—that's so stupid, Dee.

"This party tells more about people than I want to know," I said in Russian-ese.

"You want to whip Donny?" Porno Scarlet asked, drawn to the punch bowl too.

"You whip him for me," I said.

"Ah'll be raght baaack," she said in her drawl and walked up to Bette. Feeling Sascha's touch on her shoulder, Bette turned and surrendered the whip. "You betta drop those drawers," Sascha said to Donny, "'Cuz, honey-chile, I'm gunna whup you senseless."

Zac, I thought. Where is that rat? And how did he get back here? What was going on? I backed out of the room into the dark peace of the corridor. Outside the wind and rain bludgeoned the island, but we were oblivious. Safe, too, I guess.

"Dallas," Oscar said. I looked up at him and took his proffered hand. He pulled me up and into his arms. "You're shaking. Why? What is wrong? Talk to me, trust me. Just a little."

This big man was begging me, and I was so sorry. "It's not your fault," I said. "It's me. It's not you."

"What? What are you talking about?" He looked down into my face. "You drive me mad."

"And we barely know each other, so that can't be good." I wasn't completely joking.

Oscar dropped his hands and stepped back. "Fine," he said, holding his hands up. "Fi—"

"Ohmigosh," I interrupted him, shaken out of my daze. "Your hands! What happened?" The palms of his hands were tortured: blisters and calluses, burn scars and knife cuts. I looked up. Oscar was grinning. "What happened?"

"My battle wounds," he said, pointing them out. "That is from picking up a pan with no towel, which taught me to squirrel them away in the rafters. That's from deboning a pheasant while shouting obscenities at a purveyor who was cheating me. The rest are just hazards of the job."

"You never did tell me how you became a chef," I said, my gaze still on his beat-up hands.

"It's a long story."

"I'm here," I said. "Just waiting for a hurricane to pass."

"That'll be a while," he said.

I touched his chest. He was solid beneath the tropical-weight wool jacket and finely woven shirt. "I'd really like to talk," I said. "Learn something about you."

He looked down at my hand, and then followed my arm with his gaze. "Here's your jacket," he said, and pulled it from the door handle where'd he hung it. "Do you want some coffee?"

"Always," I said.

"Then come on." He took my hand and led me through a narrow passageway to the back of the kitchen. We walked down a smaller corridor to the pastel kitchen. He lit a few hurricane lamps and pulled out a chair for me. "Take your ease," he said.

I watched him pour coffee grounds into an Italian-style espresso pot. He patted them down and screwed on the other half. He added Evian to the top and lit the burner on the stove. Then he poured milk from a glass jug into a saucepan and started to stir it. With a gesture he turned on the espresso machine's steamer. "While we still have electricity," he said.

I took the chair and buttoned my coat so that my breasts weren't on a plate in his face.

He stirred the milk as he waited for the coffee. "I told you I was an anthropologist before I was a cook, right?"

I nodded. "Then we were interrupted."

"Yes, by Bette," he said. "An amazing woman."

Bette? I thought. She had amazing eyes, but . . . Bette? "So how did you get from bones to deboning fish?" I asked.

"The coffee fumes are starting to work on your wit," he said.

Damn. That was probably the last clever thing I was going to manage today. "What kind of coffee?" I asked.

"Blue Mountain," he said with a glance over his shoulder. "It's preferred by royalty."

"So I shouldn't get used to it?"

"Not unless you're robbing the cradle of some royal house, no."

Conversational lull. I watched him stir—such controlled movements, so graceful. What was I doing here talking to him when I really wanted to just be lost in his skin? Bad plan, Dallas.

"Anthropology isn't really about bones; it's more about societies and their movements," he said.

The silver pot started to gurgle and he swept it off the fire, then poured both the milk and coffee at the same time. He put the milk saucepan under the steamer and frothed away, then dolloped it on my coffee. A sprinkle of spice on top, and I was dazzled. I'd never seen anyone move in a kitchen like that, it was almost like watching ballet. Every movement was exactly right, measured, slow to watch, but then I realized how quickly he had gotten the coffee from the pot into my hand. It only looked slow because he was so precise and relaxed.

"I always cooked," he said. "I was a bad kid, in a bad school, with teachers who didn't really care, except my drama teacher."

"Where?" I asked.

"Listen to me," he said. "Where do you think this accent comes from?"

I hadn't noticed an accent, just his tendency to speak pirate-ese from time to time. "I have no idea."

"Upstate New York."

"Oh."

"I was always in trouble with the cops. Then one day I was before the judge, yet again, swearing he would never see me again, and he said, you're right. I won't."

"Juvenile hall?"

He shook his head. "Put me to work in the kitchens of the nicest restaurant in town, as a dishwasher."

I sipped my royal coffee and nodded.

"It was amazing to watch the chef, the way people bowed to him, the respect he got. He also got the best women and best drugs," he said. "I mean, it was the early seventies, and that's how success was measured in my world."

What was I doing in the early seventies?

"I got lucky and started to read. Then I got lucky and got into college on a drama scholarship," he said.

"Pirates of Penzance," I said. That was the way he talked, formal and flowery.

"Ah, the lingo. No, that was from the restaurant," he said. "It was the way everyone spoke." He mixed his own coffee, added half a cup of sugar, then sat down across from me. "In college, I studied anthropology, but what I did when I was tired or bored or frustrated or anything else, I cooked."

Oscar leaned back and put his feet on the table. Booted feet. Flamenco boots, with a little heel, in the most succulent black leather. The shoes tell so much about the man.

And everything I was learning made me want to learn more.

"Enter girlfriend, stage left," he said.

I giggled as I savored my coffee.

"She was studying to be a pastry chef, I met her at the restaurant, where now I was eating instead of working. I had started on my graduate degree, she had started with the CIA." He looked over at me. "Culinary Institute of America."

I knew that.

"I kept her fed, I read her books to her, I did all of that. When I left on my first field study, she gained twenty pounds because the only thing she ate was pastry from her classes. Anyway, out in the field, I always found myself in the cook's tent. Usually sharing his pot and swapping recipes, or suggesting we try something the way the natives had done it."

"Did you have a specialty area?" I asked. "I mean, a culture."

Oscar took another swig of coffee and nodded. "These island tribes, the Arawak, Lucaya, and Carib Indians."

"Did everyone like your food?" I asked.

"They did. After the group came back, I found myself offered all of these great opportunities to go places with my profs. Mostly so I would cook. My pastry-chef girlfriend graduated and moved on. Suddenly my life felt very empty."

"You were in love with her and missed her?" I asked, as I tried to be sympathetic.

He sat up. "No, I missed cooking for her."

Ouch, for the girl.

"Do you want something to eat?" he asked. "Some fruit? A little something sweet?"

"Uh, sure," I said.

Oscar got up and surveyed the bins, talking the whole time. "When I told my committee that I wouldn't be pursuing my dissertation, that I was going to open a restaurant instead," he chuckled, "well, they found the money for me."

I had tasted his food; I understood how even poor profs would dig up the funding.

"I paid them back in two years, then sold the restaurant to a chain. The chain, of course, changed everything and killed it." He popped up, holding two mangoes. "Have you ever eaten a mango?"

I shook my head. "Then what happened?"

"You can't leave the islands without tasting fresh mango," he said. "Well, after the restaurant sold, there were other girlfriends, a lot of debt, bad cooking, good cooking, bad drugs, good drugs—" As he spoke, he took the end of a huge knife and beat the yellow-red fruit a thousand times.

"Is this therapy?" I asked as he continued to bludgeon the mango.

"It's called p'onging," he said. "I'm trying to save your costume, unless you want to eat your mango in the nude?"

It thundered outside, and the wind picked up. "I didn't think so," he said at my silence, and continued to beat the fruit.

"What about cod?" I asked. "Where does Basque fit in?"

"My father is Basque, the Spanish side. My mother is Swedish. They met in New York, and we spent summers in Basque with my grandparents and cousins."

"And cod?" The mango had to be ready by now, surely.

Oscar gripped the mango in his hand, testing it, then beat it some more. "Codfish is one of the many unifying elements between these islands and the Basque. I was reading about codfish when I was a child, and got interested in these islands then. Then I read about the Amerindians and knew I wanted to know more."

"Which led to the almost-doctorate in anthropology?"

"Exactly." He clipped the end off the mango and handed it to me. "Suck."

"Excuse me?"

"See?" he said, putting the mango to his mouth. "You have to suck the juice out."

I watched him, aware that for the moment, I was living in a XXX flick, watching his mouth on the mango. Oscar handed my mango back to me, and it was still warm from his hand. He started to beat another one. I tasted the fruit; luscious.

"See why I p'ong it?" he asked, looking up at me. I glanced up, engrossed in sucking my mango and caught the expression on Oscar's face. He turned back to his mango; I had been the porn queen for a minute. I continued to mash and mangle the inside of my mango, sucking the juice.

"What's Ziren?" I asked.

"My restaurant," he said, turning his mango around, intent on his labor. "A Basque sort of spelling on Siren."

"Is the cuisine Basque fusion or something?"

"Nouvelle Basque? No. It's just whatever is fresh, and whatever meets the requirements of my imagination at the time. Sometimes it's more French, sometimes more Spanish, sometimes Indian."

"Feather, not dot, right?"

"No, there's a lot of dots around here," he said. He clipped the end off his mango, and we sat in harmony making ridiculous noises to the background of the storm. He finished first; his mango was flat.

"I think you p'onged yours better than mine," I said. Mine was still lumpy in places, and I couldn't get the juice out. Oscar pounded it a little more and handed it back.

"You don't have to watch," I said, finishing the mango.

"Why the hell wouldn't I?" he said with a laugh.

"How do you know the Diva?"

"She proposed to me."

Oh. "Did you say yes?"

"I was recently divorced, so I told her I wouldn't marry her, but I would cook for her. She, and Cattie Abramson, whom I know from high school actually, became my partners. Since then, la Diva has made this island paradise mine, whenever I want it, and its guests have been my laboratory."

Somehow, his marriage had gotten skipped in his story. My hands were covered in mango juice, my face as well. I licked my lips, but my tongue wasn't that long. Oscar laughed and handed me a towel. "You know my story," he said. "Tell me what it takes to be a stylist."

The lights, no joke, went out right then.

"And that, ladies and gentlemen," Oscar said, "was the backup generator."

We weren't in total darkness; the lamps were burning away. "Should we do something?" I asked.

"Pray this isn't Hurricane Andrew's evil little sister," he said. "The ninety-two season about obliterated this fair spot."

"Mama said the hurricane was going to be a bitch," I said. "But she didn't sound worried. Where are they, the islanders?"

"If they're not at the shack," Oscar said, "then they're on

the other side of the courtyard, telling stories and drinking beer. They're fine."

"You," I said, against all good sense, "look wonderful by lamplight."

"Ms. O'Connor, are you making a pass at me?"

My rum punch had worn off, the mango juice was sticky all over my face and my hands. And I was a coward. I shrugged.

"Refill your coffee?"

"No," I said. "I'm good."

He filled his own cup, warming milk on the gas stove. "Your turn. What does it take?"

"To be a stylist?" I said, thinking out loud. "You have to love clothes. You have to be very, very organized. You can't have much ego, or it will be trampled, you have to know everything there is to know about fabric, construction, and fit."

"Why is that?" He stirred the milk, his back to me. He had a great back, with broad shoulders that narrowed to a trim waist.

"To know how to handle it, how to make it look the best on the model, and what it's supposed to look like," I answered in order.

"What challenges you the most?" he asked.

"The follow-through. Energy and excitement and enthusiasm can get you through the weeks of shopping, the days of the job, but at the end, the returns, the paperwork, the calculation and the filing. . . . That's the tedious part, because you've already done the fun part." I licked at my fingers; they were sticking together.

"What's your secret?" he asked turning around with his coffee.

"Excuse me?" I said, looking into his amber eyes.

"What gets you through, how do you survive?"

Had anyone ever thought to ask me that before? "I run."

"You are as predictable as the sunrise in the morning," he said. "Will you go running this morning?"

"If I can," I said.

"Do you like what you do?" He sipped coffee.

"Sure." I squirmed.

He sat forward. "Does it satisfy you?"

I looked away, and nodded.

"Could you do anything else?"

I shrugged. "I've been asking myself that lately, I guess everyone did after nine-eleven. I have done a lot of things, been a lot of things. I'm not sure if I'm ready to switch careers again, or what I'd switch to."

"I'm still hungry," he said, and turned away to the bins again, searching for something. "Are you?"

"Sure." It was quiet as we listened to the storm rage outside. I didn't have my watch on, so I had no idea what time it was—and I had no idea what meal he was preparing. I watched him, back at the stove, pouring and stirring. Did this man have any idea how sexy he was? Such economy of motion, never off target by a millimeter.

When you do what I do, and time is truly money, competence and efficiency become some of the most appealing traits around.

"Fate will knock on your door if you are willing," Oscar said. "I mean, if you're open to opportunity, opportunity will present itself."

"You really believe that?" I asked.

He looked over his shoulder. "I do." Then he turned around with a bowl and a spoon. He scooped a spoonful and presented it to me. I could feel it was cold, ice cream, with a peppery, minty smell.

"Izarra means star," he said. "This liqueur is the green Izarra. I drizzled it over the ice cream, which I made with the yellow Izarra, because it is sweeter. It has honey in it."

I opened my mouth, and he fed me a bite. I put my sticky

hands on the collar of his jacket and pulled him to me. "I want to taste all the Izarras," I said.

I slid my hands down to cut arms to his cuffs, skimming the buttons on my way to his lapels. *Buttons.*

I froze; he pulled back and looked into my face. "What?"

"I um,—" I lifted his cuff and looked at the button, but I couldn't see it.

Oscar was watching me like I was crazy.

I angled his shirt and read the letters. *T. Charles Bespoke* was carved into the shell of the button.

Chapter Twenty

"What is going on?" he whispered. "Dallas . . . Beautiful," he said. "Talk to me." He tried to get me to look into his eyes.

I couldn't.

It was just a jacket.

Just a button.

Just a body on the beach.

Someone had taken that picture. I thought it was someone wearing those shoes, but it didn't have to be.

"Dallas?"

"Were you here before I came?"

"On the island?" he asked.

"Yeah," I said.

He sat back, the ice-cream dish between us. "I come here a lot."

"This time?"

"Maybe beat you here by a few hours." He looked at me, puzzled. "What the hell is going on?"

"Do you know what wrestling shoes are?" I asked.

"I've seen wrestler's shoes," he said. "Is that the same thing, or is this a fashion quiz?" He touched his collar, tugged his cuffs straight. "I tend to be a uniform kind of guy. This outfit or my chefs' togs."

"Nice choices," I said. Tobin Charles did make the best. "The ones I'm thinking about would be yellow and white. Does that sound familiar?"

"A pair of shoes someone was wearing?"

"Or maybe just had? Have you seen those shoes?"

He was stiffening up. "No."

"How do you know Zac?"

"He's here periodically. I know him through Ladeeva. What's with the inquisition?"

"Unexpected?" I snapped.

"You never expect the Spanish Inquisition," he smarted back.

If the lights hadn't come back on, I might have fallen in love right then.

I returned alone to the drawing room. It looked like the aftermath of an orgy. The lights had gone on in here too, and everyone was in disrobed disarray. I avoided looking for Donny or Jillyian—that situation was too twisted. I stood there, and Teddy stirred. "Is it over?" he asked.

"It's quiet out," I said. "Superstill."

"It's over! We survived!" Teddy crowed.

"Yeah. We should make up some T-shirts, 'I Survived the Hurricane of Castle Cay Island,'" David, his arm currently around Zima, said. She blinked sleepily at him.

"Dat is not it," Mama Garcia said from the doorway. "Dis be de eye ob de storm."

"You mean we've been in the hurricane?" Eladonna asked.

"We be on de middle ob it. De *loa* is strong for us today."

"There's more?" Teddy asked.

"True-true. We hab a break, mebbe half hour, mebbe hour," she said. "Breathe dat air, eyestorm air is good for fixin' magic."

"I don't want to go out there," Jillyian said.

"You need to go most ob all," Mama Garcia commanded.

Jillyian huffed, but she followed the rest of us out. We opened the door, emerging cautiously, like post-Apocalyptic survivors. "What a perfectly lovely day," London said.

⟍ It was just dawn, and the sky was brilliant blue, as flawless as fresh enamel. The air! It was like breathing pure oxygen— the shallowest of breaths, and you got dizzy.

"I'd hate to be in Florida in a few hours," Eladonna said.

"Yeah, Miami must be battening down the hatches," Jillyian said.

"Better plan to just take those boats out of the water," Zima said.

"What do you mean?" Ka'Arih asked.

"Battening down the hatches is a nautical term. It means to prepare for a storm," Eladonna said.

"Thank you, Ms. Lifeline," Jillyian snapped.

"Let's all take ten," Donny said. "Get cleaned up and then come back, get something to eat and work a little." He looked at his watch. "This afternoon."

Like dutiful little monkeys, we trooped to our rooms. I traded my costume for jeans and trusty linen shirt over a crocheted halter top, with my Nikes. Then, and only then, did it dawn on me that I had wanted to talk to Palize. Or he had wanted to talk to me. He said he'd meet me here, but that had been hours ago.

I checked my messages, and there was one from Lindsay. "Darling, I hope you are okay. I . . . well, you have a sense about these things, as freaky as I think it is. It took some finagling and quite a bit of creative talking, but . . . a Gerald McCrander took off for Bimini five days before you arrived. He hasn't returned, at least not paying with the Centurion.

"However, there's more. I looked through some books and found Gerald's agency. According to them, he said he was going to South America on holiday. I was acting like I wanted to book him, but they said he'd booked out indefinitely. Verrrrry interesting. Well,"—I heard her drink something—"I'm so glad you have a long mess—" It hung up on her, but she was the next message, too.

"Damn, well. I spent a bit of time on the Internet tracking down that agency. They are fairly new and don't really mingle. Darling, do you remember that guy—of course you remember him. The long-haired gent who you will not work for, even though he offers you indecent amounts of money? His return addy matches the agency's addy. Darling, I think—"

I swallowed and plopped down on my bed. My thoughts followed her path exactly, even as she said it. "—your friend Gerald is employed at Tobin Charles, courtesy of Thom Goodfeather."

My phone felt like a lead weight as I listened to the rest of the message. "So, Dallas, get your lovely arse out of there right away! Do you hear me? I'll call, I'll leave some message about a dying relative—anyone you want me to pick?—and you fly home straightaway. Call me from the airport if the money isn't on your card. I'll invoice these bastards immejitly and . . . just come home! Call me! Love you, darling!" She hung up.

AT&T asked if I'd like to keep or erase the message. I just terminated the call.

Zac. He was here, somewhere; even he couldn't leave in the middle of a hurricane. Whether it would blow his cover or not, we had to talk. This was serious. Thom Goodfeather. Damn!

I was never going to be hired again if people kept showing up dead on my sets. Except Gerald hadn't, I mean it was just a guess that his body was the one in the surf. No one else—"Stop it, Dallas," I barked at myself. The skies started to rumble again. The peace of the eye was passing. I dashed back down to the dining room before the storm broke.

Ka'Arih was in the courtyard, looking around, a little frantic around the eyes.

When she saw me, she smiled. "You crazy girl," I shouted to her through the rising wind. "Are you coming in?"

"I think I'll just breathe a little more fresh air," she said. "You go on without me."

"Don't be silly," I shouted. The wind was starting to tear at the door in my hand and lash the trees. "Get inside."

"I can't, Dallas," she said. Then she took a deep breath and I saw the tears in her eyes before the rain even began. "I lost something."

"Out here?"

She looked around and shrugged helplessly. "It may be here, it may be inside."

"Come here!" I commanded her and yanked her into the shelter of the house. I closed the door and locked it just as the rain hit. Her eyes were wide and I had a sinking feeling. "It's not something, it's someone, isn't it?"

Ka'Arih nodded, miserable.

"Your pet . . . ?"

"He's a snake. Just a little baby. And he got out of his box and—"

I stopped before I betrayed myself. "You think he's in here?"

"Well, I've been catching frogs and feeding them to him, but I knew the storm was probably upsetting—I mean, animals can sense so much—so I got him out for a little walk . . ."

"You take your snake for a walk?" If my Granddaddy could hear this conversation . . .

"He has the cutest little leash," she said, smiling. "It has rhinestones around the collar—"

"Ka'Arih—where did you take your snake for a walk?" I could barely keep a straight face, saying those words.

"Outside, in the garden. Then I thought I heard someone call me, and I picked up the end of the leash and put it just inside the door while I went to see, and—"

"And when you came back, snake and leash were gone?" She nodded again.

"Have you seen Zac?" I asked. I had to talk to him about maybe a murder. And she was one of the potential murderers, though even in my wildest dreams, I couldn't imagine that. "Ka'Arih," I said, "do you know what the other people are, in the enneagram?"

"Dallas, can we talk later? I have to find Willie."

"Willie?"

"I named him after Willie Nelson, 'cuz he's a white rattler."

If my Granddaddy could hear this—"You have lost a baby white rattlesnake that is wearing a rhinestone collar?"

"And leash."

"Holy Saints and Mother of God," I said, doing my best Oscar imitation.

My oldest sibling, Sherman, who became a professional disappointment (according to Grandmama), had played with the idea of becoming a veterinarian. All through my childhood he'd found broken animals and tried to fix them. However, what he deemed was worth saving and what my family generally considered to be either a delicacy to eat or a pestilence to shoot, were often the same. But not even he had ever had a pet rattler. "Holy God," I breathed.

"He's a baby," she said apologetically. "But that means his venom is the strongest right now, so if you find him, just call for me. But if the girls find him, well—"

He's gonna be boots. "Does he move fast?"

She nodded. We heard footsteps before Teddy appeared. "What are you two doing?" he asked. "Oscar is serving dinner."

The lights flickered as a particularly brutal crack of thunder broke over our heads. "I lost Willie," Ka'Arih said.

Teddy looked around. "Is he on his leash?"

"You knew about this?" I hissed.

He nodded. "I'm the trainer and choreographer. It's kind of like being part psychologist and part confessor."

Then there were three of us, looking in the dark corners of the hall, seeking the warmest, driest spots where a one-foot, rhinestone-collar-wearing, highly poisonous baby rattler would be hiding. "Folks, don't try this at home," I muttered as I peered into the shadows.

"Keep quiet and we should hear his rattle as we approach," Ka'Arih said. "Whatever you do, don't pick him up. He's gonna be scared and ready to strike."

"You do not have to worry about me trying to pick up a damn snake," I said. "Do you have his cage?"

She shook something that looked like a long, skinny sock. "He'll feel safe in this."

"I think I've got him," Teddy whispered. Sure enough, we heard the rattle, the closer we got.

"Do you have a snakebite kit?" I asked, while I mentally castigated myself for not packing mine in my first-aid kit. But with a baby rattler, it was about over if you got struck. "Are you sure you should—" Oh God.

Ka'Arih made this weird noise and held out what looked like a thick string. The snake struck it—I whimpered and jumped back—and she grabbed it by the head and stuffed it into the bag. "Gotchababy," she said.

Teddy's color wasn't any better than mine. "I need a drink," he said.

"I'm going to return Willie to my room," Ka'Arih said. "Then I'll be right down."

"Teddy, go with her," I said.

He must have heard something in my voice, because he looked at me, then followed Ka'Arih, with her bag trailing a leash through the hall. I must confess, I leaned against the wall to steady my pounding heart. What brain-dead idiot would bring a snake to an island, or worse, have a snake to begin with? How in Hades did she get it through Customs? I'm sure the Bahamian authorities would be delighted to introduce a new poisonous reptile to their own collection. "Mother of God," I said, closing my eyes—probably in prayer.

"Are you going to eat with us?" Donny asked a minute later.

"Uh, sure," I said, opening my eyes. "On my way."

"Dallas," he said, laying a hand on my arm, "are you okay?"

"Sure."

"I'm sorry about this. I thought the hurricane season wasn't until August, or I would never have agreed to come here now."

"I figured that was why this was such a high day rate," I joked. "Hazard pay."

We walked into the dining room and it looked like the set for a horror movie. Shutters covered the windows, and the light of a thousand candles glinted off the red of the feathers, the napkins, and the wine in the goblets. The black tablecloth was just creepy, and the dark china was lost on it. The group was there, talking quietly over silver dishes filled with food.

There were no lights in the kitchen. Donny pulled out my chair and I sat down.

"Try this," he said, and handed me a serving tray. It was room temperature. "It's really good. Here, I'll serve you," he said and put something on my plate.

No! My brain screamed. You can't trust these people! They lied! Who knows what else they did?

"This is great," Eladonna said and handed me another dish.

"Don't you want some?" I asked her.

"Oh no," she said, "I ate before you came."

"London?" I offered

"No, I'm not really hungry," she said.

Ka'Arih and Teddy rejoined the group and I passed the dishes down to them.

"Ka'Arih," Zima sad, intercepting the food they'd been trying to feed me, so that no one else got it, "you won't like this."

That couldn't be good.

Was this how it began for poor Gerald McCrander? One minute sitting, eating, next minute dead? It was how the Dixie Chicks had written about murder in "Earl Had to Die." Poisoned black-eyed peas. I shivered.

"Dallas, you aren't eating," Donny said.

"I'm not really hungry," I said.

The storm blew around the building, and we huddled into each other.

"Wine?"

I looked at the open bottle. "I'll get another bottle," I said and skipped out to the kitchen. It was dark, and I fumbled for the light switch. No one was in here, but a few bottles were coming to room temp. Where was Zac? I claimed a bottle for myself, uncorked it, then tore the label so I'd be able to recognize this, the safe bottle, in the dark.

Should you just go hide? I asked myself. The storm will be over soon, and if you make it through this night, you can get back to Miami safely. Had they killed Gerald? What did Thom Goodfeather have to do with it? Was someone his agent here?

Or were they all?

If Gerald worked for Thom, then . . . My brain ached. This made no sense.

I turned off the light and returned to the dining room. Jillyian was singing in the darkness—they'd blown out a few million candles—so only a little light remained. I couldn't see shit. Her voice continued through the blackness, calming and soothing, and the girls picked up the background vocals in perfect harmony. Sascha's back was to me, and as I walked by her, I heard her singing. Exactly the same pitch as Jillyian.

Pity struck me.

Her voice was as good, as strong, as Jillyian's. In fact, it was a dead ringer for Jillyian's. I was asking myself why she hadn't tried the stage when I remembered her terrible fit, and realized that indeed, the stage might have been her dream, but her body, her seizures, would never allow its fulfillment. How it must hurt to spend time with these girls and be as good, but know their destiny could never be hers. I sat down with my bottle of wine and they stopped singing.

"Oh, come on," I protested. "I'll go stand in the kitchen if you'll just keep it up," I said to Jillyian.

She laughed and held out her glass. Reluctantly, I shared some of my private stash.

"Now what?" Zima asked. "We wait for the storm to end?"

"I can think of ways to take your mind off the weather," her musician said to her, and we all chuckled.

"Where's Oscar? Zac? Palize?" I asked. "There's a lot of missing parties at our party."

Donny looked around. "Oscar and Palize were fighting, shouting at each other, before they put the food on the table."

"Zac go to his suite," Sascha said. "He is too good to stay with us."

Everyone laughed.

"He has a suite? Where?"

Sascha shook her head at me. "No, no, Dallas. He is trouble."

"He is trouble," one of the musicians said.

Was Zac in danger, too? "Well," I said, "if it's the same to everyone, I'm going to go lie down."

"Where? Remember, Mama said to stay in these two rooms, in case it gets bad," Donny said.

"Then I think I'll just stake out one of the couches in the drawing room," I said. "Don't wake me up."

"Good night," they called, and I walked down the hall.

Chapter Twenty-One

First, I built a fake-me-out of mannequin and a blonde wig beneath a blanket on the couch. I stepped into the dumb-waiter. I knew how far it went one direction. One would think it would go the same distance the other way. Meaning the next stop should be my tower. I pulled switches and slid until I found myself in an unknown lobby. I took the elevator up and found myself in . . . Donny's room. I went into his bathroom, and entered my bathroom through a connecting door.

I saw a note on my bed: *"Your room, 20:30h."*

Palize? Had to be. I counted on my fingers: twelve plus eight equals twenty. He'd be here at eight-thirty. It was eight now. Time flies when you are paranoid and waiting out a hurricane.

I watched the storm moving across the beach. I put on another layer of clothes and did a few pushups to move some blood through my body. It was getting downright chilly. I even brushed my teeth. By eight-fifteen, I was pacing.

At eight twenty-five I wondered if he was going to come up the secret elevator in Donny's room. I opened the connecting door in the bathroom.

At eight-thirty, I stood with a wooden box in my hand, waiting. The box was to bash him over the head if I needed to.

By eight-forty, I lowered my arm to wait.

By eight forty-five, I was pacing again. It's a bad storm, Dallas. He's Spanish, Dallas. At least I thought he was. Anyway, lots of reasons to be late.

By eight fifty-five, I was downright nervous. The hurricane had died down to a plain rainstorm and Palize still wasn't here.

At nine, I closed all the doors and went out the front door, down the stairs, toward the kitchen.

Where else does one find a missing chef?

The wind howled around the castle walls as I hurried through the courtyard garden for the safety of the kitchen. Palize was late; and he'd set the time. My imagination turned the black branches of the dancing trees into skeletal fingers clawing at the window. Everyone else should still be in the drawing room, I guessed.

The dining room shutters had come open and banged on the outside walls. Rain poured into the pool, lit up by the frenzy of electrical power in the skies. The lights were back on, but I bet it wouldn't be for long. The kitchen was still dark.

Where was Palize's room?

"Hello?" I called, in Spanish and English, as I swung the kitchen door open. No one—the echoing silence of no other breath, no one else being in there filled my ears. But something was in there, I could smell it. A sewer was not the way the kitchens usually smelled.

I fumbled along the slick tiled wall for the light switch and turned it on.

Well. Late certainly described him now.

Palize was pinned to the table with a knife through his

chest. The blood looked fake it was so red, and it covered everything, the white tiles, the shiny steel, his gray-checkered pants and his white coat. He wouldn't be talking to anyone now.

I stepped closer and looked. The knife was huge—it had taken a lot of strength to push a blade like that through. Damn. I blinked away tears as I looked around a little more. A cloth on the floor, burned black. I sniffed it and knew what had warned me before I even turned on the light.

Cordite. Someone had shot through the napkin, scorching it.

And someone had stabbed him? Had Palize shot the gun?

I looked around me. Like a killer would just leave the weapon hanging around.

I raised my head in the sudden silence. There were no windows, but it sounded as though the storm had just stopped. In that silence, nothingness screamed. Then it dawned on me: I was in the kitchen with a corpse, freshly killed. Someone had done it recently, maybe in the last ten minutes?

That someone might still be here.

I ran for the knife rack and grabbed another heavy German blade. I couldn't see myself stabbing someone, but I am a survivor, so if it came to a choice—I looked around. The door to the kitchen was moving just slightly. From me?

I heard a muffled step and turned my head, raising the knife. That hallway led to the two dumbwaiters. Anyone could come through there. And farther back was the pastel kitchen with a door that led outside the castle.

A crash.

Utter blackness surrounded me.

I ran for the body; this one was not getting away.

Now I had proof. Now I had a case. All I needed to do was summon the participants.

I opened my mouth and proceeded to scream my head off.

* * *

Oscar burst into the room, with a blinding flashlight. He halted when he saw me, and swore.

He walked up to the body and ran the light over it.

Oscar owned a gun, I reminded myself. He'd held it on me. Did he still have it? Had he used it?

Teddy and Eladonna came running in next.

"Ohmigod!"

"Dallas, are you all right?"

"Don't say anything—I'm sure it was self-defense—" Eladonna said, already in legal mode.

Ka'Arih and Zima were on their heels.

"Oh shit, man," Zima said.

"He's dead?" Ka'Arih asked.

Mama Garcia came in with Zac.

"Chile! Quit that caterwauling!"

"I'll be damned," Zac drawled.

Then, and only then, I stopped screaming.

"In here?"

"I'm the one with the knife," I said. "I'm making the rules. Everyone in here, now."

"But—"

Jillyian, Sascha, London, and Donny showed up, the musicians behind them.

I spoke over their exclamations of horror and surprise. "Sit down," I said. "Make yourself comfortable; we're going to be here a while."

"Who killed him?" London asked.

"All will be answered in good time," I said. I had all the facts now, and the proof. And the FBI.

"We're staying in here with the corpse?" London said.

"This is so gross—"

"I think I may vomit—"

"I want to go home—"

"Shut up!" I shouted. "You have a lot of nerve being grossed out by the dead!"

"Who's she talking to?" Ka'Arih asked.

"You all! You're killers, or accomplices, all of you. And we're going to discuss it right here and right now before another corpse gets away or before you kill again!"

"You've seen too much TV," someone said.

I stabbed the table with my knife. "I only watch hockey. Now shut up!"

Oscar's flashlight stood on its end, its light reflecting off the ceiling and down on the people. A very weird angle for lighting, about as flattering as Dilliard's changing rooms. Other than that, and the myriad reflections on the steel and glass, it was dark. Oscar had sprayed some room freshener, but there wasn't enough in the bottle. I needed to talk fast, or I would be the one getting sick.

"This is the second corpse," I said. "The first one belonged to Gerald McCrander, a stylist."

I took a breath, to wait for a confession. Nada.

"Palize said he was going to tell me everything. Since he'd been on the island the whole time and admitted to it," I said, looking at Oscar and Teddy. "I wondered if he was going to confirm the death of the first man.

"Why kill this man? I asked myself. What did he do? Well, I came to realize it wasn't what he did, but what he knew. What he threatened to reveal, possibly to the Mafia."

They watched me; I definitely had everyone's undivided attention.

"Maybe he realized that the band isn't what it seems to be," I said. "Maybe it dawned on him that there was fraud going on—"

Someone whimpered.

"Maybe Gerald figured out the kinky sex roles being played. Maybe he was going to sell the story, or blackmail the participants."

"Bitch," someone muttered. I didn't recognize the voice.

"Regardless, you concluded that he had to die. Then you tied him up and tried to sink him. But you didn't get rid of the evidence. You left his styling kit. You left the shoes you used the shoelaces from, though why you didn't use ordinary rope, I have no idea. Or tape. Tape would work really well, but anyway, you also overlooked a Polaroid."

A squeak of disgust from someone.

"Not to mention that y'all did a sucky job of sinking him. Ya need weight. Bodies float! That's the purpose of cement shoes. Anyway, I guess a few days after you got rid of him, you realized that you did really need a stylist and hired me. Why me? Because someone around here knew me, had worked with me before, or was in touch with someone who had, and who was making suggestions that no one could ignore."

An expression of surprise.

I figured that "someone" was Thom Goodfeather, but I was saving his name for shock value at the end.

"Enter Palize. At the rate people have come and gone around here, it could be a few days before someone working at this castle would realize that one of the guests was actually missing, not just departed."

"Dearly departed," someone said. Oscar, I think.

I glared at the group. "A few inquiries and when things didn't add up, Palize began to wonder. Maybe he called the mainland and heard about Gerald's sudden "South America" trip that was going to last for a long time. Maybe he caught one of you being slimy and you couldn't explain your way out of it. Or maybe he just made you mad with his insinuations. He threatened every one of us last night, said that we were going to be sorry. Maybe he'd decided to blackmail all of y'all. I don't know."

"What do you know?" Zac asked.

"Thanks for asking," I said. "One. Jillyian is not who she appears to be."

Gasps.

"Neither is Donny."

More gasps.

"The band is a fraud."

"Oh no!"

"And . . . I can't explain any of it. I mean, why."

"Then what are you trying to do?" Eladonna asked.

I turned on Oscar. "We'll start with you. You know Bette. You've been on this island a dozen times. Palize was closest to you, though y'all were constantly trying to kill each other. But something changed in the past few days. You've been especially angry at Palize, threatening him every time I saw the two of you. Palize was making a fool of himself with the guests? Palize knew the secrets of this place? Palize was going to replace you? Did you finally lose it, and come into the kitchen, and y'all had a fight and you shot him, then stabbed him to make it look like a . . ." I ran out of steam. "To confuse the issue?"

The expression in Oscar's eyes was flat.

"Or do you have another boss who had instructed you to get rid of a pesky stylist, and your second-in-command had seen you do that? Were you the one, Oscar, the one who killed Gerald? Then when you were looking for rope you came across the shoelaces and used those instead? Afterward Palize tried to blackmail you, and you had to stage a fight to cover up killing him? Are you even now covered in blood, Oscar?"

He didn't look away from me. He didn't try to prove he wasn't bloodstained.

"Do you have another employer, Oscar?"

"I work for myself," he said. "I have a restaurant and I work for myself."

"What about your partners?" I said. "Those people who've given you money, made it possible for a reformed drug addict to get a start on a new life?"

I killed any possible relationship then. I saw it in his eyes.

"Ladeeva," he said. "A famous photographer. From time to time, a consortium of university professors."

"No one named Thom Goodfeather?"

Silence.

Oscar just stared at me. I broke the eye contact.

"If Oscar did the murder that way, then why didn't he just get rid of Palize's . . . body?" Eladonna asked. "It's his place, he knows his way around it. Why leave the body like this?"

She had a really, really good point.

"Because," I said, "as mad as Oscar can get, I don't think he did it." I glanced at the man. "He's painfully honest. He has integrity. Oscar would kill someone and then turn himself in, cursing the whole time. He has a temper, but he has great appreciation for life, for beauty. If he killed Palize, he would have been stoic or been sobbing, standing in the middle of this room for whoever found him."

"He's an adventurer," Ka'Arih said. "He isn't a liar."

"So I'm looking for a liar," I said. Bette dropped her gaze, Eladonna too. Jillyian didn't look away, and Donny looked bored.

"I'm looking for someone who has a lot to lose. Anyone, I've been told, can get away with one murder. Two murders, and you're pushing your luck. Who would kill once without qualm, and then kill again out of desperation?

"And why would you all lie? I have a photograph that is proof you all knew someone else had been here. Why lie to me? All of you."

No one, except Sascha and Donny, was meeting my gaze.

"Teddy arrived the same day I did, so he's off the hook, at least for the first murder. The musicians are pretty boys, brought in for their charms and skills. They aren't players.

Bette? She knows everything, but she's not going to jeopardize her lover."

She made a choking sound.

"Who's Bette's lover?" Ka'Arih asked.

"That's not mine to divulge," I said.

Oscar made a rude noise.

"Me," Eladonna said.

"Oh. Y'all are together?" Ka'Arih asked, pointing to the two of them.

Eladonna reached for Bette's hand and glared at us all. "We are."

"A defender and a nurturer. It's a good combination," Ka'Arih said. "Congratulations."

"Thank you," Bette said.

"Why didn't you tell everyone? Or am I just—" Ka'Arih looked around—"the last to know?"

"We were going to tell you all after the video premiered," Eladonna said. "I needed to talk to my parents first."

"I—"

"Could we get on with it?" David, the musician, asked.

They turned back to me. "Not Bette, though she did lie. Understandably, I think."

"And she wouldn't do anything to hurt Eladonna, and several of those things did," London said.

"Right." I'd forgotten about that. "The voodoo and the poisoning." I stood for a moment, thinking.

"You were talking about liars?" Zac prompted me.

"Liars. I kept looking for who would lie and why. Sascha? Poor Sascha. She'd been here on makeup and had been made to be the stylist, and she wouldn't even complain." I smiled. "That in itself was a giveaway. I've never met anyone in this business who didn't want credit where it was due. Not in a bad way, but if you are doing two jobs, not only do you want to be paid for it, you want to be acknowledged as a goddess. The client isn't likely to do that, but your colleagues would.

She wouldn't even tell me she'd had to do it. She didn't want to say anything against any of you.

"Obviously, she was scared."

Sascha was looking down.

"Fright could have triggered the attack she suffered. And when I heard her sing, I realized she probably did makeup on videos because her dream had been to be a singer, but epileptic performers aren't widely accepted. That's right, isn't it, Sascha? You always wanted to be a singer?"

She nodded, her eyes wide and her face dead white in the lighting.

"In fact, you have an exquisite voice. As good as Jillyian's."

She made choking noises, and I was sorry I'd made her cry. "Not Sascha." I looked around at them. "I knew I wasn't guilty, so that moved the circle in closer. To the actual members of the band.

"Eladonna has a life to go back to. She's been a student; she can return to that if this explodes. Zima hasn't said three words, but I gather that she is very internal and just wants to write music and be in love. If she's a songwriter, she can be a songwriter, regardless of what happens with this band and contest. Things like fame and money aren't unbelievably attractive to her because they are peripheral." I sighed.

"Ka'Arih has some strange hobbies, but she's got a life, a support system, and probably a future outside of music. She's also at peace, more so than most anyone I've ever met. She wouldn't get riled up enough to kill someone. London? She's blown through her millions; she's no longer recognizable as the supermodel she once was; she is gambling everything on this chance.

"But London, according to Ka'Arih's observations, wants to live life big. The money, the clothes, the cars, and more importantly, the ups and downs of romance. I knew she wouldn't sleep with either Gerald or Palize, because that would cross boundary lines of class."

"Not to mention taste," London offered, tossing her hair over her shoulder.

I grinned. "Yes. And neither of them could give her the accoutrements of romance. Dozens of flowers arriving daily, jewelry, and privileges like private jets and limos. They were both working boys. She wouldn't risk living the rest of her life in an orange jumpsuit for someone who couldn't treat her 'right.' " I made little quote marks with my fingers. "If this blows, London will become a millionaire's wife, or maybe mistress." I paced a little. Of course, all my theories discounted a crime of passion. There were many reasons I wasn't an attorney. . . .

"Which leaves Jillyian and Donny. Strangely enough, these two seemed to like each other the least out of the group. They were rarely affectionate in public, and where an outsider would expect the leader and the manager to be almost inseparable, they were never together.

"Except," I said. "I was next door to Donny's room. He's a sexy man with healthy appetites, and Jillyian can't hide her cries of pleasure—"

"What?"

"Are you crazy?"

"That's sick!"

"Gross!"

"Jillyian and Donny?"

The reaction from the band girls was instantaneous. "Donny and Jillyian," I said with authority, "are lovers!"

"They're brother and sister!" Ka'Arih shouted.

I spun on my heel to look at Donny. "You are one sick bastard," I said. "Your sister? I thought she was your wife and you had arranged this for fame and fortune. You're banging your sister?"

Donny looked around at the faces watching him. Slowly he closed his eyes. "Oh shit," he said.

"Ohmigod," I said, and leaned back against the table.

There was motive. BIG motive.

"You can't let her keep going," London said.

"You've got to level with her!" Zima shouted.

The girls pleaded with him, but Donny crossed his arms and glared at me. "I'm not telling Dallas anything. I want to hear this constructed fantasy of lies. Not even lies, absolutely ridiculous . . . hallucinations," he sputtered. "Keep going. You say I'm having incestuous sex—"

"Understandably, you don't want anyone to know your . . . uh, connection," I said. "Maybe the contest was rigged? Maybe you have cut her a bigger piece of the pie than the other girls? Maybe she got you the job instead of vice versa? Anyway, Gerald finds out y'all are related. You off him, but Palize sees you. Blackmails you for a chunk of change, and since you got away with it with Gerald, you kill Palize too.

"Or maybe you work for Thom Goodfeather?"

No reactions anywhere.

"He set up this whole thing, and Gerald discovered that. Another good reason to kill him. Then, because Donny, you really do have to produce the videos and CD, you have to hire another stylist, and Goodfeather suggests me."

Though why he'd do that, I didn't know. Unless it was to involve me in such a mess that I couldn't ever go to the cops without incriminating myself in some way. My head was starting to ache. Again.

"Or maybe it was different than that. Jillyian, your . . . singer and . . . sister," I said. I couldn't even use "lover" and "sister" in the same sentence aloud. "She confessed y'all's relationship to Gerald, because they were friends or lovers, and then they broke up. She had to kill him so he couldn't tell, and you helped her get rid of the body. Then Palize came to

blackmail her. He upset her, which we saw as the two of you
fighting from time to time—" in between y'all having sex
loudly, in the room next to mine—"and then you killed
him." A woman, outside of the WWF, couldn't pin that man
to the table with a knife. Especially the women here. "You
shot him, then stabbed the body to make the murder confus-
ing."

"What about Zac?" Eladonna asked. "You haven't accused him."

"Zac was in and out so much, he couldn't have been very
involved." I said that even though I knew he could have
killed both of them. Why, wasn't I suspicious? Because he
was FBI, but the last time I checked they were the good guys.
Zac had worked hard, I'd presumed, to get undercover. I
wasn't going to blow that even if I was angry. (For no good
reason I had my anger.)

"Well, in your grand ruminations," Oscar asked. "What
about the poisoning?"

"And the voodoo?" London asked.

"Neither were meant for Eladonna," I said. "They were
warnings to Jillyian."

"Oh God," Jillyian said.

"The food got confused at the last minute, and Eladonna
ate Jillyian's portion. What might have made Jillyian sick almost killed Eladonna." I shrugged. "As for the voodoo, the
green dress was the giveaway. Eladonna was in purple."

"Yeah, freakin' voodoo practitioners always have time to
appropriately clothe the dolls," Oscar said.

I ignored him. "But why do it? The doll was ineffective, so
juvenile, so obviously designed to cast blame on someone
else. I think Donny was feeling jealous," I said. "He just
wanted to send Jillyian a message. It was obviously an action
by a lover. The hair, the dress—"

"It was done by my lover," Jillyian said; she was crying.
"My real lover."

Donny dropped his head, and we waited.

"Who?" I asked, finally.

"Palize," Oscar stated.

Jillyian sobbed as she nodded. I looked at Donny. As either her husband or her brother/lover, that couldn't be good news.

Chapter Twenty-Two

Stunned silence, as we sat in the flashlit room, with the rainstorm outside, and Jillyian's sobs inside.

Then Mama Garcia started to laugh. "Oh, chile, if I'd be knowin' what sip-sip was runnin' tru dat pretty haid o' yours, I coulda set ya straight right away."

"Well, I'm sure I made some errors," I said. I'd hoped for a little support. "But the gist of it is accurate."

"And that gist is?" Zac asked.

"Donny and Jillyian are . . ." I fumbled for a word that wouldn't bring *Inside Edition* to mind. "Partners. They intended to do this contest and video CD tour thing and then retire with a bunch of money. Jillyian's voice is extraordinary, and Donny is talented with people." I shrugged. "They rigged it and won.

"Here, on the island, Thom Goodfeather sends one of his minions to check up on his music, which is the company that is producing this CD, and the flunkie calls back to tell Thom that it's hinky, and everything is going to go to hell once the media gets hold of the real story. Only Gerald, the spy, doesn't actually get to make the call. He's killed instead."

"Who killed him?" Zac asked.

"Donny, I think," I said. "But I don't know how he was killed."

Zac nodded once.

"Palize sees it happen. He starts talking up Jillyian and . . . I guess you fell for the Prince-of-the-prisonyard vibe he had," I said to her. "Maybe you wanted to get away from Donny for a little while, so you, uh, entertained them both." Jillyian looked at her brother, sending him a pleading expression, but he stayed silent. "Palize knows about the killing, maybe you even tell him about the band—"

"Oh, Jillyian told all right," Donny said. My first confirmation.

"Then you and Palize break up—wait, was he the one who made you cry?"

Jillyian nodded.

"And he sent the food to you as a warning, but Eladonna got it?" I asked.

"Oh God," she whispered. "He tried to make me sick, too?"

"The little bastard," Oscar shouted. "We were fighting in the kitchen. I had just found out about him and Jillyian, and was setting him straight about sleeping with the guests and . . ." Oscar looked at the corpse. "He distracted me, to put something in her lunch."

"And I got her lunch," Eladonna said.

"And I found the doll," Zima said. Her musician hugged her closer.

"The doll that was meant for me?" Jillyian asked.

"So beware, misspelled, was for real?" I asked. And that's why Palize had looked triumphant, even after Oscar whupped him.

Jillyian nodded. "English was like Palize's fifth or sixth language."

"What was his first?"

"Filipino," Oscar answered.

A sudden buzzing in my ears. "Palize was Filipino?" I asked. I leaned against the table. Against the table with the Filipino corpse.

"Dallas, are you okay?" Oscar said, standing up. "Dallas?"

I looked straight at Zac. "Palize was Thom Goodfeather's guy?"

Zac nodded.

The Filipino Mafia strikes again: the long arm of Thom Goodfeather. I looked at them all in a suddenly, completely, different light. "You guys have killed a Mafia man," I whispered. "We're all in trouble now."

There was a moment of silence, then:

"I killed Palize," Oscar blurted.

"I'll take the heat," Donny said.

"I did it," Zac said.

The three men looked at each other. I put my hands on my hips. "The essential part of lying is to at least agree on a story," I said. "Who killed Palize?"

Sascha spoke. "I did."

My friend crossed her legs and I looked at her feet for the first time. I'd never been to her room, never seen her closet, never looked for her shoes. But I have an eye that calculates sizes as a practice. "The Chanel wrestling shoes," I said as it dawned on me. "They were yours."

"It was my fault," she said in soft, normal English. "I should have tossed the shoes, but I bought them when we all were in Vegas for the contest, and they brought us good luck."

"You used laces to tie him up," I said. "Why?"

"We were on the beach; there was nothing else around," Sascha said.

"You killed him on the beach?" I asked.

"I didn't kill Gerald," Sascha said. "I killed Palize."

"You fired the gun. Through the cloth."

Sascha nodded.

"And your accent is gone?"

She nodded again. "I have two sides. I was born in Vladivostok, and I did grow up in Russia, but I did it while listening to American music. My mother was from Nashville and my father was from the Soviet Union. I was there until I was fourteen."

"Why did you kill Palize?"

"He was going to tell everything."

"He was blackmailing you?"

"Don't say anything else—" one of the girls said to Sascha.

"She's flat wrong so far—" another said to her.

"Shut up, Sascha—" Eladonna said. "She's got nothing."

The girls pleaded with her, and then I remembered something else Sascha had said. "*You* were in Vegas for the contest?"

She nodded. "I was singing in a bar there before I met . . . Donny."

"You aren't a makeup artist?"

She laughed, and she sounded like the Sascha I knew, even though I couldn't reconcile her words, her confessions, with the friend I thought I'd made. "In Vegas you have to be something else as a backup," she said. "I sing in bars, but I make my living as a makeup artist for showgirls. I did get my start with Estee Lauder. Not in Moscow, but in Memphis, at a department store."

"What about the epilepsy?"

She looked away. "You're right. It's the reason I am not recording as myself, today."

I felt so sorry for her, and looked at Zac. "Palize was a bad guy, right? No one has to know Sascha did this. It—"

Zac shook his head, slowly, back and forth.

"You said you killed him?" I asked Zac, trying another angle. "Won't the authorities just write that off, or something, since. . . ." Silence in the room. "Sascha shouldn't go to jail for killing scum," I said.

"Palize wasn't scum," Jillyian said, defending her ex-lover.

"He sold you drugs, and he apparently was Mafia. What would it take for you to call him scum, little sister?" Donny snarled.

"He did what he had to to make ends meet!" Jillyian said. "Sascha sells makeup on the side, Palize just sold what was readily available. He couldn't help it that drugs were what was available."

"Did you know this?" I asked Oscar.

"Palize hasn't been in my kitchen long, but he always showed up, and he always did a great job. What he did on his private clock was none of my concern. Except when it involved sleeping with guests. Not one-night stands, they're fine. But not long and involved."

"It was long and involved?" Donny demanded of Jillyian. "You told me you had just fooled around one or two times and he'd stolen the CD from your room—"

"He stole a CD from the studio," I said as I realized that fact. I hadn't fit that piece in at all before, but now I was sure of it. "I caught him in there. He said he was looking for a sweater to return to one of the girls."

"You gave him the key code to the studio?" Donny asked Jillyian, his voice getting louder.

"No! I swear it! He must have stolen it while I was . . . sleeping or something," Jillyian said.

"Stoned out of your wits," Donny snapped. "Jillyian, God, I could wring your neck!"

"Stop it, both of you!" Eladonna said. She looked at me as though I was the enemy. "Nothing's lost if you two will *just shut up*."

I looked at Zac; did he know what was going on? He was looking at Sascha, a puzzled expression on his face.

"So for the record," I said, trying to clear my mind, "Sascha killed Palize, and one of you men came in here and stabbed him to the table?"

"Palize hurt her," Donny said. "He was going to hurt me."

"You were here, too?" I asked Donny.

"I wasn't letting her meet with this scum by herself," Donny said. "Palize grabbed her, to hold her hostage, but she got away. I guess she got the gun while he and I wrestled. She shot him, just bang, right against his skin." Donny looked a little green. "We started to clean up. We thought he was dead." Donny looked up. "I didn't know. Palize came around enough to pick up the gun—we'd just left it there—and to shoot at Sascha."

"Are you okay?" Ka'Arih asked Sascha.

"He nicked her," Donny said. "Then I attacked him with the knife, and finally I pinned him. He kept coming after me, so . . ." he gestured toward the table. "Not anymore."

Donny held his hand out for Sascha, and she came to him, took his hand, and sat on his lap. Only then did I notice the patch on her shoulder. The wound.

"Well," Eladonna snapped at Donny. "Thanks for the memories. You did it."

"Shut up," Zima hissed at Eladonna.

Donny kissed Sascha's forehead, and she melted against him. Jillyian watched with sympathy, as tears streaked her cheeks.

I looked at Zac. Could he believe this?

He watched Donny and Sascha, frowning.

Ka'Arih was watching me. "Trust her," she said to them. "We don't have anything to lose."

My feelings of claustrophobia were becoming intense. On one side I had a blackmailing, a Thom Goodfeather-paid-for Filipino drug dealer, and on the other . . . a threesome?

"Wait a minute," Zac said.

"Just tell her," Ka'Arih pleaded. "Dallas is one of us."

Jillyian and Sascha exchanged a glance, and then Jillyian opened her mouth. For the first time I was getting to hear her sing live. You could tell she'd been crying, but her voice still gave me chills. She could sing live? This was the secret?

I looked over at Sascha, and her mouth was moving too.

Wait!

Sascha was Donny's lover.

And—

Jillyian was his sister.

Jillyian closed her mouth, but the singing continued.

Sascha was Jillyian's voice.

Chapter Twenty-Three

That was the fraud, the secret, the mystery.

"How . . . ?" I said, sitting down in Teddy's lap. "I never, I—"

"It was a simple enough situation," Donny said, his voice rough. Sascha had laid her head on his shoulder, and he stroked her hair as he spoke. "The record company set up the contest, but they had to have big-time winners. They had already scouted and practically handpicked the girls before I even arrived. But they were missing a lead singer. We needed someone who could sing, dance, lead, and be beautiful and smart in interviews. Someone to really represent and guide and hold the group together. Of course, I thought of my half-sister, Jillyian."

"You work for the record company?" Eladonna asked Donny.

He looked miserable. "I did work for them. Now I work for you."

"You lied to us?" Ka'Arih said.

Donny nodded, and glanced at us all. "I lied to everyone. But these lies, well, the record company had no problem with me getting my sister. They just asked that she not use her last name. Then the problems started. We tried, but even with training—"

"I can't sing," Jillyian said.

"But she writes—" Ka'Arih said.

"And she dances—" London said.

"She plays—" Eladonna said.

"And she makes the rest of us look cool," Zima said.

"All I needed," Donny said with a sardonic chuckle, "was a voice to substitute for Jillyian's. This realization hit me while we were in Vegas. This group had to win the contest, that was the word from the record company. The execs already had a plan for CDs, videos, a concert tour; they just needed the names, faces, and voices. The machinery was in place, even a shot on TRL."

"Logical," I said. "Promote a band you haven't even signed."

"Promote a band that didn't even exist," Donny said. "It was a big gamble, but it was a matter of marketing. And coke habits of the rich and powerful." He sighed. "Well, our group was going to lose. I went for a walk and wound up in this local bar. A woman was singing at the piano. She didn't play very well, but her voice—"

"Tanya Butler," Zac said.

We all looked at him.

"I've been in this business for a long time," he said.

Donny nodded. "Exactly. I recognized the voice of Tanya Butler."

"You?" I asked Sascha. "You're Tanya Butler?"

She uncurled from Donny and stood up. "I was a one-hit wonder when I was fifteen years old. The Debbie Gibson of my generation, until I collapsed on stage one night. The audience panicked, and two kids were trampled to death leaving the stadium. I was dropped instantly. No sponsors, no record deals. According to them, it was my fault those kids were dead."

"I heard her voice, and suddenly it looked like a way out," Donny said. "I went backstage, and—" he smiled as he looked at Sascha—"I fell in love."

"What was the story with the recording in your room?" I asked.

Donny grinned. "We were working on the CD in the early morning. Once Sascha said you thought she was Jillyian, we decided it was mine and Jillyian's excuse for not being around. It strengthened the lie the group was based on."

"Did everyone else know that Sascha was Jillyian?" I asked.

The musicians all nodded. "We knew something was up, Jillyian was so particular about recordings," David said.

"They didn't tell us, but we're professionals. We figured it out," John said. "We just didn't know who the voice was."

"The record company owns us all, so we'll keep quiet," Derek said.

"What about concerts?" I asked. "How—"

"Don't be dense, Dallas," Teddy said. "No one actually sings live anymore. It's all on tape. You can't move like that, unless you're as fit as Madonna, and still sing."

"We make the right CD, and Jillyian lip-syncs, just like every Backstreet Boy," Donny said.

"But Gerald found out?" I asked, still confused.

"No, Gerald was found out," Zac said. "The FBI took the body."

Everyone looked at him. "How do you know?" Donny asked.

"I'm here a lot," Zac said. "Half the boats in the water are DEA, and those guys aren't subtle when they're asking questions."

He was going to maintain his cover. I glanced at Oscar; he wasn't swallowing Zac's story.

"Who was Gerald?" Teddy asked.

"An informant?" Eladonna asked.

"Like, was he made or something?" Zima asked.

Zac shrugged. "I ran into some guy in Miami. He was trying to get here; he was supposed to meet Gerald."

"He was FBI?" Sascha asked.

Zac chuckled. "You know those guys, they're obvious. He tried to play the part of the bonefishing fanatic, but he was so Fed."

Oscar was as amused as I was. Zac was just lying away. *He* was the Fed.

"Apparently, this guy Gerald just vanished. The Feds suspected the Mafia got to him."

"Did they know who he was?" Eladonna asked. "I mean, if he was their informant, they must have—"

Zac raised his hands in defeat. "I had to read between the lines, you know? This guy wasn't forthcoming, if you get my drift." He glanced at me.

"How do you know the FBI took the body?" I asked, playing along.

"They were lookin'," he said. "I left that morning, and I saw 'em pick it off the beach. I guess they were going to take it back to the mainland."

"And make me look like an idiot."

"We all knew," Eladonna said. "We just hoped he'd wash back out."

"God, he would not stay sunk!" London said.

"You did kill him?" I said.

No one said anything.

"No, we didn't," Donny said after a minute. "But we found him, dead, on the beach."

"Like three times," London said.

"That boy just would not wash out to sea," Zima said.

"You knew who I was talking about?" I asked them.

The flashlight's brightness dropped a notch.

"You knew he was on the beach?" I asked them again.

"Gerald had told me," Sascha said, "before he left by

boat, that he was in trouble with the mob and they were after him. When he washed up—"

"The first time," London said.

"I guessed that he had gotten caught," Sascha said.

"Why didn't you—" I started.

Eladonna spoke. "It wasn't a crime scene. He'd been killed someplace else."

"We couldn't afford the publicity," London said. "The media would start digging into our backgrounds, and they'd learn who everyone was, especially Sascha—"

"And the gig would be up before you began," Zac said.

They all nodded. I continued. "Let me get this straight. You're on the beach; you find the body—"

"Again," London interrupted.

"Sascha strips her shoes of laces, and you throw him back in?"

"That time his luggage washed up, too, so we put rocks in it and tied him to it," Ka'Arih said.

"Not well," Zima said.

"It seemed like he was gone," Jillyian said. "The problem was removed."

"You didn't wonder about who killed him?" I asked. "Didn't worry they would come after you?"

"We were doing the Mafia a favor by dumping the body," Zima said.

"We didn't think there was any harm," Ka'Arih said.

"Palize must have been freaking when I talked about a body on the beach," I said. "He is the one who shot Gerald, then?" I looked at Zac out of the corner of my eye. He put his finger behind his ear and pulled an imaginary trigger. Standard Mafia style.

Donny shrugged. "I don't know. We didn't do it. We were just protecting ourselves."

"We didn't do anything criminal," Eladonna said.

I refrained from looking at Palize, who was stretched like a butterfly on a board and dead as a doornail.

The only remaining piece in the question was who owned the record company. I wasn't sure this was the place to ask.

"Well," I said, getting up and stretching. "That clears all that up. Now what are we going to do with the body?"

"I wouldn't suggest trying to sink it," London said.

The first big problem we had, the *first*, was that no one knew how Palize had been communicating with his contact. "My suspicion," Eladonna said, "is that he was a bottom-feeder, hired to do this one job. Maybe he also passed along some drug money, but he was no one in terms of the organization. Just another set of eyes and ears."

Zac was mute. Did that mean she was right?

The lights had come on twelve hours ago, revealing who was bloodstained and who wasn't. We'd cleaned up, eaten, and reconvened in the drawing room to make our plans.

"Palize didn't call the mainland," Oscar said. "Not from these phones."

"Did he go to Alice Town often?" Teddy asked.

"Cigarette runs. Tuesday and Thursday," Oscar answered.

"Yesterday was Tuesday," Eladonna said, looking at her watch.

"His contact will assume the weather prevented his call, but will be expecting him to communicate immediately," London said.

"They'll give him twenty-four hours or something, right?" Zima asked. "I mean, drug running is not no science."

"What if he just never shows up?" Ka'Arih asked.

"If it be some island mon who is Palize contact," Mama said, "he gonna assume de storm got him."

Zac looked at Oscar. "Maybe the storm did get him," Zac said.

"Wouldn't be de firs' time dat no body ever showed," Mama said. "De *loa* ob de sea, sometime dey jus' take de body away."

With that covert agreement, people scattered to their rooms. I hung behind until it was just me, Zac, Mama, and Oscar.

"Are you sure about this?" I whispered to Zac.

"I had a crush on Tanya Butler when I was a young man," Zac said. "And my job was to eliminate this mob contact if he interfered, anyway. It's a little tangled the way it happened, and I'm really sorry I didn't catch Gerald—save that boy's butt. Why the hell he didn't stay put . . . anyway, it's the same in the end. Washington has their body, and the sea will have another. I can live with that. Can you, baby?" he squinted at me over his cigarette's smoke, and the sunlight from outside glinted off his wedding ring.

It was a little alarming to learn that I could live with it. I knew somewhere Palize had a mother. Somewhere a girl would miss him. He had been a person, not just a gangster, but he'd killed before and had been preparing to kill again. Oscar had found a gun in Palize's bedroom.

Live by the sword, die by the sword, my conservative grandmama would say.

Lindsay called me at noon, demanding to know if I was all right, if she needed to fly a plane in and rescue me herself. I had to shout that I was fine before she stopped to listen. "What is going on? What—" she said.

"We'll have a nice long lunch when I get back to Dallas," I said. "Make reservations, and you're paying."

"What would you like—"

"Lindsay, I'll see you in a few days." I hung up.

I was painting my toenails when I heard the whisper of my name at the door. "Come in," I said. I couldn't walk to get it; I hadn't brought my pedicure spacers.

♪ Sascha poked her head around the door. "Good morning."

"Are you on the second floor of this tower?" I asked her as she kissed my cheeks. "I never saw you go into Donny's room."

"Yes, I'm right below; we planned it that way. You know about the elevator?"

I nodded.

"At a time like this, you paint your nails?" she asked.

"I have a friend who is a writer," I said. "She gets long-lasting pedicures, until the last few weeks before a book is due. Then, she says, every time she can't think what to write, she paints her toenails."

"She has many colors?"

"Once she said she had fourteen layers of color on."

"Good thing Chekov did not try this," she said and sat down on the bed and picked up the polish. "May I?"

"Sure," I said.

She began to paint her nails in quick, short movements. "It is a relief that you know now."

"I'd ask why you didn't tell me, but that's stupid. I was an unknown quantity."

"Then you started asking questions. I thought to make the wrestling shoes disappear also, but that was after you saw them, and it would have made you more curious."

"Why did you keep Gerald's kit?" I asked.

"He said he'd be back," Sascha said. "If I'd known he'd talked to FBI and they were waiting for him, I would have tied him up alive to keep him that way, until they got here. But he said he had to go, go then, go now, and then he was gone. He said he'd be back, and if he didn't come back, then just leave his stuff here to help whoever else did the job."

"You were going to hire another stylist already?" I asked.

"I have worked in this business for many years; I know I cannot style. Look! I barely dress myself."

"You always looked perfect."

"Donny," she said with a smile. "He dresses me."

"Ohh . . ."

She blew on her nails. "Paint my toes?"

"Sure," I said as she took off her shoes. How I missed the size of her feet, I didn't know. They were long and skinny, like skis. She shook the bottle and started on her toes. "I love him." She looked at me. "I used many men to get places, but Donny I love. He is so gentle, so kind. When I thought Palize was going to kill him, I picked up the gun and I . . . just shoot. Is very easy. Donny is my man."

"Stand by your man," I muttered.

"He is good man." She looked at me. "He was trying to make everything right for everyone. His sister, the company, the other girls. He is good man." Sascha's hand started to shake as she painted her toe. She was crying, soft tears.

I patted her back, and she turned to me, hugged me. "He will never forgive himself," she said. "He did nothing wrong, but this will eat at him and he will be unhappy forever."

I hugged her, rocking her as I would one of my nieces. I couldn't imagine what a horror it must have been to stab someone through. Of course, I'm the girl who can't even slice a ham. Something about cutting through flesh, even if it's a dead pig, that's just creepy. "It's only been a day," I said. "Maybe he'll be okay once he's out of here."

"He can't even make plans to finish CD or bideo," she said, her Russian accent creeping back. "Bette, she asks him and he . . . he can't answer. I am worried, bery worried."

After Sascha left, I put on my shoes, grabbed my phone, and went for a run.

The island looked as if it had been raked, then pulled through a doggie door backward. The sea was murky, with seaweed lying like black lace at the water's edge. Trees and vines had been yanked up—it looked like giant hands did that work—and colored polka dots were sprinkled on every surface.

They were flower buds that had gotten caught in the wind and nailed by the rain.

I ran on the dry sand. The hard-packed surface was a great way for working my legs and calves, especially after days of being cramped and tight and still. I started slowly, shivering in the cool breeze. The sun was up, but it was a watery yellow that didn't feel warm at all. I ran halfway around the island, dodging debris, then I looked back at the castle. From here I could see the island workers removing the shutters from the windows. I could see into Jillyian's nest-room, and I could see the backside of my own tower. I paced.

Chapter Twenty-Four

I dialed my brother. "Hey Beaubro," I said. "S'Dallas."
  "Well, hey, little sister. How are you? Where are you? I got some e-mail from Mom about Miami and I told her she had to be wrong, you wouldn't take an out-of-town job and miss a Dallas summer."

  "Ha ha. Hear me now and cry later. I'm in Bimini."

  Beaumont whistled. "If you're working on bikini models I'm gonna have to come out there as your assistant."

  I laughed.

  "What," he said in an affected lisp. "You don't think I can pass for gay?"

  Beaumont worked as a flight attendant, but he was really working at being a rodeo cowboy. "Darlin'," I said, "Unless you were going to wear lead pants, those girls would know."

  "Oh jeez, Dallas, you don't have to get so . . . personal." He was so easy to embarrass.

  "Question for you."

  "Yup?"

  "If someone tried to kill me, or Christi, or Ojeda, or Mineola, and you killed the guy instead, how would you feel?"

Beau was silent for a second. "Damn proud. I'd defended my women." He was the most liberal of my brothers, but he was a strong, proud Texan, true to type.

"You don't think that's kind of . . . ?"

"Kinda what, Dallas? I'd feel the same pride if I killed someone who was tryin' to kill Houston or Sherman, or Grandmama or Mom, even Dad. It's family. You do stuff for family."

"Would it bother you if someone else didn't understand?"

He snorted. "They'd have to be a misfit or an only child not to understand. It's natural. You see it with lions."

"Lions eat their enemy," I said.

"That's not entirely true, they fight their enemy and kill 'em. Only occasionally do they eat other lions."

I should never use examples from the animal kingdom with him; he lives with the Nature channel. I watch the next door neighbor's cats for my information.

"It's okay, then?" I said.

"Have you killed someone, darlin'?"

"No."

"I love you little sister. Tell me if you need anything."

I was closest to Beau; we were eleven months apart. My mother called us her almost-twins. "I love you too, Beau. I'll be home at the end of the week."

"Good, it's about time we hit Billy Bob's."

I laughed and hung up. He'd been trying to get me to Billy Bob's since I first moved to Dallas a decade ago. To me it is like the West End and Southfork; for tourists only.

After stretching, I kept running around the island. A quarter mile from the other side of the castle, I found the answer for dealing with Palize. A broken boat, washed up on shore. I raced back to the castle.

Donny was sitting in the little garden outside my window. He wore one of his suits, but it was rumpled and he was barefoot. Donny had his head in his hands and his shoulders were slumped. I put on some long pants, because it had gotten cooler, and went down the steps.

He sat up. "Hey."

"Hey."

"Those are some funky pants."

"Marc Jacobs."

"I like those colors. They're very seventies' rocker."

I was wearing cords striped in a turquoise the color of the shallows and a blue the color of the deep. They *were* very seventies, especially with my knotted leather belt and ever-present linen shirt. I touched my choker, then sat down. "You wish you could undo it? Have Palize alive and Sascha dead?"

"No." His answer was instant. "She's worth a hundred of him. No, I don't. I wouldn't change my actions."

"Then why are you choking on this, when you've actually walked away with it? The cops aren't going to come after you; you have the girls, the music, the promo plan in place. Now you're dropping the ball?"

"I scared myself," he said. "If I can summon up that kind of fury, am I really sane?" Donny looked at me, and I didn't see his cute face, his sexy curls, the way his designer clothes fit his frame perfectly. I saw a man who hadn't slept, who was scared to look into a mirror, who didn't trust himself.

"You've heard that story about the kid who gets hit by a car?" I said. "He's under the wheel and his mother, who saw the whole thing, comes running up and lifts the car off the child."

Donny nodded.

"The mother is usually some little five-foot-five, one-hundred-thirty-pound ordinary woman. Not Chyna, not even particularly fit. But it's her child, and so in those circumstances she can do whatever is necessary to protect her own."

"You're saying I'm like that mother? That this was extraordinary, and so that's why I could do it; but just like the mother doesn't lift cars all the time, I won't just lose it and start killing people in Yankee Stadium?" he said.

"No," I said, looking at him through the weak sunlight. "I'm saying just because she can lift a car doesn't make her a weight lifter, and just because you defend someone by ending the attacker's life, it doesn't make you a killer."

Donny dropped his gaze, and I patted his shoulder and stood up. "I'll see you later."

He nodded, still looking at his hands.

I wanted to say more, to encourage him not to blow this strange chance the Universe had given him. But I didn't. I walked away. He had to do what he could live with; he had to. The dining room was empty, the table wasn't set, and the kitchen was still bare.

Oscar was the next person on my list.

I found him on the beach, his checks rolled up to his knees, his jacket open and blowing in the wind. He wore a wife-beater tank and a St. Christopher pendant. He glanced at me, but didn't say anything. We'd been working in concert, but not talking.

"Are you flying into Miami tomorrow?" I asked.

He nodded. "I need to check on the restaurant before I meet my mother."

That was right; he was sailing away. I was managing to dodge the bullet of a relationship with a wonderful man who had an "a" on the end of his name, values I believed in, and a personality I liked. I was triumphing.

Yeah, right. "They've asked me to tour with them," I said. "If Donny pulls out and gets with the program. We're supposed to shoot tomorrow night in Miami, but—"

"He'll shake it off," Oscar said. "And you'll get a world tour. How exciting for you." His voice sounded anything but excited.

"I was in Paris when this whole thing began," I said. "I've never been anywhere else except there and Mexico."

"It'll be good for you, then."

I took a deep breath. "Did I out you?"

"Yup."

I wanted to curse myself on the spot, but it was too late. "You were so open with me," I said. "I—"

"I was open with you because I wanted you to know everything about me. I would have told you anything about my life, my finances, my ties, my family. I've spent my whole life being private, but I wanted you to know me." He still faced the sea.

"But that information wasn't for general consumption." Duh, Dallas.

"No." He chuckled. "No, you see the rest of the world respects me. It sees me as a responsible man with a great restaurant and a good life. My past is my business. I pay my bills on time, I'm there for my family, I have close friends with whom I share laughs and a few drinks. Only Bette knows the truth."

"Bette?"

"Years ago," he glanced at me, "after my white-bread-blonde-haired wife had left me and took my son, I was in bad shape. Bette and I saved each other's lives. We've been in the trenches together. When I say she's tied me to the bedposts, I don't mean that sexually. She did that so I wouldn't harm myself when the pain was too bad."

Ohmigosh. "I thought there were centers for withdrawal."

"Yeah, well, not when you are so messed up that you've spent all your money, when you've sold your car for more drugs, when you haven't cleaned up for months. We didn't even care enough to brush the roaches off each other. It was bad."

"Bette saved your life?"

"She got clean first, then she dragged me into it. We've helped each other out all the rest of the way."

"I had no idea."

"Nor does anyone else, unless you open your mouth again."

I deserved that.

He sighed. "In there, I thought you were playing some psychological game, and telling my secrets was all part of the plan. Or maybe you thought I'd killed Palize. I guess I threatened to do it enough. Either way . . ."

"So when I saw in your eyes that I'd blown it with you, I was right," I whispered.

"You just came to the island for a good time, right? You didn't want me to care, you just wanted me to want to see you naked." He shrugged. "I guess the battle is yours."

It was a soft, peaceful afternoon. Music sound drifted across the sand, a sexy samba that went with the gentle breeze and the smell of flowers. The island was recovering, despite the debris on the beaches, the torn-up vegetation. It would be fine, better than fine. Nothing had happened that was irreparable.

"I have to prep dinner," he said, and turned away. I watched him slip into his clogs and walk back to the castle, a long, lean figure, braids blowing in the wind. I sat down on the sand and exhaled.

Then I looked back. Oscar stood, watching me, twenty feet away. I couldn't see his face, his eyes, but I rose to my feet and walked toward him. He stayed, watched me come.

Nothing had happened that was irreparable.

I held my hands out to him, and he took them, looked at my palms.

They were as messed up as his.

"That is from stabbing myself with the needle when I was hemming evening gowns the other day," I said, pointing to a bloody, gross cuticle. "And those burns are from the iron and the steamer. The ironing incident was three weeks ago, it's scabbed over pretty fast. The blisters are from hauling stuff, from all the carrying I do," I said. I pointed to a white line on my forefinger. "That's from slicing my finger open with a box cutter, while I was working on a household shoot. The AD fainted at the sight of the blood. There was a lot of it. The photographer had to drive me to the Doc in the Box. I severed the nerve or something," I said, and wiggled my finger. "They're not pretty hands, in fact, I think they're the only part of me that's not long." I turned them over, and let Oscar see the little white marks that marred my tanned hands. Memories in every knick and scratch. "Spatulate is what my mom calls them. Useful. My granddaddy has hands like this."

"What happened there?" Oscar asked, and touched the ring finger on my left hand.

I heard the wind and waves, felt the waning sun on my back. Was I going to be real here, or hide out, waiting for some perfectionist ideal that would never happen. Perfection, I realized all of a sudden, was a concept, a personal resolution, not a day-to-day reality. "I couldn't make myself into the person that the man I'd promised to love needed me to be. I ran away."

"He was Latino?"

I nodded and looked up at him. There was no guile in Oscar's face, no anticipation either.

"I know what I want," Oscar said. "My restaurant. A warm person to come home to. Nights when the moon is full and the sea sings."

I didn't say anything.

"It used to be that what I wanted was my next fix, my next fu-, lay, and then my next fix." He didn't break eye contact. "I have a fifteen-year-old son. He lives with my ex-wife. Now it's all very friendly. I spend a lot of time with my mother; she lives in Miami. My father passed away when I was sixteen.

"I have a good life. I control the menu at Ziren, and I take home a salary that lets me play in the ocean a couple days a week, fits me for a nice retirement plan, and allows for enough extra to escape for an eating tour of some other country at least twice a year. It's better than I deserve.

"What do you want, Dallas?" he asked, his voice soft.

I brought his mouth to mine and kissed him with all the words I couldn't say, didn't dare say. "I'm scared," I whispered. "I know time is important to you, but I'm . . . I'm sorry."

"Ah, lass," he said and hugged me tight. He was shaking as much as I was. I felt the muscles in his back, from the width of his shoulders narrowing in a V to his waist, and the strength of his legs close to mine.

"Time doesn't have to start now," he said. "When it does, the past, yours and mine, won't matter."

I nodded.

"I'll do anything for you," he said. "But, Dallas," he pulled back and looked at me, "don't . . . don't be callous about my feelings. Emotions are fragile, and once damaged they can recover, but they are never as lithe and elastic again."

I kissed him again, and it was almost a promise. Hopeful.

"I really do have to get dinner together," he said, his tone regretful.

I laughed. "I really do have to figure out what these girls are wearing in their concert tomorrow," I said. "I'll probably work through dinner."

"I'll see that you don't starve," he said, and then kissed me again.

Tenderness was replaced with raw want, and I responded the same way. I felt electrified as I pressed closer and closer to him. We broke apart, staring at each other with wariness and appreciation. "I hope 'time' starts soon," Oscar said.

I laughed and we walked back to the castle.

Oscar held the kitchen door open for me, then followed me in. No one was there, but the specter of Palize's body was memorable. "Later," he growled in my ear.

Work.

The workroom felt like a new place; I was seeing it with new eyes.

I sat down and made a list. "Femme" was definitely Zima. "Uptown" London. "Natural" would be Ka'Arih. "Diva" Jillyian, and Eladonna would be "Eclectic." I labeled five racks, and started through my bags of clothes.

About midnight, the bookcase opened. Oscar brought me food and made me dessert. Then he joined me for my 5 a.m. run as the sun came up. Rather, he fished while I ran. Oysters for breakfast was the promise.

As I was walking into the courtyard afterward, Zac was walking through. Alone.

"Dallas," he called. "C'mere."

"Is everything okay?" I asked him. "With, you know—"

He took a deep breath. "Yeah. Bodies are taken care of, authorities are notified and questions have been answered." He smiled. "It's all good."

"Good."

"Baby, I—" Zac looked around the garden. "I was coming after you, on your run that morning, the morning you found the body."

"Okay."

"I, I, well, we—"

"Zac, just spit it out." He was making me jumpy.

"I'm here with orders," he said.

"From the FBI?" I whispered.

"From my wife."

Huh?

"Dallas, baby, I married Dieta."

My eyes started to fill with tears.

"You know I've been married before, you know I didn't trust in love, but she made me want to try again," he said softly. "She makes me believe in miracles every day."

"Dieta?"

She was the dearest soul; positive and vibrant, she transformed the life of every person she met. She'd changed me. She was so good, so giving. I considered her one of my closest friends, though for reasons of Dieta's health and safety, we couldn't meet face to face. I had to pretend she was dead.

"Dieta and you? That's why you've been trying to see me?"

He nodded. "We're having a baby."

"Oh, Zac!" I was crying for real now.

"We got pregnant a month after our honeymoon. It all happened so fast, I mean, we were together all the time, and it wasn't twenty-four hours after guarding her when I realized . . ."

"It's perfect," I said. "Dieta is just perfect for you."

"I'm becoming a full-time musician," Zac said. "No more guns, a lot more studios. Dieta and the baby will tour with me—"

I hugged him. "I'm so happy for you."

"Oh, baby," he said as he hugged me back, and I knew it was a term of endearment. "Dieta wanted me to ask you something though," he said. "I gotta look at you."

My eyes were blurry, but I smiled into his black-fringed eyes. "Yes?"

"Can we name our baby girl Dallas?"

I was in the kitchen, eating coconut *suspiros*, on a break from organizing clothes. The girls were in the tower (that sounded so weird) finishing the CD. Mama Garcia was boiling coffee, but she asked me to watch it for a minute, and left.

She came back just as it was on the second boil. She handed

me a little pouch and then got the coffee. "For yo' good-good charm," she said over her shoulder. "In dis next times, you be needin' it."

"Mama, where are you from?"

"My mama, she Haiti, my poppa, he be Cuba. Long ago, chile."

I looked at the beaded pouch in my hand, sniffed it. "Thank you," I said. "It's for wearing?"

"'Round yo' neck."

I reached for another *suspiro*, and she poured me fresh coffee. We exchanged a smile, and she poured herself some, too, then spiked it with rum. She winked at me and I chuckled. "Mama," I said, "why did you call me the face of death when I got here?" I put the necklace on. It was pretty craftsmanship.

"Because you seen a lot of deat', dealt wi't a lot of sperrids, chile, and it show on yo' face," she said, then took a sip of her coffee and grimaced. "You know you was preparin' to see more, and dat showed on yo' face, too. Dat is what I saw and dat is what scared me, 'cuz I doan wan it to be none of my chirren or lob'ed ones." She poured another half cup of rum in her coffee.

"Death was on my face?"

"Destiny, chile," she said as she sliced open a watermelon. She sprinkled it with pepper.

"I don't believe in destiny. My future is not decided," I said. "And it has nothing to do with death." I didn't sound convincing, even to myself.

"If you t'ink dat, you is allowed to. But you be wrong." She sliced the watermelon into ribbons, almost faster than my eye could see.

I inhaled, tried to remain calm. "So, then, in your opinion, what should I do?"

"Go wid it, chile, embrace it. God ain't gonna let no bad t'ing be happenin' to you. You is one o' his favorites."

"But I don't like messing around with murder," I said. "I keep trying to avoid it, and it keeps finding me." Though this time, at least I didn't go through the heartache of losing someone I cared about. Heavens, Dallas, you are so cold. *Zac and Dieta wanted to name their baby girl after me.* I couldn't believe it.

"Den you can answer yor own fool question," Mama said, and handed me a sliver of pepper-sprinkled watermelon. "Can you change your destiny? I don't t'ink so, chile."

"Death is my destiny?"

"No," she said, banging the knife against the cutting board for emphasis, "dat is neber what I have said. You only hear what you want to hear."

"What are you saying, then?" I said. "I don't think I'm getting it." I focused on her, and she laid the knife down and looked at me with her spooky, confessional eyes.

"Deat' is in de world, chile, it be here like the birds in de air, de fishes in de sea. It be a part of livin' and it ain't bad. Deat' is a good t'ing when you is go'wn to be wit' de Lor' Jesus Christ. But when de *loa* wanna take you, dat be different. But sometime, de Debil, he let his chirren take de people away and den dere is much sorrow. Maybe you be de one to give comfort to dere families, so dere mamas doan cry for dem no more."

I sipped my coffee, flabbergasted. "I never looked at it that way before."

"I know you di'n't, chile, which is why I get dese ol bones up to wish you good bye-bye. Now go."

"Thanks Mama," I said and hugged her.

"T'ank you. And doan be afraid, chile. You always have a home here. De *loa* in dis place like you. Now go'wn."

Chapter Twenty-Five

I kissed Oscar good-bye at 10 a.m. "You have my numbers," he said, and smiled. "And the clock."

Then it happened, as surprising as falling through the floor, or soaring through the ceiling, as identifiable as an Irving Penn photograph or a Jimmy Choo shoe, I realized I loved him. Boom. Just like that. I didn't, and then suddenly I did.

Where my sudden bravery came from I didn't know. I didn't care. I wasn't going to seize up and walk away because this man's name bore a striking resemblance to other names that represented failures in my life. I wasn't going to judge him on what he'd done or been. I could laugh with him, I could argue with him, but most importantly, I could trust him.

Oscar reached over and touched my cheek. "I'll never break it," he said, reading my mind with a soft smile. "Welcome to the party."

By 10 p.m., I was checking into the hotel under an assumed name, surrounded by bodyguards and dodging media.

The concert was tomorrow night; tomorrow was my last day of shopping to make the girls' wardrobes perfect.

I have two Miami habits, well, three, actually. It depends on when I arrive. My cousin just moved to South Beach, but she didn't know I was going to be in the city so I was just going to avoid her altogether. I love her, but it was going to be crazy enough already.

So with cousin Gigi (Georgina Grace, shortened to GG for her modeling career) out of the way, my habits could remain in place. Except I didn't need to do number one—visit the water. I'd been on the water for weeks. Number two was either Cuban coffee at the News Café (pre-tourist hours) or a mojito at Tap-Tap (post 5 p.m.) and then the newest, trendiest pedicure.

I couldn't decide between Burberry or Pucci; either way, it would be trés bling-bling and totally deductible.

Shopping first.

˟ I'm never going home, I thought. Dallas O'Connor, meet your new residence. South Beach, Flo-ree-dah. It was a common refrain when I sat here. Nothing to do with a handsome Basque chef wandering the seas. I always said it, no matter how many times I visited Miami.

The waiter at the News Café put down my Cuban coffee, and I looked across Ocean Drive toward the mighty Atlantic. From here, with a salmon, gold, and cadet blue sky, elegant palms, and the myriad shades of aqua on the horizon, this view could be on a postcard. I sipped the heavy sweetness of my coffee and groaned out loud. Cappuccino was exquisite, and I loved café au lait, but for my rush, nothing came close to coffee Cubana.

This sweet silence was amazing. I saw the "regulars" stroll in, pick up coffee, greet each other, and leave. As Versace had done, I thought, then shook my head. Such talent, shot down on the steps of his own house, not a few blocks away. Now the enterprising Floridians were turning it into a six-star hotel.

That's right, six stars.

A few runners moved along the sidewalk parallel to the beach, across the street from me. Two guys skipped rope, and I'd already seen their boxing gloves. What a way to start the morning. Some older folks strolled, already in swimsuits, hats, and sunglasses. I'd done my run that morning, on a treadmill.

So not the same.

My own shades were on my head, and I wore one of my Cavalli shirts over my bikini, with that miniskirt I really, really would like to throw into the ocean. I needed to buy *me* some clothes.

Critically, I looked at my thong-sandaled feet. A smudge of self-tanner glared orange between my toes. A quick swipe of lemon would take care of it, but this was too public a place to do it. I crossed my legs the other way.

Prep for this evening would start about three. I needed time for a few embellishments on the clothes, not to mention fittings on the girls. I needed to buy one of those handheld sergers if I was going to do this international tour with them. I sipped my coffee and tried to imagine mornings like this in London, Paris, Madrid, Rome, Prague, Lisbon, sipping coffee in a café and planning my day.

It was time for me to get out and see the world, and what a way to do it. Then after the Europe tour, there would be the States. If I was interested.

I pulled out a notebook and started making a list. What I would need to do in order to get out of Dallas for six months: evict renter, find replacement. Did I want to sublease my place? I could call one of the modeling agencies and see if they needed a long-term residence for one of their girls. Which would mean I'd need to pack up some things and stick them in storage. I'd given up my storage unit. I nibbled on the end of my pen, gave up, and started another list.

What I'd need to take, to pack. I was deep in my list when I heard my name. "Dallas O'Connor, don't turn around."

I didn't.

"I don't want to alarm you, but I want you to pay your bill, get up, and walk over to the black Mustang on the opposite side of the street," the voice said. "Get in it, the keys are there, and drive down to Third Street Beach."

There was no way in hell I was doing this.

"I'm FBI. Goodfeather's agents are across the street. They have a weapon. I'm trying to save your life, Ms. O'Connor." The woman sighed. "Zac sent me."

Zac?

"He said you were stubborn, but to tell you . . . Dee-et-tah? . . . would want you safe."

I threw down five dollars, picked up my bag and crossed the street. The Mustang was new, shiny, and a convertible. I got inside and the keys were there. Was it going to blow up? I winced as I pushed in the clutch and turned on the ignition.

It started.

I stayed in one piece.

The street was clear, so I pulled a U and headed south on Ocean Drive.

There was no one following me, no one that I could see.

A girl on Rollerblades swung out from a side street and hitchhiked on the back of the car. "The Big Pink," she called to me as she turned toward the Third Street Beach. An FBI agent in-line skating? I passed a park on my left, and turned right. The Big Pink was on the corner. I pulled the car into a space, grabbed my purse, and turned the engine off. Was I supposed to take the keys or leave them?

I looked both ways before crossing the street, and then walked into the restaurant. A long table was filled with bicycle cops. A smattering of locals sat at other tables, but no one alone.

"Dallas!" a stunning blonde called to me. "So good to see you!"

I smiled and acted like I knew who in the world she was. We exchanged cheek kisses and I sat down. "Have you met Fred? I don't know if I was dating him then or not," she said as Fred slid a badge across to me.

"Hi, Fred," I said, going along with this. If they knew Dieta's name, it was either because Zac had been tortured to death—but probably not even then—or it was legit, and Zac knew using Dieta's name would make me act.

The girl slid me a card. "*Order,*" it said. "*Then go to the men's bathroom. The cleaning sign is up.*"

I ordered waffles, they were divine here, and coffee, and excused myself to the ladies' room. Instead, I crossed over the sign that warned about slippery floors, and stepped into the men's room. Another woman was waiting.

"Hello," she said, and extended her hand, "I'm agent Cass Rodgers."

I shook her hand; I mean, I was just going through the motions. "You were the one in the café?" I asked. "Your voice is familiar."

She nodded. "Goodfeather put a few things together, and when we saw his agents sitting outside, with weapons, we thought getting you out of there was a good idea."

"You're watching me?" I asked. "What did Goodfeather put together?"

"We weren't watching you, we were looking for an opportunity to approach you."

Oh.

"Goodfeather is looking for the same chance. He figures you messed up his plan on the island and he wants you to join forces with him."

I shuddered. "I could never do that."

"We need you to, Dallas."

Chapter Twenty-Six

My jaw hit the floor. "You want me to—"
"I'll make this quick. Zac is retiring. He's going into music full time."

"He wasn't an agent full time?"

"No, he worked for us, but he did it on a case-by-case basis. We would like you to do the same thing."

"I don't know anything—"

"You know Goodfeather's world, fashion. You know brands and styles and—" the agent shrugged. "Look at me, I buy clothes at Penney's. I couldn't mix in that milieu without three years of training. You already know that environment. You know weapons, too. You're a good observer, you have an eye for detail, and you already know a lot of what is going on."

"You want me to spy on fashion for you?"

Agent Rodgers cocked her head. "I want you to think about it. Goodfeather is going to approach you with some kind of arrangement. He's been pursuing you for a while."

"Why? I don't want anything to do with him."

"Because if you are in his pocket, it's one less eye and ear he has to protect against. You work in a billion-dollar industry, you know that. A lot of that money is going to very disreputable places. We need to stop it, but to do that, we need evidence. You can get that for us."

"He won't believe me if I suddenly give in."

"He'll be persuasive. And he thinks everyone has a price. You'll know how to handle it." She looked at me. She was right, she would never pass in the fashion world. She was dressed fine, she had on makeup, and her hair was done, but she wore it all like a costume or a uniform. "Think about it," she said.

"How do I get in touch with you?"

"We'll be in touch. Be safe."

Great, sure, I thought as I went back to my "breakfast."

The girl there talked on and on, about the newest restaurant she and "Fred" had gone to (C.H.A.I.R.), about the opening of the newest club (B*tch), about the cutest pair of jeans she'd ever seen (Santini Mavardi), and about the rad new DJ (ReGeaux). All in all, I ate my waffles and smiled and laughed at her jokes, and then we pretended we'd see each other again, they picked up the tab, and I went back outside.

Was I supposed to ride or walk? I was standing in indecision, when my phone rang. I looked at the time with shock. Ten-fifteen? I had to get moving. I walked by the car, saw the keys were still in it, and drove back to the News Café. I parked the Mustang where it had been, then put on walking/shopping shoes and hit the streets.

The "concert" was going to be at Purdy Lounge, a laidback local bar with hand-shaped chairs, a pool table, and original local art. The mixture of people would give the record company a great sampling to gauge a reaction to Fate of Paradise.

A musical taste-test.

There wasn't much in the way of dressing rooms, so the girls got dressed before they arrived. A hard-core rock-star look would be too precious for such an intimate setting (the stage was within touching distance of the floor), and the lighting was sexy, not dramatic.

Zima had become the easiest to dress. She wore a Dior kimono over Levis and a white sleeveless turtleneck with red wedge sandals. Sascha fixed her hair with chopsticks and gave her a "bamboo" manicure.

Short skirts were also a little bit of an issue; the stage wasn't raised, but anyone sitting could look up the girls' skirts with a little effort. None of the five wanted to feel awkward, so either tights, or no minis.

Ka'Arih wore a Marc Jacobs innocent top over a knee-length black skirt and black gladiator boots with a black cap on her curls. Eladonna wore purple Juicy cords with lace-up front and pin-tucked seams, and a Custo Barcelona top in burgundy, purple and gold, with Lucite-and-cork sandals. I put London in a pair of Guess jeans with a black tank and Casadei lace duster and some ebony-studded Gucci ankle-wrap sandals. Her hair was in ringlets, cascading over her shoulders.

Jillyian wore a vintage puzzle dress (and matching tap pants) with Mizrahi boots and Baby Phat jewelry. Sascha straightened her hair and gave her doe eyes and pink punk streaks.

Anyone who knew clothes could look at the girls and know where I'd been shopping, but it didn't matter. They were comfortable. They were wearing the clothes, the clothes weren't wearing them. No Fashion Victims here. They looked the part of talented PYTs, and I had no doubt that once the crowd heard them, it would be over. Stars born, and all of that.

As the girls were stepping off the RV, they hugged me. "We're going to be rock stars," Jillyian said, but the braggadocio was gone, and she sounded dazzled. "We just got an invitation to be on TRL."

Zima walked out next, with Eladonna. Zima hugged me and then jerked away like she'd been shocked. "Atlantis!" she shouted.

"What?" Eladonna asked, London crowded behind her. "It should be the album's name!"

"That's brilliant!" London said. "Tell Donny," she said and turned around to get Ka'Arih's attention. "We can be mermaids on the CD cover!"

"This could be the Atlantis Tour!" Zima and Eladonna walked off, talking excitedly.

The others hugged me and I whispered good luck to them. Ka'Arih kissed me on the cheek. "Willie's safely in the bathtub at the hotel," she said. "I probably should ship him home?"

"Probably."

She smiled.

"Good luck, little peacemaker."

She stepped down the stairs, then turned around. "He's an adventurer," she said. "An exact balance for a perfectionist."

I smiled even wider. "Break a leg."

She hurried to catch up with the other girls. Sascha and I hugged each other. "I feel like a mother hen," Sascha said.

She didn't seem to mind that it was her voice these girls were going to be selling. I doubted I could be that generous, or calm, or whatever it was that made her able to smile as Jillyian lip-synched along. Of course, they were Jillyian's words, and Jillyian was playing the keyboard.

I wandered over to the bar, feeling it was club soda time.

"Buy you a drink?" I turned to see a pretty Latino in workaday-world clothes: dark pants, white shirt, Kenneth Cole square-toed lace-ups.

"I'm not drinking," I said.

"Is that every day, or just tonight?" he asked.

"Just tonight," I said.

"Is there a reason?" he asked.

"I want to remember it."

He fell silent, and then spoke again. "I'd really like to buy you a drink . . . Dallas O'Connor."

There was a definite pause.

"Should I be surprised that you know my name?" I asked.

"We have a mutual friend," he said.

"I doubt it."

"You don't consider Mr. Goodfeather your friend? He thinks the world of you."

This was it. "I don't," I said. "Now if you'll leave me alone, I'd like to listen to the band."

The Latino shrugged. "I won't bother you any longer, but," he slid a key card across the bar, "if you change your mind, he's in your hotel. Just go to room eighty-nine." He tapped the key.

"I'm leaving tomorrow," I said, and slid the plastic card back. "Thanks anyway."

He pushed it back to me. "In case you change your mind."

I turned away. A moment later, he left.

The key was still there, on the bar.

If I picked it up, I would be getting into a whole other world. The FBI? Thom Goodfeather and the Filipino Mafia? What about Oscar? What about my home, my life in Dallas? I watched the girls onstage; they'd taken a lot of risks to get there. When was the last time I'd taken a risk?

This job, for one. The job in Washington. They'd both become dangerous, but I hadn't known that from the start. I'd always been able to blame anything but myself for being in whatever precarious position in which I'd landed.

If I did this, started this game, then I'd have no one to blame but myself. I'd live in a haze of worry, of rushing adrenaline. I'd be responsible for my predicaments.

But I'd be doing something worthwhile.

Shakira's lyrics were imprinted on my mind, telling me that my real life had just begun, that I was ready for the good times, that whenever, wherever. . . .

I picked up the key, watched the stage, and wondered.

GREEN

MYSTERY

Green, Chloe.
Fashion victim

$ 22.00

JAN 2 3 2003